BLOOD OF THE LOST KINGDOM

BLOOD OF THE LOST KINGDOM

DAUGHTER OF ERABEL ~ BOOK TWO

KRISTIN WARD

Blood of the Lost Kingdom
Daughter of Erabel Series, Book 2
By Kristin Ward

Editing by David Taylor
Cover Image by JD, JDCoverDesigns

ISBN 978-1-7327923-6-4

Visit https://www.kristinwardauthor.com/

To those whose hearts beat to Celtic drums.

PROLOGUE

The candle guttered, its flame flickering atop the waxen heart—a sickly yellow mass made from the fat of a newborn. Crackles and pops erupted in the darkness, in time with the echo of that squalling innocent. The ghostly wails, so like the cries of Haegna as she pleaded from beyond the dank cell, begging for a word, a taste.

The mage rocked, muttering in cadences strange and sinister, his body swaying with words of power. His pale face lay shrouded in a cloak so black it melted into the darkness, concealing all but the skeletal hands that sifted through runes strewn about the single table of the dank cell. A lone figure sat upon a plush chair brought into that foul space, tucked into the damp corner of slick rock and rusted iron— far enough away from the acrid stench of the mage whose captivity did not allow for bathing. Eyes bore into the rocking form as though the observer could learn the secrets of that dark magic simply by watching as they were spun from nothing.

Slamming his hands upon the rough wood, Xander lunged backward, the tendons in his neck bursting in stark relief as wide eyes stared into the nothingness above him. His voice rose, seeming to double and treble, growing louder, the din forcing the man who sat but a short distance away to cover his ears. Words spat from a mouth of rotted teeth, vile and vicious, curling in the air, thick with meaning and malice.

The noises reached an impossible crescendo as the watcher pressed his fists against his skull to escape them.

And then, abruptly, it stopped.

Silence smothered every sound, even the rapid breathing of the figure whose aching fists dropped to his lap. Slumping upon on his worn stool, Xander dropped his head, the hood of his cloak wrapped itself around his face, embracing its master like a thing half alive. The watcher lowered his hands, flexing fingers that had grown rigid under the onslaught of what had transpired only moments before.

In an otherworldly voice, the mage hissed, "The Aos Sí have risen. Look to Dorcha Wood. The daughter of Erabel has come. But do not fool thyself into thinking she is easy prey. The Cù-Sìth protect her, and her lost kin are assembling. They are of one mind. One purpose."

"Tell me," snarled Lord Darragh.

"Vengeance."

CHAPTER ONE

rulan tore through the low hanging branches, limbs that reached out to snag Fiadh's clothing and flesh as she clung to his back. He stretched his legs, claws gouging the earth, tearing chunks of soil and debris and sending them hurtling in his wake. Fiadh, head pressed against the base of his skull, gripped his fur until her knuckles turned white, the joints standing out in stark relief beneath the grime that coated them. Her eyes were clenched against the world, too grief-stricken to watch their violent passage through landscapes she had traveled but days before, days that had not held such wrenching heartache. Behind her closed lids, Fiadh saw Gideon's face, his mask of betrayal, his venomous expression, and the words. Words, spoken with such malevolence that their memory sent spasms of pain and anguish through her body.

What was left for her now? Mother was gone, murdered by the people of Felmore when they imagined villainy in the good works of a woman. They had turned on Riona, unleashing a vengeance so great that her mother had burned within their rage, torched upon a platform that had gone from innocuous to evil in the span of a heartbeat.

And Gideon.

She had found him just beyond the wood, wounded and too weak to go on, needing to be nursed by herself and Riona. She had given him everything: her heart, her love, her soul. And, for his part, he had taken her broken spirit and offered her a chance at a new life, one she had tenuously reached for, only to have it ripped from her grasp as her fingers held its fragile promise.

Everything was gone. The life she knew. A future with a man who had awakened a part of her she had never known. Gone. All that remained was the cold hut of her youth, an empty shell of the warmth it used to hold. Thinking of that barren hearth, the silence of that small space which had once held so much laughter and love, sent flares of resentment coursing through her. *I should have left him to his fate,* Fiadh thought. If she had walked away, would Mother still be alive? She could be wandering the woods, communing with the creatures that lived there, ignorant of feelings that refused to be ignored now that they had been aroused. But there was no turning back. The dead could not be resurrected. Love that had felt the fatal bite of betrayal could not be revived.

Fiadh reached beyond herself, feeling the strength of Dorcha Wood in her veins. The voices of all manner of life flared in her mind, so clear, as they had always been. Focusing on that subtle flow of power, she sent thoughts into the ether, calling to the mother of all things. *Danu,* her mind pleaded, *everything is lost, as I am lost. Help me.*

The wind whipping through her hair as Krulan's stride broke through trees and brush took on a new quality. No longer random, it began to coalesce, funneling around her even as she moved at speeds that brought waves of dizziness when she opened her eyes. The air itself seemed to whisper, washing over her scalp with tingling awareness, smoothing her worried brow in sweeps of movement so at odds with their frantic race through the forest.

Fiadh's heart stuttered, its rhythm becoming fragmented as she took in the sensations. *Great Mother. Show me the way.*

Fear not, the wind sighed, lashing softly against her with a warmth that contrasted with the air around her. Fiadh let herself go, her weight and worry leaching into Krulan, through his pelt and muscle, into his heart where he felt it and took it in.

All will be well, little one, his mind called to her.

And, at that moment, she believed it. She had to believe because to go down the path of misery that was set before her could only lead to ruin.

Deeper into Dorcha Wood they traveled, past game trails and small bodies of water that few but Fiadh had explored and into its forbidden heart. The landscape changed with subtle shifts, shadows eclipsed weak rays of light that pierced the branches overhead.

Where are you taking me? Fiadh asked, turning her head to the side, her voice muffled against dense fur as she peered from weary eyes.

Erabel, Krulan told her, the echo of his thought resonating through her mind.

Her chest clenched for a moment. *Are you inviting me into your territory?*

Erabel does not belong to my kind. We are but the keepers of it. It is the realm of the Aos Sí. The kingdom lost to them in the time of the Great War.

Fiadh gaped. *What? Is it not Cù-Sìth land? I thought…*

There is much you do not know, but the time has come for you to learn.

I don't… this makes no sense. Humans may enter the realm of the Aos Sí? Wouldn't places like that be protected? she asked.

Awful visions of her body torn asunder flooded her mind as she imagined being repelled by some unseen force that protected such a sacred place from interlopers. Stories spun from the lips of countless tellers, paraded through her head. Tales of horror and wonder that had reached her young ears as she sat hidden within Dorcha Wood, spying on village life she could never be part of. All of those tellings ended in a bloody culmination. Men and elves were two peoples whose history had tainted any possible future.

And she was caught in the middle, in a sticky web of secrets that Krulan had hinted at but not divulged. Unable to enter the close-minded society of Felmore, shut out of a future with Gideon in Belfirth, reluctant to begin years of isolation in the small hut she had called home, Fiadh had no place in the world.

Krulan was taking her to a location so forbidden that its name had been buried in a bloody history when elven culture was wiped from the earth. Erabel. That mysterious realm could not possibly be her future.

You may enter, Krulan said matter-of-factly, offering no reasoning. Just the simple statement as though that would ease her lingering worry.

Fiadh thought about the meaning behind the words and offered, *So, any human may safely cross into that place?*

Not… exactly, he replied.

Kept behind a mental barrier where Fiadh could not hear him, Krulan's thoughts churned as he wondered if she would guess the truth of it. Riona had entered those sacred lands, not because she was Aos Sí, but for the purity of her human heart, her connection with Danu. Humans called the goddess their Great Mother, but, for most, those words were an echo of what they had once been. Long ago, mankind had become separate, turning their backs on their mother. Unfortunately, they were not the only ones to do so.

Fiadh wanted to grind her teeth in frustration at his cryptic response but huffed instead, turning her face back into his fur. The coarse texture abraded her skin, but it was a good pain. It kept her grounded as his body swayed with his pounding feet. *I cannot tell if your words are meant to ease my worry or spawn more questions. I do not understand this. I have no place in your world, yet you insist I am somehow part of it. It makes no sense.*

All will be revealed by those whose knowledge surpasses human understanding. You will be safe.

Was he suggesting the Aos Sí lived? If so, Fiadh had to wonder how they had survived and where they had hidden for decades, unseen and growing in numbers so vast that they slaughtered hardened warriors like a scythe through stalks of wheat. She had not found a slain elf among the masses that littered the earth beyond the borders of Gideon's home. Not one. Had none been killed? Or had they taken their dead, ferrying them away to some hidden place?

People were told the Aos Sí had been killed. Lord Darragh even outlawed telling stories of them. To speak of them was to court death, she told him.

Burying the truth does not alter its veracity.

Then, Erabel was a kingdom of the Aos Sí, and some survived? Do they still live there?

None reside within its boundaries, but they are coming. I feel it in the wind. I sense it in the thrum of hooves behind me.

Fiadh arched her body, craning her neck to look behind her, scanning the blurring landscape for movement as she was jostled. Her head began to swim the longer she held the position as she strained to see something beyond the rush of forest on all sides. Waves of dizziness, as foliage became chaotic swirls of texture and colors, caused her stomach to begin to heave. Clutching Krulan around his neck, she hugged herself to him, pressing herself so tightly against him that, for a moment, they became one. The beat of his heart. The pull of his lungs. The tightening and release of his powerful muscles. And then the connection severed, leaving her feeling a rush of air upon her back once more.

Is someone following us, Krulan? she asked, her thoughts strangely lethargic.

There is one who follows.

Alarm flared, and her eyes popped open, which proved a

mistake as another bout of wooziness overcame her. Clenching them closed again, she asked, *Should I be afraid?*

You have nothing to fear. He has heard of your coming and is seeking you. But you will meet him in Erabel, not in the world of men.

Whoever is following us is Aos Sí? she questioned, fear lacing the thought.

He is.

Krulan's declaration did nothing to ease the worry that was now beginning to peak into panic. This was not right. She should not be here, perched on the back of a mythical animal from children's nightmares, followed by a being whose kind was supposed to have been exterminated long before she was born. The events that had led her to this moment tumbled through her mind, as did other memories. Her mother's worried face was prominent in flashes of recollection that collided with the harshness of recent events. Fiadh struggled to capture snippets of conversations from the past, those times when Mother's features had become guarded, as though a veil fell over her eyes, shutting away secrets that had never come to light.

Krulan, did you know my mother? His silence spoke loudly. The blood drained from Fiadh's face, and she felt cold and unsteady as she gripped his pelt. *Krulan?*

All will be revealed in time.

"I am done waiting!" she yelled, wrenching her body backward.

The motion brought Krulan to a sudden halt, sending Fiadh to the ground. She rolled and got to her knees, glaring at him. Then, balling her fists, she stood, feeling the strength of Dorcha Wood thrumming through her muscles as leaves and dirt began to churn at her feet. Within a part of her mind, she felt bear and wolf, hawk and badger, come to her as though she had called them without conscious thought. The sounds of their coming permeated the forest around the pair and, though they remained unseen, she could see that Krulan sensed them as well.

Do not set your beasts against me, Fiadh. It will do naught but get them killed.

She began to pace. *I have no desire to hurt you, Krulan, but I am weary of your half-truths.*

Krulan chuffed. *You are too impatient. Too naive.*

Her eyes flashed. "Do not speak to me as if I know nothing of the world! Mother protected me from much of it, that is true, but I am not some ignorant peasant. Why won't you just tell me whatever it is you've been hiding? I deserve to know!"

I cannot, Krulan told her, eyeing the disturbance of forest debris at her sides that had begun to form a tiny funnel.

The air around her settled as she heaved a mighty sigh. "What? Why?"

Many magics bind me. My place is to protect Erabel and... he paused, choosing the words carefully. *And Her people. It is not for me to share what you ask. However, if I am released from that bond, I will tell you all that I know.*

Fiadh made a face and looked around, noting the pointed snout of a badger poking through the underbrush. Crouching, she held out her hand, and they came to her. All of them, even a fox and wildcat she had not immediately felt within her mind. Each creature eyed Krulan, who stood stiff-legged, his yellow stare flicking from one animal to another. She sent them off, watching for a few moments as they melted into the trees.

Thank you for telling me that much, Krulan. Scanning the forest of her youth, she balled her hands into fists. *It's not good enough, though. You are leading me as though I am some beast of burden, a tethered horse with no mind or will.*

I bring you to your destiny.

"I will choose my fate, Krulan. Not you." She glared. "I am done being led at your whim, kept from the things you know and refuse to share." He growled, and she slashed her hand through the air. "I care nothing for whatever stills your tongue! I need to know why this happened to me! Why am I here? You know!" she yelled, jabbing her finger toward him. "You know, and you refuse to tell me! You're supposed to by my friend. You're all I—" she shook her head and gulped down the sob that threatened to crawl out of her throat.

Krulan huffed and bumped his head against her shoulder. *I am your friend.*

Friends don't keep secrets. Swallowing hard, she pinned him with her watery stare. *Do they?*

His eyes looked pained for a moment. *The secrets I keep are not mine to tell.* He watched her stride away, listening to her soft mutters. *I understand your frustration, Fiadh, but you have waited all the years of your life to hear what you seek. Another short span of time is not too much to ask.*

"I cannot accept that," she said, showing him her back.

Anger flashed in his yellow eyes as he straightened his massive body to his full height and stalked to her. She turned and took a step toward him, tilting her neck to meet his piercing stare.

You wish to know all?

She jerked her head in a curt nod.

Then await the one who follows.

She cast a glance over her shoulder, unease flashing across her features. *He comes? This man you spoke of?*

He is no spawn of mankind.

Fiadh glared at him. *You speak of my race as though we are little more than vermin.*

There is much you do not know.

"Then tell me! Why all the secrets?"

Krulan lowered his head until his muzzle was mere inches from hers. *I cannot break my vow. It is binding.*

She made a sound of frustration. *I feel trapped.*

I am sorry for that, but it changes nothing.

Her eyes flashed to his, lip curling. *You are making it very hard to like you.*

Krulan swung his head with a throaty growl. *So be it. Shall we carry on or stay and await him who follows?*

Fiadh paced with indecision. *The Aos Sí who follows…*

Aye?

Is he close?

We are farther ahead and will enter Erabel before he arrives if we leave now.

Releasing a long-suffering sigh, she climbed onto Krulan's back. *I am not giving up,* she reminded him.

He huffed and launched into a run. She let herself be caught in the rhythm of his strides, fighting the urge to look behind their racing forms, and tucked her forehead into Krulan's thick pelt, shutting her eyes from the world.

Could Riona have known of the Cù-Sìth? Memories of

the time Fiadh had begun to confess her first encounter with them floated through her head. Those confessions had always ended in silence, there on the tip of her tongue until any hint of it left her mouth as a shadow fell across Mother's face.

Had Mother, perhaps, been protecting her from Krulan himself? Had she somehow known whatever Krulan was hiding and chosen to keep it from her? Is that why so many questions had been diverted or simply cut off with no explanation? And, if so, why would she have felt the need to hide such things? They had lived an isolated life. Whom would Fiadh have told? It hurt to imagine something so profound hidden from her, but Fiadh had trusted her mother and knew that whatever was concealed, it must have been for a reason. Perhaps Mother would've one day confessed such things. She would never know.

Krulan's stride ate up the forest floor as he took her into the craggy hills that she hadn't dared enter since the first encounter with the Cù-Sìth years before. They had looked so massive as they emerged from the trees, menacing shadows that stood hulking over her as she waited for a death that never came. So much had changed since that day. Krulan's body coiled, leaping up steep climbs, sending shards of rock tumbling. Pressing her cheek into his fur, Fiadh watched the landscape change through squinted eyes. It appeared to grow more vibrant as they hurtled through the underbrush. She caught a sudden flash of movement and zeroed in on its location, trying to discern the shape beyond the shadows.

Fear not. That is Rivya.

Who?

My mate.

Fiadh leaned to the side, her eyes hopping from location to location, but their speed was too fast, and Rivya never came into the light. Abandoning her search, Fiadh shifted and listened to the steady pounding of paws upon the earth. Soon, a numbness crept over her body, beginning in the palms of her hands and spreading outward until her mind grew fuzzy. Eyes fluttering, she let out small meu as she slipped from the waking world and into another.

CHAPTER TWO

Murmuring filled her mind and brought Fiadh to awareness. Where there had been only Krulan, now there were others—male and female in tenor—creating a cacophony of thoughts. And beyond the Cù-Sìth were hundreds more, every lifeform, even the trees, adding to the din. It was beyond any connection she had felt in Dorcha Wood. Louder. Stronger. Her head buzzed with it, the clamoring making her mind flinch. Breathing deeply, with sounds like sleep, she shut them out until they became a dull hum and concentrated on what Krulan and his pack passed rapidly from one to the other.

Reluctant to reveal her awareness to them, Fiadh quieted her mind, trapping her thoughts in a web, and focused on the content of their speech. Krulan's voice was distinct, not only for its familiarity but within its quality, as though the weight of his rank imbued the tone of his thoughts with authority.

Veren has crossed the border. The time has come.

Fiadh didn't recognize the speaker. Its deep resonance. Its overt maleness. Cracking her left eye, she steadied her breathing in the slow rhythms of slumber as she spied on the Cù-Sìth that formed a loose circle a short distance away. The musk of their bodies filled her nose, and her nostrils twitched, not in distaste so much as a desire to inhale air that wasn't infused with the heavy scent. They were massive, their greenish-black fur covering muscular bodies with broad chests and powerful muzzles. Long, bushy tails swept back and forth as they conversed silently, the only sounds were claws scraping the ground, and soft rumbles punctuating things said in their soundless dialogue.

She still bears the scent of the son of Belfirth and may not welcome Veren's presence. She is new to this world, young yet and untried. We should be cautious, a female told the assemblage.

There were soft growls followed by Krulan's concurrence. *Rivya speaks truth. The girl has been through much and is yet unaware of her heritage and all that comes with it. Her connection with Danu is tenuous. Now that she has come, it will grow, and that awareness and power must be nurtured if she is to reach her full potential.*

A male snarled. *You cannot keep her from Veren.*

Krulan swung his massive head toward the Cù-Sìth who stood across from him. His wolf-like body seemed to grow, shoulders stiffened, legs elongated until Krulan looked down on the almost equally muscular beast who had spoken. *Do you accuse me of refusing to fulfill my vow, Vaymir?*

A tense silence filled her mind as all voices stopped, waiting for the outcome of the confrontation. Vaymir's yellow eyes swung past the others in a rapid sweep before resting again on Krulan. *I make no such accusation.* The statement was followed by a lowering of his head and torso in a bow of obeisance.

When the girl has risen and been fed, they will meet, and we will stand with her.

A rumble of agreement followed this pronouncement. The Cù-Sìth slowly broke away from the gathering. Their hulking bodies swallowed into the undergrowth as though they had never been. In moments, only Krulan and Rivya remained. Fiadh watched them surreptitiously from her prone position, marveling at the complex relationships between beings whose reputations labeled them as nothing more than mindless killers. Every snippet of information she had gleaned in her youth about these creatures was wrong. So many stories spun in the fearful hearts of men and spread from ear to ear until truth lay buried under layers of fear and hatred. She must have let down the veil hiding her thoughts because Krulan's ears swung back, followed quickly by his head. He pinned her to the ground with his golden stare, sending pulses of thought into her mind.

I sense that you have heard much. A low growl emanated from his chest. *It appears you are learning to mask your awareness from me. Interesting.*

If he wore the face of a man, an eyebrow would've cocked as he looked down at her. As it was, the muscles beneath the thin layer of fur covering his features shifted and settled as he slowly approached. Quickly sifting through the last few minutes, she couldn't recall how she'd shut her mind from Krulan. It had simply been a desire to do so. It confused her to hear him imply that blocking her thoughts was curious.

Shrugging, Fiadh levered herself into a sitting position and rose to meet him, her heart thundering as Rivya trailed his form. It was not fear that coursed through her veins as the two regal creatures crossed the distance and stopped before her, their heads lowered to look into her face. Rather, it was the knowledge that she stood on an invisible precipice, and all she need do was leap into its vastness to find the truth that had lain hidden.

As you have heard, Krulan began with a wolfy smirk. *Veren has come. He awaits you.*

Fiadh looked from Rivya to Krulan. *Am I to know who that is?*

He is Aos Sí, from the realm of the Oadsera.

The air around her thinned as names and places that she had never heard of sank their teeth into her mind. *What? Who? You're speaking in riddles.*

You wish to know what I am bound to keep hidden?

She nodded slowly.

Veren shall tell you.

Fiadh let out a puff of air. *Fine.* She absently rubbed her palms on the dirty fabric of her woolen dress. A fine layer of grime coated her hands when she realized what she was doing. Grimacing, she looked at Krulan. *I'm filthy. Is there a pool of water nearby? I would like to bathe.*

They glanced at one another before Rivya stepped forward. *I am Rivya, mate of Krulan. I will take you.*

She looked at the female Cù-Sìth. *I am Fiadh.*

Rivya gave a throaty chuckle. *Aye, I know who you are.*

"I wish I knew as much as you both seem to," Fiadh said, frowning.

Ignoring her comment, the Cù-Sìth asked, *Have you no other coverings?*

Fiadh sighed. *I have nothing but what you see.* She spread her arms in defeat. All her possessions lay scattered on the hill overlooking Belfirth, abandoned when she fled from Gideon's anger.

Very well. Come.

The Cù-Sìth nudged her arm, then looked at her mate, sending him some message Fiadh could not discern. Turning her head, she watched Krulan leap away, eating up the ground beneath his paws until he disappeared in the distance. *How far must we travel?*

Rivya eyed the clusters of trees. *Not far. Do you wish to hurry?*

I wish to dispense with the secrets Krulan keeps hidden.

You have a fire in you, Rivya observed.

Fiadh shot her a look of surprise.

It is good. You will need it.

Fiadh followed the Cù-Sìth, curiosity overpowering the frustration burning in her heart. The landscape beneath ancient bowers was rich and, though it remained hidden from view, teeming with life. She reached out her senses, as she had always done, and sent tendrils of thought, waiting for them to be caught by whatever moved through the brush and towering arms of the trees. From a low branch arching over her head, came a response, a soft caw. Fiadh stopped and looked up, a crooked smile splitting her lips as she spied a beautiful, black raven perched above, staring at her. Bobbing its head and shuffling its feet along the limb, it sent her a series of unusual calls. She cocked her head, listening with more than her ears, marking the violet glow from the animal's eyes as it held her in its gaze.

"Dasha? Is that your name?" Fiadh asked, forgetting for a moment that Rivya was by her side.

The raven flapped its wings and tapped at the branch in a series of rapid knocks. She laughed, the sound filling the forest for a moment before it was lifted into the air and carried away. Swooping in a graceful dive, Dasha circled her head, releasing a garbled collection of croaks and gurgles. Fiadh listened to the sounds and tried to make sense of them. Dasha canted his wings, landed on the ground at Fiadh's feet, and stalked toward her, leaning his head forward in invitation.

She crouched, running her fingers through his dark plumage. "Does this mean we're friends?"

Dasha clacked his beak, inching closer and tilting his head to the side, the purplish hue of his irises holding her fast. Time stopped as though the forest held its breath, and in those moments, Fiadh's mind fused with Dasha's, forming a link so intimate that her perspective shifted, and she suddenly saw her face looking down at her. The sensation threw her off balance, and she toppled to the side, her stare fixed on the raven who crept closer, giving off high-pitched croaks that suddenly had meaning. Tearing her attention from him for a moment, she looked at Rivya.

"What just happened? It was like I was... him."

That is the bond.

Fiadh's mouth worked for a moment. "Bond?" Her eyes swept back to Dasha, who waited patiently at her feet, beak opening and closing with tiny huffs.

It has come to pass many times. The bond is a connection unto each other.

Why hasn't this happened to me before? I've always had a link with the animals of Dorcha Wood.

Rivya's lips twitched and curled, teeth flashing along her muzzle. *You are awakening.*

"Huh. That really doesn't explain anything," she muttered, watching Dasha hop in a circle, wings partially open. The bird stepped closer, nudging his head into her hand that dangled from her leg. She rubbed along the edges of his beak and behind the hidden canals of his ears, watching as his feathers puffed in ecstasy. "This bond, is it like a mate? I mean… not like *that*… but somewhat the same?"

Aye. I suppose that is one way to describe it. Rivya sat next to her, tail sweeping across the ground in a wide arc. *Think of it as a kinship that is so strong you can share his mind. With training, I have seen some who could feel the earth beneath the paws of their kindred or the wind beneath its wings. Though*—Rivya paused, her thoughts flashes of awe and fear before she concealed them from Fiadh's mind.

Fiadh glanced at the still beast at her side. *What?*

Rivya's shoulders rolled in a shrug, the action awkward in her kind. *I admit that I have never seen a bond formed so quickly. It is… unusual.*

Dasha croaked softly in his throat and bobbed his head, causing Fiadh to smile, but the action was pained. *Am I? Is there something wrong with me?*

I am no healer to say if aught is wrong with you.

Fiadh rolled her eyes. *That's not what I meant.*

Aye, I know it. Rivya let out a sigh mixed with a soft growl. *I do not know what it means, but it is not a bad thing. The bond is pure. It is a gift that not all can experience.*

Do the Cù-Sìth have such bonds with other creatures?

The bond is not within our kind.

Then which kind? Humans?

Rivya hedged for a moment before answering. *The children of Danu.*

Danu. The Great Mother. Fiadh had always felt such love for her, that guiding hand throughout her life. Perhaps this *was* a gift, and she ought to be thankful, but secrets overshadowed the gravity of the moment. This place. Herself. The beast at her side. Even the raven. All were cloaked in a veil of secrecy, and she was tired of being left in the dark.

Everything was so different here, as though every lifeform was imbued with… something. Trees, shrubs, rocks, and earth filled the landscape, as it did throughout the Dorcha Wood, and yet each of these elements was unlike the forest of her youth. Fiadh's gaze swept the scenery as she attempted to distinguish what it was that felt so different, slowly realizing that the vibrancy of the colors surrounding her imbued everything with a depth and lifeforce unlike any she had seen or felt.

Rivya, why does this place feel so different?

It is Erabel. What you feel is an untainted land, free of the evils of mankind. It is the true realm of Danu, our Great Mother. The raven is one of her children, as are all living things within her kingdom.

You and Krulan seem to have a dim view of my people.

Rivya grumbled. *That is not… accurate.*

Cocking an eyebrow, Fiadh turned to her. *Oh? Please explain it then.*

I cannot.

She ground her teeth. *This is maddening. You both speak in riddles as though you wish to drive me mad.*

Like Krulan, I am bound. There are things I would share with you, Fiadh, but I cannot.

Fiadh nodded, though the motion was reflexive, not the surrender Rivya may have hoped for. Dasha sent her a chirping croak and flew into a nearby tree. Rising, Fiadh brushed the dirt off her soiled dress, keeping Dasha in her sights.

He will not stray far. Rivya rolled one of her huge yellow eyes toward Fiadh until she began to fidget.

What?

Try seeing through his eyes.

Fiadh made a face. *I don't know how I did that before. It just… I don't know. It just happened.* She shrugged and looked at Dasha, who had begun to bob his head.

A deep rumble vibrated through Rivya's chest. *Try.*

Focusing on Dasha, Fiadh reached her mind to him like she had done with the creatures of the forest all her life. The connection was instant and strong, causing her to suck in a startled breath. Closing her eyes, she sent Dasha a thought, a wish, a desire to see what he saw. The images began as blobs of color, fuzzy, indistinct, growing in clarity until she saw herself standing next to the huge Cù-Sìth. She gasped, body rocking, as Dasha turned his gaze to their surroundings, showing her the threads of the trail they had traveled among the trees. When he launched into the air, Fiadh's head spun. She flung out her arms for balance, finding Rivya's massive shoulder and clinging to it. Her body felt as though it were floating, though part of her mind sensed the earth beneath her feet. The forest, stretching to the horizon, swam behind her clenched eyelids. Dasha banked to the left, and her stomach heaved, severing their connection. Fiadh's knees buckled. Gripping Rivya's fur, she rested her head against the Cù-Sìth's side, panting as she tried to quell her roiling gut.

You have great power, young one.

"I don't—" she panted, *"feel powerful. I feel awful."*

Rivya chuckled, the sound almost human, though gruff and deep. *It will become easier.*

She craned her neck, keeping her cheek pressed to Rivya's thick fur, and watched as the raven swept through a break in the trees and landed on a branch. He cocked his head, studying her briefly before preening his feathers in a gesture so ordinary that, for a moment, it was as though she had imagined the link they had shared. But the illusion was shattered as he turned his head and caught her watching him. This was no ordinary raven. This was no ordinary forest. And, apparently, she was no ordinary person.

CHAPTER THREE

From the bluff overlooking Belfirth land, Gideon hadn't seen the bodies nor smelled the death that lingered in the air. But he could see them now, smell them now. Trees rustled while clothes, hanging from lines, swayed, flapping gently in the breeze. Beyond that, all was silent. Men, women, and children lay where they had fallen, most having taken refuge in their homes, bolting doors that an invading horde had caved in. It was a massacre. Poking his head into wattle and daub hut after hut, he found only half-eaten meals, overturned chairs, cold hearths, and trails of blackened blood leading to body after body. The beating heart of Belfirth was still. Fear and dread coursed through his veins, pushing him onward. Struggling on legs that scarcely remained upright, he yelled for his mother, his voice echoing through the inner bailey. There was no answer. Even the hounds lay dead.

The doors to the keep hung at awkward angles, having been battered open. The bodies of the few soldiers who had stayed behind to protect the castle when the army had gone to war lay in thick pools of dried blood, swords useless at their sides. Few showed signs of having hit their mark before the one who wielded it had been struck down. Gideon spun in a slow circle, his heart sinking with each breath. Making his way up the stone stairs to the upper level of the keep, he walked through numerous rooms, hardly seeing the bodies anymore, stopping when he stood in the solar. His mother's embroidery lay on the floor like a discarded child's toy. The needle, still attached to thread filling the frame, a pastoral scene depicting their land, lay winking in the light from the window. Bending low, he picked it up with shaking hands, unwelcome tears clouding his vision, as he strode to his mother's body a few paces away. Gideon sank to his knees, hoarse sobs filling the unnatural quiet, as he clutched her artwork to his chest and looked at her.

Tilting his head back, he let out a roar of anguish, cursing the Aos Sí, cursing everything and everyone who had kept him from his family as they were slaughtered. Fiadh's stricken face bloomed in his mind, and he clenched his teeth, smothering the affection he felt for her, twisting it into something cold. Hatred so fierce it made his muscles hot, flooded his body.

Whispering prayers to the Great Mother—the same entity worshipped by the hated Aos Sí—he leaned over and closed her eyes, which lay fixed, the soft gray of their stare leeched of life. Placing her embroidery upon her chest, he said his goodbyes, vowing vengeance for her brutal death, for the deaths of his brother and father. For the murder of all his people. Coming to his feet, he determined that this room would be her tomb as he didn't have the strength or will to carry her stiffened body to the crypt. Righting the damaged door and anchoring it to the frame, he pressed his hand to the wood, letting it limply fall as he turned and made his way to his bedroom.

Gideon's feet echoed in the quiet, and he paused as the oak door to Doran's room came into view. Pushing it open, his stomach clenched. His brother's chest of clothes stood open, rifled through before they had marched on Felraine Vale. The bedding was still bunched and rumpled, visible between the heavy curtains surrounding the frame to keep the chill out. Stepping inside, he walked to the open chest and looked at Doran's possessions, smiling sadly when he spied the hilt of the wooden sword he had made for his brother on his sixth birthday poking through piles of clothing and trinkets. He leaned forward and tugged it free, running his hands along the blade, feeling where countless blows had marred the wood. Happier times. Never again would he hear his brother's laughter or see his shadow striding at his side. Tucking the sword into folds of clothing, he closed the lid, the soft thump filling the quiet with finality. With muffled footfalls, he walked to the door, looking back for a moment before shutting it, knowing he would never set foot in that space again.

Gideon stared about the dim hallway, trying to piece together what may have happened here following the battle with the Aos Sí. The elven army had come, though it was horribly clear that the attack was only a few days old. For whatever reason, they had waited rather than storming Belfirth immediately after the battle, which decimated his father's army. If only he hadn't found himself on Darragh's land, wounded and senseless. If he had left that accursed wood and the woman it held and gone home, perhaps he could've warned them, done something. But his mind had not been his own as he left the battlefield and wandered onto Lord Darragh's lands in search of a woman the elven king had wanted within his grasp. Daggers of blame found their mark in Fiadh, though common sense told him she had nothing to do with the slaughter. If not for her… if he had come sooner, not let her keep him those extra few days, then maybe… maybe… he shook his head, a quaky sob catching in his chest.

Had anyone been able to sound the alarm when the Aos Sí attacked? The thought made him pause. There were so many bodies, but he began to wonder if some of his people may have seen the danger coming and hidden somewhere, perhaps in one of the caves carved into Viliock Mountain. Picking up his pace, he strode with renewed determination to his bedroom and rummaged through his trunk, pulling out a fresh set of clothing, a warm cloak, and a leather satchel into which he stuffed a few spare items.

He stopped at the larder in the kitchen, grabbed food-stuffs that had not soured, and headed to the armory. Gideon chose a quiver, arrows, and bow, then slung every-thing onto his back. Looking toward the stables, he cocked his head, listening. From their depths, he heard rustling. Pulling his blade from its sheath, he quietly set his baggage on the ground and stalked to the stable entrance. Shadows filled the space, coating the smell of old hay and horse drop-pings in a film of darkness. He darted inside, pressing his back to the wall as soft thumps carried to his ears. Gripping the hilt of his blade, Gideon ran toward the noise, his feet pressing firmly on the dirt floor with little sound to mark his passing. At the end of a row of stalls came a loud snuffling, stopping him in his tracks. The sword lowered as disbelief filled his mind.

"Aridius?" he called out.

A low nicker answered him, and he watched, mouth gaping, as his warhorse stepped from his stall. Aridius trotted to Gideon with a whinny, rubbing his forehead against his master, trying to relieve an itch under the leather strap of his bridle. Hands shaking, Gideon rubbed the horse, speaking softly as he removed tack the poor animal had been wearing since it had fled the battlefield. Patches of skin, rubbed raw from days and nights wearing the stiff leather, marred the gelding's black coat. Picking up a currying comb and a jar of ointment, Gideon treated the wounds and brushed the horse, speaking softly as his hands stroked the animal's familiar body.

"How did you come to be here, my friend?"

In response, Aridius nickered and grunted, the sounds bringing a smile to Gideon's face. Fetching water, oats, and fresh hay, Gideon settled in while the horse had his fill after days of little to sustain him. When finished eating, the animal was led to a grassy area away from the corpses and blood, well beyond the outer bailey, where he rolled for a solid span of minutes, rubbing all the sore and itchy areas. Gideon watched, taking heart in the sight. If Aridius had survived and found his way home, perhaps there would be others.

Tethering the horse in a patch of shade at the base of the mountain, he took off into the forest, unease washing over him at the closeness of the trees, the noises of unseen things scurrying about in the underbrush. The deep shadows all around him could be hiding an Aos Sí scout. The hair on his nape prickled, and he held his breath, eyes darting, but there was nothing more than the beasts of the forest and rustle of leaves in the wind. The ground was steep as he began his ascent, straining his leg, and he often stumbled, cursing himself for his weakness. Halfway up, he stopped and rubbed his leg, feeling the lump of cloth from Fiadh's dressing beneath the fabric of his leggings. An image of her soft smile flared in his mind, followed by a lump of regret. He struggled for a few moments to dispel the vision and all that came with it. Looking at his leg, his hand shook as he made to lower his leggings and rip the dressing from his body, but he clenched his fist and left it.

The trek to the first cave was slow and laborious. Peering into the darkness, he looked for signs of movement, tilting his head to listen but hearing nothing beyond the trill of birds in the woods surrounding the opening.

"Hello?" he called out, wincing as his voice echoed in the darkness. Minutes passed with no reply. Stepping inside the mouth of the cave, he called again. Silence.

Turning away, Gideon made his way to the two remaining caves, his guts knotting with each step. Sweat poured down his face, his limbs shaking so violently he wondered if they would give out beneath him as he struggled up the final leg to the largest of the caves and the most remote. If he had fled a horde of elves, this is where he would have come. Tucked beneath the boughs of a massive oak, the opening of the cave looked like a jagged wound in the rock. Wide at the base, it tapered to a narrow crack that spanned the height of three men before becoming solid stone. Ducking his head, Gideon entered the cave, stopping just inside to allow his eyes to grow accustomed to the darkness.

"Is anyone there? It is Gideon," he said into the dark. From the depths of the cave came a scuffling, like that of a body brushing against a gritty surface. "Hello?"

Shuffling footfalls came to his ears as hope flared. Waiting for what felt too long, he was rewarded by the sight of a young girl. Casting his eyes around her shaking form, he looked for another individual, but all was silent and still behind her. Kneeling, he held out his hand and coaxed her to him. She looked uncertain for a moment, then flung herself into his arms, her body quaking with sobs. Picking her up, Gideon left the cave and carried her to an overturned log a short distance away.

"What is your name, little one?"

"Aishling," she whispered.

"Where is your family?"

She shrugged, sniffling with wet tears, and picked at her dress—a coarse gown streaked with layers of dirt and smelling of urine. Gideon looked her over, taking in her fair face and youth. She couldn't be much more than six. A memory stirred. He recalled seeing her playing in the bailey with a boy not much older than she. "Have you a brother?"

Aishling nodded. "Keiran."

"And where is he?"

She looked toward the woods. "He left for food. We were hungry."

Gideon's heart picked up speed. "Were others with him?"

"At first, but they fell down, and then it was just Keiran and me. Papa said to run and hide."

Masking his disappointment, he asked, "How old are you, Aishling?" She held up five fingers. He grimaced. She's too little to tell me much of anything, he thought, then said, "When did Keiran leave?"

"He said to wait in the cave." She glanced back at its entrance. "I don't like the dark."

"When did your brother leave to find food, Aishling?"

"Today?" she said in a tiny, lilting voice.

She's so young, Gideon thought and sighed with frustration. Trying to get anything out of her could be difficult. "Today? Keiran went to find food today?"

"Maybe it was yesterday."

He closed his eyes, resisting the urge to pinch the bridge of his nose. Aishling sat on his lap, tracing her fingers along the stag that made up the family crest on his armor. Her small, soiled gown felt damp, whether from moisture or something else, he didn't know, but he could feel it seeping through his leggings. She needed a bath, a clean dress, and food. Looking toward the base of the mountain, he contemplated taking her to the castle.

As if to confirm his thinking, she whined, "My tummy hurts. I'm hungry," she said again.

Reaching into his satchel, Gideon pulled out a loaf of bread and a small wheel of cheese he'd grabbed from the larder. Tearing off a hunk of each, he passed them to her, pulling her hand away from her mouth when she began to stuff the food between her lips. "Slow down before you choke."

She nodded, chewing slowly before swallowing what was in her mouth. Gideon watched her nibble the remains of the food he had given, his mind racing as he considered how she had come to be here alone.

When she had her fill, Aishling looked around, eyes fastening on his satchel. "I'm thirsty."

He took his leather wineskin, which he'd filled with water from the castle's well, and offered it to her. Aishling took a long pull, wiping her hand across her mouth when she'd finished. "Are you taking me to papa now?"

"Nay. Which way did your brother go?"

She pointed, fear making her features spasm.

Lifting her from his lap, he set her on the ground and said, "Stay here while I find your brother."

Her face crumpled, bottom lip began quivering. "Keiran left. He didn't come back."

Gideon took her by the shoulders. "I'm going to come back, Aishling. I promise." She gulped and nodded. "Have you been alone for a long time?"

"It got dark out," she said in her tiny voice. "The dark is scary."

Trying to piece together how long she'd been alone was a struggle, but he realized it might have been more than a day, and if that were true… he sighed. "I'm sorry Keiran didn't come back, but I will return, all right?" He wanted to find the other child and leave this place. Already, he could feel the weight of an assessing stare, though no matter how hard he looked, he saw nothing but forest.

Her eyes glistened with tears, but she held herself together, impressing him. Nodding, Aishling let go of his hand as he rose, craning her neck to look at him. She was so small. He couldn't care for her, and there was no one left to take her in, but he certainly wouldn't leave her to her fate up here on the mountain. It was a quandary. He shook his head, putting the worry aside. "I will be gone a short time while I look for your brother. You stay just inside the cave," he said, jerking his head toward it.

She padded to the entrance, looking back at him before stepping into the darkness, legs trembling. "Maybe his hurts got bad. Do you have hurts?"

"Hurts?"

Nodding, she pointed to her shoulder. "Where the arrow got stuck."

His mouth dropped, and he strode to her. "Keiran was struck with an arrow?"

"Aye. When we ran away. Papa said to run." Aishling looked to the side for a moment. "Mama wouldn't get up. Is she still sleeping?"

Gideon's heart sank. Nay, he wanted to tell her. "Aishling, how did Keiran get hurt?"

"They had arrows. People fell down a lot."

"Who had arrows?"

She shrugged. "Lots of people. They looked funny. Keiran made me leave." Putting a dirty knuckle in her mouth, she said, "Papa said go." She paused, her face puckering before she whispered, "I maybe cried."

If Keiran was struck with one of their arrows, he was likely past saving. Gideon grimaced as he remembered the effects of their poison-laced blades, how it stung and left him writhing. Aos Sí arrowheads were likely no different. A child would not live long if wounded by one.

Herding Aishling into the cave, Gideon gave a final reassurance and struck off in search of the girl's brother. It didn't take long to find his tracks. Following them, he came across the boy lying on his side beneath a lip of rock. His back was caked in blackened blood from a wound on his shoulder where the broken haft of an arrow jutted through the fabric of his tunic. There was no movement. His lips twisted in anger and sorrow. Too young. Kneeling by the boy's body, he said a small prayer to the Great Mother, then cast about for some branches to cover his form. It wouldn't keep scavengers away for long, but staying to build him a small cairn felt too risky. The forest was closing in on him, feeling more dangerous with every moment, and he acknowledged that Aos Sí scouts could be prowling the mountain, picking off any who survived and came out of hiding. He needed to get to open ground, away from the woods.

As he trekked back to the cave, he tried to piece together what Aishling had experienced. It sounded as though his worst fears had come to pass. Belfirth's folk had no warning when the Aos Sí army swarmed their land. From what the girl had said and the evidence he'd seen, the elves slaughtered everyone, even children. It was monstrous. How Aishling and her brother had managed to escape when no others had was a mystery. Reaching the cave, he called out to her, girding himself for the inevitable task of trying to explain Keiran wasn't coming back.

Aishling emerged, looking about for her brother. "Where's Keiran?"

"He's gone, Aishling. Your brother is with your mother and father now."

She looked confused. "Why didn't he come back?"

He swallowed hard. "He couldn't. Let's go now," he said, holding out his hand. She took it, though her eyes kept darting to the forest as though she expected to see her family emerge from the trees.

"Did they take him too?"

Gideon paused. "Take him?"

Aishling nodded, her eyes huge saucers. "They taked one. The funny-looking people."

"Who did they take?" he asked, grabbing her thin shoulders. She tried to pull away, fear washing over her features. Loosening his hold and masking his emotions, Gideon repeated the question with a tempered voice. "Who did the strange people take?"

She shrugged. "He was big like you. But old."

Her description did nothing to narrow down who may have been captured. Gideon flipped through his memories of the bodies strewn about the great hall. Was anyone of importance missing? He shook his head. There were so many bodies. He couldn't even recall identifying any of them in his haste to find his mother. "Aishling, I need you to think about what you saw. Did the funny-looking people take someone from the village or the castle?"

"I seen him in the castle. He had gray hair."

"Was he a soldier, like me?"

Cocking her head, she considered him. "His belly was big," she said, puffing her cheeks and sweeping her hands out from her middle, "he was bossy. Keiran likes to boss me."

Faces and forms raced through his mind, stopping as one was snagged and held. His steward? Could she be talking about Reece? She wouldn't know the man by his name, but the description fit. What would the Aos Sí want with his steward? The man was hardly a target for ransom, not that they would be interested in holding him captive for coin. Reece managed the estate and knew every detail of its management… Gideon sucked in a breath. Reece would be a wealth of information should an Aos Sí army wish to march on other fiefdoms. He knew the inner workings of Belfirth, from the structure of the castle to the running of the lands, and had often met with other lords who visited the castle when he, his father, and brother were on a campaign. If the Aos Sí wanted to storm another holding by exploiting its weakest points, who better to tell them where and when to attack than a steward?

CHAPTER FOUR

They traveled down the mountainside, Gideon on edge at their slow pace. Just before leaving the edge of the forest, he knelt in front of Aishling. "I'm going to pick you up and take you into the castle."

"I don't want to go," she whimpered.

Gideon knelt, taking her small hands in his. "It'll be alright. I will be with you."

Aishling darted a glance toward the opening in the trees where the castle grounds lay, huge trusting eyes looking up at him. "There's bad people there."

"The bad people are gone. I promise. It's safe now." He tugged at her, impatient, but she stood rooted.

"I'm scared," she confessed, whispering the words.

"I know you are, but there is naught to be scared of. Do you think the bad people would dare show themselves with me at your side?" he asked, making his chest swell and putting a grim expression on his face.

She gave him a wobbly smile. "Nay. Have you a sword?"

He slid it from the scabbard, pushing her hand away when she tried to touch the blade. "Careful, it's sharp."

Gideon let her look it over, then replaced the blade and picked her up. "You must close your eyes."

"Why?"

He wracked his brain for a moment. "Because we are going through a secret passage. Do you know what a secret is?"

She nodded. "I have a secret. Want to hear it?"

Gideon grimaced. "It wouldn't be a secret if you told me. Now, close your eyes."

Aishling did as she was told, and he cradled her against his chest, stalking from the trees and into the open land surrounding the castle. Bodies lay scattered. "Are you keeping your eyes closed tight?"

"Aye," she said, then wriggled. "It smells bad."

"I know."

"What is that smell?" she asked, reaching a hand between their bodies to plug her nose.

"Nothing you need worry about," he told her, his eyes skittering from those of a dead woman who lay on her back. "Don't open your eyes. We're almost to the secret passage."

Gideon halted momentarily as they passed into the great hall, trying to recall where his young cousins had stayed when they came to visit. Once inside the room, he bolted the door and set Aishling on her feet. She opened her eyes and smiled at him. "I didn't peak once!"

"Aye, I know it. You did well."

She puffed up her chest and looked around. "Is Papa here?"

"Your family is gone, Aishling." Gideon watched her mull that over, hoping she'd make sense of it while dreading the tears that may follow.

"I won't see them again?"

He shook his head. "Let's get you some fresh clothes and be on our way."

"Are they dead?"

Gideon sighed, shoulders sagging. "Aye."

A sob shook her chest, followed by the tears he knew would come. Wondering briefly if he should hug her, he settled for patting her back awkwardly, letting her cry for a few minutes, and wiping away the mucus that dripped from her nose with the cuff of his sleeve. It didn't last long, and Gideon said nothing more about it. Helping her tug off her soiled clothes, he gave her a new set, slipping the tiny shift and tunic over her frail shoulders before handing her stockings and helping to lace a pair of soft leather boots. Riffling through the remaining items, Gideon pulled out a woolen shawl, knowing she'd need it at night, then rose.

"It's time to go."

Aishling took his hand and let him lift her into his arms, burying her face beneath his chin.

"Are your eyes closed?"

She nodded, having remained quiet since receiving the news about her family, and he walked out, closing more than the door softly behind him.

Leaving the land of his birth left a hot coal of hatred in Gideon's chest. It burned with every step they traveled, scorching him until his mouth felt dry with a thirst for retaliation. He would avenge his people.

His steward, Reece, would likely be dead. Not that he had the power to rescue him from the Aos Sí if they'd truly captured him. But if they had taken him, the steward could provide valuable information to an invading force, having been privy to everything from the size of holdings to close allies. The steward was loyal, a good man, but not loyal enough to withstand whatever horrors and tortures Rygeil's folk would use to extract the information they needed. Others should be warned, but he was one man and, with a small child, he could do naught but get them both killed, for he would not leave the girl behind. Pulling on Aridius' reins, Gideon halted their progress and considered where to go. He could travel south to Taigon and seek an audience with King Stephan, but that man was weak and twisted and had no love for the rulers of Belfirth after a particularly vicious confrontation his father had over taxation that had hobbled his people. Besides, the wheels of the monarchy turned slowly, with too much talk among advisors and no action. He had not the time nor patience to wait for weeks while the king discussed whether or not to heed Gideon's warning. No, he would not go to the king.

Looking west, he squinted. The soldiers he and Fiadh had seen on their journey had been traveling toward Felmore. As the strongest ruler of the western reaches and far from the recent slaughter, perhaps it was time he visited Lord Darragh and took the man's measure. If he was as ruthless as Fiadh and her mother had thought him to be, then all the better for it. It would take ruthless men to turn back these Aos Sí monsters now. And if Fiadh had fled to those foul woods she loved, the Great Mother help her, because he would not.

Nudging his steed's sides with the heels of his boots, they set off, Aishling clutching Aridius' mane as she sat in front of Gideon. Her eyes were wide as they left the bluff over-looking Belfirth's land, and he watched her try to look back once, twisting her body to see beyond his.

"There is nothing for you there, Aishling. You must look to the future, not the past."

She nodded, though he knew her understanding of the message in his words was lost on her.

As nightfall came, they made camp, Gideon teaching his small charge how to brush, feed, and water his mount. He made a small fire, roasting the hare his arrow had skewered earlier and watched Aishling poke at the coals with a long stick as she crouched by the flames.

"When will it be ready?"

He chuckled. The hare had cooked for only a few minutes. "When the fat drips and the flesh browns, it will be ready. Keep turning the spit, but mind your tunic."

She scooted forward, tucking the hem of her clothing over her knees. "Mama only let Keiran mind the fire."

"Hm. Well, I think you're old enough to learn the way of it."

Giving him a shy smile, she reached for the end of the spit and turned it, shooting Gideon glances as she awaited his nod to stop the rotation. "Well done, Aishling."

They sat listening to the snap and pop of the fire, its glow bouncing off features layered in grief and fatigue. When the food was ready, Gideon showed her how to use a small knife to slice the meat from the bone. She was a ready learner, though he acknowledged she was likely too young to do any of what he was teaching on her own. They ate in silence, licking meaty juices off their fingers until there was nothing left of the meal.

Aishling cast her eyes about, zeroing in on his satchel. "Have you any cheese and bread?"

"Aye, but we must save it for tomorrow."

She frowned. "I'm still hungry."

"As am I, but we need food for the morning." She sighed, and he continued, "We are near Lord Crommack's land, and there we'll gather more food before we move on. Maybe their cook will give you a sweet."

"Sometimes Keiran and I would make a honey pull."

"Oh, aye? My brother and I did that too, though I always ended up getting stung."

She giggled. "You got to use smoke first, silly. It makes them sleepy."

"Ah, that must have been what I did wrong."

She scrunched her shoulders with pride at having taught such a strong man something. "Bees don't sting me. We're friends, and they don't mind sharing their honey. They don't like Keiran, though."

Gideon smiled as she rambled on about her many escapades. If this small child survived, he knew others must have as well, and perhaps one day he would find them and rebuild Belfirth to its former glory. But that future would never come to pass as long as elves and their creatures roamed the earth. He would use Lord Darragh and the strength of his soldiers until the work was done and that vile race obliterated.

The soft sound of Aishling's yawn pulled him from his thoughts. "Come," he said, shaking out a blanket and laying on the ground. "It has been a long day and we must rest."

He tucked her into the folds of the fabric. "Goodnight, Aishling."

Snaking a hand from beneath the covers, she grabbed his wrist as he made to rise. "Will you tell me a story?"

"A story?"

"Aye, Mama always told me one when I was scared so I could sleep."

He made a face, unsure if he'd be able to dredge up one of the tales his mother had recited when he and Doran were boys. Settling next to her, he rested his hands on his knees and wracked his brain, finally landing on one about a waterhorse. It was a fanciful story of a young boy who'd taken his father's boat without permission and become stranded during a violent storm. As the story went, a waterhorse came to his rescue as waves toppled his tiny craft, plunging him into the frigid lake. The creature took him to shore, and from that day on, the boy would visit his rescuer, often riding on its back. It was a friendship that lasted a lifetime, and when the boy had grown into an old man, he came to the waterhorse one last time, clinging to the back of the creature and disappearing beneath the surface forever.

Aishling's eyes fluttered closed as he finished the telling. He watched her sleep, feeling the gravity of the responsibility he'd taken on by bringing her with him. She had become a link to his past, and though she wasn't family, he had no one else, and neither did she. Listening to her slumber reminded him of another's soft sounds of sleep. Memories of Fiadh clouded his mind, hours and days spent together threatening to encompass him fully. He slammed a mental shield down, severing them from conscious thought. Though, they lingered in parts of him he couldn't reach, as if she had stained his very being with some elven sorcery, laid claim to him like a brand, burned so deep it couldn't be cut out. He wanted to free himself of it. Of her. And yet, part of him clung to her memory, aching for her sweet smile and soft touch, the taste of her mouth on his tongue. He ground his teeth and stood up, stalking into the darkness, where he took deep breaths to clear his head. She had revealed her true nature in the end, a nature that he had been too blind, or blinded by her, to see. If she had truly meant well, she would not have concealed it from him, not have deceived him.

At midday, they came to the edge of Lord Crommack's lands and looked at what lay before them. The Aos Sí must have come in the night, ambushing the guards on watch as the castle and village slept. The ground was scorched, a black sea leading up to the keep itself.

"The bad people are there," Aishling cried as she tried to burrow into Gideon's tunic.

"Hush, now. They are gone."

"I want to leave. It's scary here."

Gideon knew he couldn't move on just yet. Not only must he collect more provisions, but he also felt a need to see proof of what had happened and by whose hand. He found a hiding spot under a large jut of rock on the outskirts of Lord Crommack's land. Pulling out a short knife, he said, "I must see if anyone lives, Aishling."

"Don't leave me," she begged. "If you leave, you won't come back."

"I will come back. I promise I will always come back." He tugged her hands away from where they clutched his clothing. "Here," he said, placing the hilt of the blade in her palm, "you keep this with you to feel safe."

She looked at it, tears pooling in her eyes. "Please, don't go," she whispered.

"I will only be gone a short while," he told her, shooing her into the darkness of the overhang. "Don't make a sound until I return." He rose, hardening his heart to her pleas, and headed toward the castle.

Like Belfirth, none were spared, slaughtered in their beds. Easy pickings. With slow steps, he walked among the ruins of the village to the keep, coming to a stop at the doors that led inside. They were whole. Unscathed. Yet, he knew that within the stone walls, all were dead, as no life stirred. Walking the castle's perimeter, he found their entrance point, so like that of Belfirth, a small opening leading into the cellar. His home had a similar passageway, a safeguard should the castle be breached, and those inside needed to flee unseen. One his steward knew well as he would've been responsible for safeguarding the family should the unthinkable occur. Gideon's heart sank.

In the great hall, lying on his back alongside the corpses of every member of the household who could not escape, was his steward, Reece, an ornate dagger piercing his chest. He looked at the markings on the hilt, unmistakable in their design and origin, the strange steel seeming to glow subtly. Seeing it protruding from his steward's chest felt personal, as though whoever left it meant for him to see it, and if that were so... Gideon shook his head.

Did the wanton slaughter of his people have something to do with Fiadh? What was she to Rygeil? Why had the elven king not come for her himself? If an Aos Sí army could lay waste to entire fiefdoms, why could they not simply enter Dorcha Wood and take a helpless girl? It made no sense.

The wind whipped through the sky, snaking through the narrow slits in the walls and causing the tapestries to flutter. He felt his skin crawl, alarm flaring in his mind at the thought of Aishling being discovered while he stood there among the slaughter. Gideon strode from the great hall, not wishing to tarry, save to grab a pastry left sitting on a silver plate. Sending a prayer to the Great Mother for his faithful steward, Lord Crommack, and his people, Gideon hefted himself onto Aridius, who he'd tethered under a copse of trees, away from the sights and smells of death that made him fidgety. Clutching the reins in his hand, he searched the horizon, sensing the weight of an unseen gaze from the trees that bordered the keep.

Gideon kicked Aridius into a gallop, giving a low whistle

when he neared the place where Aishling hid. Hopping to the ground, he stalked to the rock, peering into the darkness. "Aishling, 'tis Gideon."

She came running to him, the knife he'd given her clenched in her fist. "Gideon!"

Plucking her from the ground, he briefly admonished her for running with a blade, then placed her onto his mount, swung up behind her, and headed west.

"I'm hungry. Did you get more food?" she asked after they had ridden in silence for a time.

Reaching into his tunic, he brought out the pastry he had grabbed and handed it to her. She beamed and took a bite, cheeks bulging as she chewed. After she swallowed, Aishling looked at the sweet roll in her hand and said, "Where is yours?"

"I was so hungry I ate mine on my way to fetch you," he lied. "Besides, I'll hunt, and we'll find some late-season berries."

"Where are we going now?"

"To Felmore, in the western reaches."

She thought for a moment. "Is it far?"

"Aye, but when we get there, you'll have a roof over your head and food in your belly." Aishling clapped, her enthusiasm lifting some of the weight Gideon felt pressing on his shoulders. They rode, eyes fixed on the west.

CHAPTER FIVE

Rivya's stride matched Fiadh's as they walked, shoulder to shoulder. A slight motion from the corner of her eye caused Fiadh to stop in her tracks. Leaning forward, she peered into shifting shadows, gasping when a tiny form emerged. Covered in moss wrappings, it was no taller than the length of her palm and bore a strong resemblance to a man, though on such a diminutive scale that she gaped at him, trying to make sense of what she was seeing. Sensing her perusal, Rivya stopped and swung her head toward Fiadh. Eyes wide, Fiadh glanced at Rivya, limply waving her hand in question at the minuscule figure that watched her with a beadlike stare.

That is Darrow, guardian of the gruagach.

"The gruagach?" Fiadh asked.

The people of the Coll.

You say that as if it means something to me.

Fiadh glanced at the copse of trees just beyond Darrow's form. Clusters of nuts hung from branches.

Hazel trees. That's what they were. Perhaps, people of the Coll simply meant people of Hazel trees? Darrow stepped toward her; the dark pools of his tiny eyes utterly captivating as he made his way into a shaft of light. Bending down to be at eye level, she smiled, and he cocked his head, gazing at her. There was no white in his eyes, only darkness that seemed to absorb the light and reflect nothing. Wiry brown hair capped a head with an angular face, sharp chin, and pointed ears. Darrow's skin was a deep reddish-brown and weathered where it was visible on his arms and spindly legs. Glancing down, Fiadh noted his limbs were disproportionately long for his torso, with four fingers or toes on each appendage. The tales Gideon had told her had gotten nothing right. This was not a silly trickster living among people, wreaking havoc in houses, or accepting food offerings in exchange for chores. He was an intelligent being who took her measure as she stood before him.

Rivya made a small noise, so much like the clearing of a throat that Fiadh remembered her manners. "Good day to you, Darrow. I am Fiadh."

The tiny being looked into Fiadh in a way that felt strangely intimate, as though there was a window into her mind that only he could access. Opening his mouth, he let out a rapid succession of words that had no meaning to her with their lilting cadence, though their intent felt welcoming —almost like a homecoming. How strange.

Cracking a smile, Fiadh nodded and looked at Rivya. "Can you tell me what he said?"

Darrow offers the heir of Erabel welcome.

"What?" Fiadh asked, her thoughts stuttering at the translation.

He gives the heir welcome.

"I don't…" Fiadh looked from one to the other, finally landing on Darrow. "I'm not… heir? Did you mean heir as in someone who inherits something?"

Darrow swept her a bow, followed by more of his strange language.

A deep sound rumbled in Rivya's chest, followed by the beginning of a warning that was quickly concealed from Fiadh.

Did you just warn him not to say something? Fiadh asked, turning toward the Cù-Sìth.

Aye.

Why would you do that? If he's willing to tell me what you're not, let him!

It is not for Darrow to share our histories.

A growl of frustration spilled from Fiadh's lips. Staring at Darrow, she said, "I would like to know what you have to say. Can you… can you speak into my mind as Rivya does?"

Darrow studied her but said nothing.

Does he understand what I'm saying?

Aye, and he can speak your tongue, but he will say no more.

"What is it with all of you?" Fiadh shouted, shame coloring her face when she saw Darrow flinch. "I'm sorry. I didn't mean to frighten you. I just… I just want to under-stand." Propping her hands on her hips, she looked up at Dasha, who had begun to caw. "Would you be able to tell me?" she asked.

The bird nodded, and images flickered behind Fiadh's

eyes like memories, though strange and muted as if she were looking through muddy water. All at once, they were ripped from her mind, her connection with Dasha severed at the sound of Rivya's startled yelp.

Fiadh's eyes widened. *He could show me?*

Rivya snapped at Dasha and stepped back. *It is forbidden. What's forbidden? Him telling me or me asking?*

A strangled sound, like a muffled gurgle, made its way from Rivya's throat. *You cannot. Please, Fiadh. You must wait for Veren. We are bound, the Cù-Sìth. If it were discovered that we shared, or allowed to be shared, what our masters have deemed secret, we would be punished.*

Fiadh watched the massive creature shudder. *Are you saying that I carry your fate in my hands?*

Aye.

She made Rivya wait for a few seconds, taking grim pleasure in the fear that flashed within the Cù-Sìth's eyes, then shook her head as though ending an internal argument. *Alright. I will wait for Veren.*

Thank you, Rivya said, the thought heavy with gratitude.

Fiadh nodded and bade farewell to Darrow.

As the pair continued, Fiadh mulled over the events of the day. There were so many pieces of her life that no longer fit together, like that quilt she had made as a girl of ten and three, all mismatched and without any semblance of continuity. The world, as she thought she knew it, was utterly changed. Stories of little people, fanciful tales that upon hearing them she had never believed possible, were now true. Only they didn't reside in the world of mankind— they were *here*, kept in a place as hidden as the truth of their existence. How many other stories would be proved real? A pressure began to build in her head, weighing her down so that her pace slowed. It was becoming too much to bear. All of this. How can one person go through so much in so short a time—have every aspect of their life ripped away, jumbled up, and thrown back together in an unrecognizable heap— and remain sound?

Be calm, young Fiadh. All will be well, Rivya's thoughts rumbled, breaching the haze of confusion.

"I feel like my life is no longer my own," Fiadh grumbled. "I don't even know what's real anymore or where I belong."

Each of us has a destiny. Yours was set before you when you lay in your mother's womb. Now, through circumstance, you are newly birthed into the world in which you were always meant to dwell. It is a destiny you cannot fight. Rivya paused, closing her golden eyes and arching her massive head toward the sky. *Reach out with your mind. Feel our Great Mother. She is here. She is with you.*

Rooting her feet to the ground, Fiadh closed her eyes and opened her mind in a ritual she had repeated in happier moments. Pulses of thought and longing traveled through her as she tilted her head back and breathed deeply, inhaling the exotic scents of this world, earthy fragrances so unlike any she had known—faintly sweet, with a peculiar tang of herbs. The smells lingered in her thoughts, subtle and appealing. When a connection came, Fiadh swayed with its power, rocking back on her heels and flinging out an arm to grasp Rivya's shoulder for ballast.

Daughter, a voice, lush and melodious, sang in her mind.

Fiadh's eyes flew open with a yelp. Rivya watched her,

her muzzle curving in what would be a grin if she could make one. "Rivya ... she spoke to me," Fiadh whispered.

In this place, she speaks to all her children, Rivya explained.

Trembling with awe, Fiadh opened her mind in silent communion with Danu. Tears fell from her eyes as she let go of the pain and grief that had dogged her every step since the murder of her mother, welcoming Danu's loving embrace of each aching feeling, letting that warm presence envelop her completely. Time ceased its slow march. She felt a myriad of life forces in all directions, and all tied to the Great Mother, as they had always been and would always be. Danu held her fast, in whirls of wind and strokes of leaves from the oak that sheltered them, finally letting her go with a gentle flow of thought.

Fiadh felt as though she was drifting back to earth, her toes touching the ground first and then her feet, becoming anchored again. Salty tears dried upon her cheeks as the last of the wind stroked her face. She sensed the moment Danu drifted away, carried on the breezes of her will. She kept her eyes shut a few moments longer, savoring the sensation of release. Within her mind, a piece of the puzzle of her life settled into place.

CHAPTER SIX

*D*asha flew over Fiadh's head, belting out raucous cries that caused songbirds to scatter. Fiadh giggled, watching him, sensing his intent as he dove from tree to tree.

He's trying to impress you, Rivya noted.

Fiadh laughed. "Impress me? He's a knave!"

As though to lend credibility to her comment, Dasha flew at the Cù-Sìth, banking to the right just before he collided with her head. Rivya growled and barked, snapping her teeth, to which the raven cawed lightheartedly.

Cease your antics before Rivya loses her good humor and does more than snap, Fiadh passed along to Dasha. The bird gave her a shrill call in response and glided to her outstretched arm.

Rivya snorted. *I begin to wonder who is training whom.*

Dasha is not for me to train, are you? Fiadh replied, stroking the bird's breast.

Rivya stopped walking, and Fiadh turned to look at her. "What?"

I did not think I would live to see one such as you. It is an honor to be at your side.

Dasha fluffed his feathers and strutted as though he were the object of Rivya's compliment. The Cù-Sìth growled, and Fiadh laughed, sending the raven into the trees.

Rivya, she started, feeling uneasy with the female's words. *I do not deserve such praise. I've done nothing but cause trouble for Krulan and your kind.*

My mate may complain, but he does not consider the protection of you to be trouble. Neither do I. You… you have long been awaited.

Fiadh huffed. *You know, unless you explain what you mean by that, it means nothing to me.*

Aye, I suppose that is true, but I cannot break the vow I swore.

She shook her head and stalked down the faint trail they walked, muttering about mythical creatures and tiny men keeping secrets. Rivya let her rant, content to listen to the unique female who knew so little of who she was.

Some of the Cù-Sìth's thoughts must have escaped her guarded mind because Fiadh turned and said, "Who am I?"

You are Fiadh.

You know that's not what I meant. You were filled with other thoughts, something about—

Cease! Do not pry into my mind without my permission.

I'm sorry, Rivya. I just… She sighed. *Never mind.*

They walked in silence for a time, their footfalls joined by the beating of Dasha's wings as he tried to pry Fiadh's attention away from troublesome thoughts. When she ignored his most obnoxious croaks, he let out three shrill caws, the sounds pummeling her brain. *Fiadh! Fiadh! Fiadh!*

I hear you, silly bird.

He swooped to the forest floor and spread his wings, hopping in circles like a trained bear she had once spied in the village of Felmore. Of course, that poor animal had been in misery, and she felt nothing but grief as he went through a series of tricks his master had beaten into him. Dasha's antics pulled her away from those sad memories, finally eliciting a light-hearted grin. He gave Fiadh a gurgling croak, eyeing her as he walked at her side in that pigeon-toed fashion of birds. She stopped and stroked her hand down his body, from his head to the tip of his longest tail feather. Dasha beamed under her affection, causing Rivya, who watched the encounter, to give a wolfy chuckle.

Fiadh turned to her. *He's a wonder, is he not?*

Aye, that he is. I admit that he is special among his kind.

Of course he is, aren't you, clever boy? He bobbed his head.

Using her mind, Fiadh told Dasha to fly and not worry about her. She would be well in Rivya's company. All around were sights and sounds that were both familiar and strange. As they always had, animals found their way to Fiadh, but they were not like those she had known and loved the whole of her life. Though ordinary at first glance, the squirrels and birds held a profound consciousness that spilled from their eyes as they came close. Bodies arched and twitched in an invitation, begging for a stroke from her hand. When Fiadh reached out to them with her mind, as she had always done with wild things, they responded in ways unlike any she had felt. Deeper. Untainted. As though they were a wholly separate species from those who dwelled in the Dorcha Wood of her youth. But it was not only the creatures that were different. *She* was different. There was something in her that felt… awake, as though this place, whatever it truly was, had changed her. And within the varied landscape, Danu presided—a goddess, not absent like those of myths, but present and observing all within her realm with a keen eye. Fiadh was deeply aware of the Great Mother as she traveled through a world within a world.

Rivya?

The Cù-Sìth paused and swung her massive head toward her. *Aye.*

Why is Erabel so different from the world I come from?

Erabel is a reflection of the Great Mother, she began. *Her being is within every aspect. You will no longer find that in the realm of men.*

The last was said with such venom that Fiadh wondered how deep the hate was for her people. *I sense your hatred for my kind, and I am sorry for it.* Rivya growled but passed no thought to her. *Why… why is it so different here? Are we not of the same world?*

Rivya thought for a moment, images and words trapped within her mind until she was ready to share them. *It would be easier for me to show you.*

Fiadh stopped moving and watched as Rivya turned her body to face her. She lowered her head and stared into Fiadh. *Close your eyes.* Fiadh's brow wrinkled. *I will share my memories with you.*

She nodded slowly, closed her eyelids, and embraced the darkness, feeling the heat of Rivya's body as it moved closer. Spikes of fur brushed against Fiadh's forehead before pressing fully against her skin. At the contact, a buzz of energy leaped from Rivya into her body. It tingled along Fiadh's hairline and slowly moved across her skull, electrifying every nerve until awareness bloomed within her mind like an explosion, encompassing every thought and impulse.

Fiadh balked at the intrusion and threw up mental walls to keep the invasion out, but Rivya's voice echoed through her head with reassurances until Fiadh let down her guard and surrendered. Flashes of light. Blurred images. Muffled sounds. Her mind swam in it.

Minutes passed while Fiadh stood immobile. Rivya held her fast as their connection grew, clarified, and revealed a wealth of memories as though a portal to the past had opened, and all Fiadh must do was step through it. Rivya's mind led Fiadh through a clutter of remembrances, scenes that unfolded behind her eyes, tugging at her as she drifted along until the journey stopped, as though an anchor had been tossed in the sea of the Cù-Sìth's thoughts. Fiadh was settled among a series of memories that felt so real she flinched as they unfolded before her, her senses fooled into thinking she could smell and feel what burgeoned behind her clenched eyes.

Dorcha Wood, teeming with life, flora and fauna reflecting those she had seen as she crossed the border of Erabel, interspersed with familiar creatures that lived in her recollections. As quickly as it came, the scene shifted, and her body tilted with the variation, falling to the side only to be propped up by Rivya's strong form. Their bond held fast through the change, and Fiadh looked upon a different landscape in Rivya's mind. The wood, which moments ago had glowed with an essence that transcended the natural world as Fiadh knew it, looked...darker. The trees bending to block the light as though they sensed something coming.

Through Rivya's mind, Fiadh stared into a copse of oak, noting their movement, feeling groans of fear, the tremble of leaves and roots, as a multitude of warnings shot from the woody tendrils below the surface like a current, passed from one to the other until the entire wood was brought to fevered awareness. And then the crack of a branch echoed through the forest, and all went silent. Fiadh sucked in a breath, waiting, searching out the direction from which the snap still hung in the air. Minutes passed, and then came the soft thump of men's feet beating upon the earth. Fiadh clenched her fists, knowing what was to come, wanting to shield herself from it, but unable to do anything but watch it all unfold. From her peripheral, a huge buck burst through the undergrowth, its eyes wild. She could feel the racing of its heart, smell the fear pouring from its body in rivers. It turned its head, snagged on where the Cù-Sìth lay hidden, and within that recognition was a knowledge that there was no hope. The Cù-Sìth were not the guardians of the myriad of creatures that inhabited the forest. They were the wardens of Erabel. Warriors for the Aos Sí should a threat come to their borders.

The buck's heart beat fiercely in a frenzied rhythm that traveled up Fiadh's spine and then slowed, acceptance washing over those intelligent eyes. It turned toward the intrusion, its back to Rivya, who lay in wait, a mute observer. Erupting from the trees, a small band of men burst into a scene that played out with grim purpose behind Fiadh's eyes. Sneers filled faces, turning to raucous banter, as they formed a loose half-circle around the deer. Blades winked in the sunlight as the men took up a fighting stance, throwing jeers at the animal whose body trembled in rigid submission of what was to come.

"Look at it," one of the men muttered, his young face covered in a scraggly beard caked in layers of dirt and particles of food, "it's not trying to run. What do you make of that?"

A man with graying hair and a soiled tunic that stretched so tightly over his protruding belly that the seams showed small tears sauntered forward and spat on the ground a few paces from the motionless buck, the yellowish glob smacking against a rock in a slimy mass. "Mayhap, he knows his match when he sees it," the man chuckled, cocking his head. "He's one of them, alright. Look at his eyes, Toby. See how they glow?"

"Aye, I see it, Conall, but I don't like the way he's standing there and not running like the others," Toby said, taking a step backward.

"Well, he won't be standing for long," Conall sneered, jerking his head to the men at his back.

They came forward as one in a slow-moving wall that unfurled to encompass the animal. The buck's heart became a rapid thrum, like that of a hummingbird, the whites of its eyes visible against the rich brown of its fur. With a subtle signal from Conall, the men lifted their swords and lunged. Metal pierced flesh, slashing through muscles and tendons. It bleated. Its body was stuck with a succession of stabs until the animal's knees buckled. The heart, that moments before had begun a terrible rhythm, stopped with a final ga-lump. Triumphant roars filled the air as the men wrenched their gore-slicked weapons from the body. Stepping forward,

Conall lifted the stag's head. The light was gone from its eyes. The glow snuffed out as surely as a candle. Hacking violently, he ripped the antlers from its skull, shaking them in his fist when they finally wrenched free with a hideous squelch.

Fiadh sobbed, jerking her mind from Rivya's grasp as the murder played out. Her guts roiled. Dasha, sensing her distress, broke from the trees, releasing threatening caws to any who dared mistreat his mistress. Fiadh shushed him, patting the ground next to her where the raven landed, and stood by her side, his sharp eyes darting about in search of a threat.

They were hunted. Slaughtered. The sounds of the men's glee as they stabbed and stabbed still reverberated through her mind. She wished she could unsee it.

Why did you show me that? It was awful!

You must know the hearts of mankind. They are an evil race.

Fiadh shook her head. *That's not fair. My mother wasn't evil. I'm not evil.*

*You are not—*Rivya started, then cut off her thought. *I showed you truth. Too long you have been in the company of mankind. You have become blind to their cruelty.*

"Blind to their cruelty?" Fiadh yelled, indignant. "They murdered my mother! How can you say I am blind to it? I saw it! I watched her burn. Where were you?"

Dasha snapped his beak and lunged at Rivya, biting her between the pads of her feet. She yelped and scrambled up, the raven following her with menacing pecks and croaks.

"Dasha, cease," Fiadh said wearily.

I do not mean to upset you, Fiadh. Please forgive me. You asked what had changed, why Erabel feels different than Dorcha Wood.

Fiadh sighed. *I'm not angry at you, Rivya.* She gave a harsh laugh. *Truthfully, I am angry at so many things that I would hardly know where to start. Some people are evil. I have seen it.* She looked Rivya in the eye. *But, I am not evil. Mother was not evil. It hurts to think you believe otherwise.*

Rivya, eyeing Dasha, who paced the ground menacingly at her feet, stepped forward and licked Fiadh's cheek. The action reminded her of the wolf who often visited when she lived in Dorcha Wood. Faolan. She touched the wetness and smiled, though it did not reach her eyes. *Thank you.*

You are not evil, Fiadh. Nor was your mother.

She closed her eyes, taking in the words and letting them cool the heat of anger coursing through her body. *Why did those men do that? What you showed me in that memory.*

When the alliance with men was severed, they came for us—slaughtering any who bore the mark of the Great Mother, forcing every surviving creature to the realms of the Aos Sí. So we left the world of mankind and have not returned.

But the Aos Sí and humans lived side by side for centuries, did they not?

Aye, but those days have long since passed, Rivya said, stretching onto the ground.

How did it all go so wrong? What happened that set us against each other? Brought us to war?

Greed.

metal door clanged shut with harsh finality, locking away one whose sordid craft had brought him to the bowels of Felmore Castle. Xander cocked his head and listened as Darragh stalked away, having been fed sufficient information to spur his anger. A feral smile curled his lips as he recalled Darragh's expression when he'd informed the man that the young woman the lord had sought in the depths of Dorcha Wood was, in truth, of Rygeil's line and not the get of a woman he'd naively believed to be a witch. She'd been hidden under his nose all these years and the fool blind to it. Arrogant human. They all were.

The children of men were nothing more than pawns on a chessboard, and he had begun to move them about, putting the game into play. So easy it had been to feign capture, to cower and beg after slaying two of Darragh's men—one must be convincing—and, in the end, he was led precisely where he wished to be. But there was something more in this dark castle than a lord who would unwittingly do his bidding. No, there were whispers of an ancient power here, squatting within the stone itself not far from where he sat—the true witch of Felmore, the lord's mother.

Listening to the receding footsteps of Darragh's heavy tread, Xander sniggered, the sound echoing off the damp walls. The flame from his single candle flickered under his harsh breath as the mage gathered up the runes that lay scattered on the scarred table. Rubbing his thumb along the surface of the most powerful, he began to mutter words of power in the forgotten language of his ancestors. Sounds, never before uttered within those walls, were disgorged into the dank cell in exhalations of breath rank with rot and malignancy. The words soared, bouncing off the rock, gaining substance and power until they were pregnant with fetid intention.

Body rocking, Xander spun a final magical web, draining heat and energy from the room. The spell spasmed and curled, birthing twisted forms that coalesced into an immense beast of scales, jagged claws, and fangs that dripped a noxious venom onto the icy surface of the floor where it sizzled. Without looking at the dragon-like creature he had conjured with nothing more than spellcraft, Xander sent out a command in a ruthless projectile of thought. It sank into the thrashing form at his blackened feet. The monster began spitting bloodied clots of foam from between needle-like teeth as it writhed in silent agony, the only sounds that of its rigid scales and claws scraping the floor in harsh metallic squeals. In moments, it stilled, turning blood-red eyes with narrow, glowing pupils on its master.

The mage chuckled, the sound grotesque and sinister.

"He thinks to keep me here." He chuckled harshly. "As if that sack of flesh could wield power enough to see me caged."

From beyond his cell came a woman's voice. "I smell you, mage. Mayhap, I will taste you soon, too."

Xander cocked his head, following the voice, and turned toward it as though he could see through the stone itself. "Haegna," he tsk'd. "Do not meddle in things beyond your feeble power. Bar your door, old woman, lest you become meat for my pet."

Haegna hissed but did as she was told. "Her blood flows in me as well, wizard. Never forget that."

Distaste flashed across Xander's face, but he put the woman from his mind and focused. Reaching for a small bag that held his belongings when he was taken from his mountain refuge—well, not taken precisely, as he had lain such a clear path to his door for Darragh's men to follow, he may as well have walked to the keep himself. Xander blew out the candle, stuffing it into his pack, and commanded his creature to tear open the door of his cell.

The pair slipped into the dark underbelly of the castle. Those few guards who were unfortunate enough to cross their path were gutted with a single swipe of wickedly long claws before they could draw breath to raise the alarm. Feeling benevolent, the mage allowed his creature to savor the last of its victims, watching dispassionately as blood and matter were slurped from the cooling body by a pronged tongue that stabbed in and out of the corpse with feverish intensity. Barking an order, Xander finally sent the beast slinking away from his spoils, and the two forms stepped beyond the dungeon's sole outlet and into the night.

Xander, with the scaled beast at his side, made his way into Dorcha Wood. The forest, feeling his presence, awoke. Trees groaned and bent, twisting their branches to grab at his limbs. Words of defensive magic erupted from the mage's lips as his monster tore at leaves and bark, causing the trees themselves to scream and writhe. Animals surrounded the pair, snarling and snapping, shrieking and dive-bombing, only to have their bodies ripped apart by claws and fangs or words of power.

They climbed, skirting an elven boundary Xander sensed but could not see, ascending to an elevation that would allow the mage to look beyond the wood and into the horizon, to another place. A dark realm tucked within folds of earth that saw scarcely any light. Men avoided it, their fear of the unknown eclipsing the truth of what it was that repelled them. Within that place was Dothur, a being born from an ancient evil—the spawn of Carmun—imprisoned by the Aos Sí long ago in a cage whose magical bonds had begun to weaken as the darkness growing among the Aos Sí became more powerful. The strength of that prison waned as surely as the strength of Danu herself.

The mage would free his master, and when the daughter of Erabel's blood was spent, Danu would be too frail to fight alongside the Aos Sí. That race would fall as they should have in the Great War. In this, mankind would prove useful. Darragh would raise his armies and unleash a horde onto the Aos Sí stronghold, cutting them down in his quest for power over a kingdom he would never possess. Once the elves were hobbled, Dothur would rise and take back the world that had been usurped, restoring it to its former glory, a time so distant that it was lost to the memory of all save the oldest and wisest of the Aos Sí. Aye, the son of Carmun would reclaim these lands, and Xander meant to be at his side when he did.

Reaching the summit, Xander raised his arms to the sky and loosed words into the air, feeling them caught and taken, pulled to the heart beating in the darkness.

Dothur, the only living son of Carmun, sniffed, his body uncoiling. Stark white skin enfolded a slender frame of elongated limbs extending to a harshly angular face. Irises of pale pink surrounded pupils whose darkness could pull an onlooker into their depths and keep them there, unmoving. Their minds flayed with such precision the only indication of his violation was blood that trickled from their nostrils before their body crashed to the ground, still and silent. Ragged, leathery wings flared out behind him, so pale and thin they were translucent, each tipped with a deadly claw that could cleave a man in two.

Dothur's tongue licked the air that filtered through the iron walls of his prison, tasting Xander's words and interpreting their meaning. *He is a powerful mage*, Dothur mused. Certainly, the most powerful left of their kind and the first to be turned from the Aos Sí scum the wizards had long been aligned with. It had not taken much to turn them once their leader had been killed in the early years of the Great War, an attack blamed on the elves, though it was he who'd slain the mage. Webs of dark magic the wizards had no power to shield themselves from had ensured their new alliance, and their feverish devotion had only grown since those days.

With a grim smile, punctuated by teeth that had been filed to points by his mother after his first suckle, he let out a roar of triumph. Rygeil's heir, Danu's last hope, had come home, and the Aos Sí loyal to her were rising. Others were rising too, he mused, readying themselves for war with mankind and each other as they sought to reclaim their sacred land and the power that dwelled there. His wait was nearly over. Already, he had reached into the void, allowing the witch of Felmore to ensnare him with her spellcraft. He fed her sips of his power, showed her what he wished her to see, and waited for his efforts to bear fruit. Men and elves would slaughter each other and when the heir of Erabel breathed her last, he would free himself of this cage. The time was drawing near.

CHAPTER EIGHT

In the great hall, Darragh sat, stewing, ignorant of what occurred beneath the layers of stone at his feet. Damn his wretched mother with her infernal meddling! *He* had captured the mage. *Him!* She would do well to remember that and cease her machinations. From the moment he had consigned the wizard to his cell, she had been whining, cajoling, pestering him for want of blood or speech or whatever else her black heart coveted. Haegna may have been the one to suggest he find and capture Xander, but she had done naught save that. He had lost two men laying siege to the mage's lair! And now he meant to have what power and knowledge that creature possessed. *He* would wield it, not Haegna.

His lips curled in a cruel smile as he imagined how he would use the latest information the wizard had imparted. The girl was young and untried, raised in secret by that witch, Riona, whom he had burned at the stake. She would be weak, not yet in possession of her full powers, or so the mage had said. Easy prey once flushed out of the accursed woods. Darragh chuckled darkly, earning him a glance from his commander, Donal, who stood at his side. It would surely grieve Rygeil when he learned of his descendant's violent death. A grieving mind was a careless one. And perhaps he would sweeten his mother's tongue with the girl's blood. He was, after all, nothing if not a dutiful son, and that wretched old woman did have her uses.

But, for now, the mage was his. Unspoiled until he deemed the creature's use exhausted. The race of elves would fall and when they did, he, savior of mankind, would be there to rule.

A noise from the assemblage before him drew his mind from those thoughts. His eyes flicked to the emissaries he had summoned, who now raised their voices on the cusp of a brawl.

"The Aos Sí are amassing," said a battle-hardened knight from the eastern holding of Dungraven. "Three of my men were slain at the hands of one of their scouts."

Another man who hailed from Ardrath, a fief in the western reaches, scoffed. "Their kind was wiped from this earth a hundred years ago. You see things that do not exist, young Rory." His comment was echoed by a handful of others, spreading through the gathering.

"Rory does not speak of fictions, Sir Saere," snarled Sir Jamie, who also hailed from the east. "I, too, have seen evidence of their kind. I passed near Felraine Vale and found what was left of Belfirth's army. All were slain."

His announcement quieted the men as unease swept through the crowd. Darragh marked their reactions.

"Who is to say you and your soldiers didn't kill them?" Saere asked. "The enmity between Lord Ross and Lord Sorley is well-known." He turned in a slow circle. "Are we to take Jamie's word over common sense?"

Rumbles of disagreement followed his question as the group of men began to fracture into those who had seen evidence of the elven army and those who chose to believe the race to be long dead. A couple even swept their hands from forehead to chest and spat on the floor, motions to ward off evil.

Saere stepped toward the group of easterners. "Fairy tales and folklore are an eastern tradition, are they not?"

Jamie glared at him and drew his sword, the slow hiss of metal filling the room. "Have care if you want your head to remain atop your neck."

Saere chuckled, rolling his eyes. "I have no wish to slay one who still believes tales from his wetnurse."

Darragh sat back and listened to them bicker, knowing full well the easterners' spoke the truth. But a wise ruler did not sacrifice his armies when others could fight in their stead. Even now, his commander, Donal, had begun requisitioning soldiers from among his people and those of surrounding lands. If they could lift a sword, they could die under one. Better he sends boys and old men, just enough to show honest desire to aid his fellows, but nothing that would weaken Felmore, and save his true soldiers for the real battle. No, his men would not be among the initial ranks in the war to come. Let the lords of the north and east be the first to face the Aos Sí horde. When all but those in the western fold were exhausted, he would make his move. The Aos Sí would be weak from weeks of battle, their numbers more than halved. That is when he would strike.

Donal stood at his side, marking his lord's eyes as they flitted from one knight to another.

Darragh leaned over. "Have you noticed how they squirm at the mention of the elven race? It is as though I look upon a gaggle of women."

"Aye, my lord. They sound no better than children still suckling their mother's teat."

Darragh barked laughter. "Ah, Donal, it is good you take their measure. We'll need their quick fists, not their slow minds."

"And you will have them, my lord."

Just then, an angry snarl ripped from Jamie's mouth as he faced off with Saere.

Darragh's voice cut through the confrontation before it escalated. "Silence!" He swept his eyes across the assemblage, marking each face before landing on the group of men from the east who had separated themselves into a small mass, ready to attack should the tension spill into violence. "Rory and Jamie have made strong claims. Whether or not their stories are true matters little." Pinning the men with a stare, Darragh continued, "What you are asking is that I spend my coin and leave my walls undefended in pursuit of little more than a band of ruffians and cutthroats."

"But, my lord—" Darragh cut Jamie off with the swipe of his hand.

"If Lords Corbain and Sorley require my protection, let them come here and pledge fealty." Masks of outrage flooded the faces of Jamie and Rory, causing Darragh to chuckle. "Let your anger go. I did not say I wouldn't come to your aid. I will. But I would have them kneel before I raise my banners."

The two men bowed, eyes flashing anger, and left the hall. Saere smirked, muttering a comment to those around him as they passed. Laughter followed, and Darragh watched it all, knowing that the lords of the east would indeed come to him and beg his aid. They would prostrate themselves at his feet, and when the war was over and the Aos Sí dead—especially that foul spawn of the witch of Dorcha Wood—he would be as powerful as the king. Maybe, even more so.

Just then, a guard burst into the room, his face ashen, eyes wild. "My lord!" he yelled, careening toward Darragh. Landing hard on his knees at his lord's feet, he stammered, "Your guardsmen... they've been slain."

"What?" Darragh thundered, shoving the man aside.

The announcement sent a shockwave through those who remained in the hall. The sounds of metal rang out as swords were drawn. Darragh rose and stormed toward the passage from which his guard had come, Saere and the others at his heels.

Darragh was the first to arrive in the dark passages of the castle's dungeons. Unerringly, he sniffed out the tang of blood that filled the fusty air, a scent that any warrior who had been in battle had stamped into their brain—that, and the screams of the dying. Loping through the darkness with a small troop at his sides, he found the first of his guardsmen. The corpse lay in a pool of blood that had already begun to turn black, torso flayed open in shreds of skin, bone, and organs. The door nearest the dead man gaped open, the interior black as pitch. Grabbing a torch from the wall, Darragh stepped inside, illuminating the cell and finding it empty, save for the table and stool at its center. Taking a few strides toward the only furniture, he held the torch over the table's surface, the light revealing an odd collection of markings that had been recently dug into the wood with fingernails, evidenced by flecks of blood and the remnants of a torn nail protruding from the deepest gouge. He spat on the markings, hurling a black oath into the empty space before storming out of the room and into the network of tunnels that comprised the dimness.

At a small opening, hiding the only outer exit from the dungeon, Saere had found the last of the slain men. A few of the soldiers at his side looked away, making signs to ward off evil, and swallowing the gorge that had begun to crawl up their throats as they muttered about how the body looked… gnawed upon.

Darragh glared, silencing the men's voices, and bellowed for them to step aside as he studied the bloody mess. The mage had not been alone, he noted. Rage at his captive having escaped made his head throb. Whatever had done this had taken its time, lapping up the blood from the wound and floor, leaving shallow streaks of deep red stains, the only evidence of a horror he could only imagine. The knowledge that the man they looked upon could have been living as he was devoured sent tremors of rage through Darragh's body. Stepping over the corpse, he ducked through the doorway, knowing even as he did that he would not find Xander. The wizard was gone.

CHAPTER NINE

Greed, Rivya had told her. Her stomach felt raw as Fiadh mulled that over, throat twinging in the aftermath of what she had seen. Having been shown Rivya's disdain for mankind, Fiadh assumed the greed the Cù-Sìth spoke of originated in the hearts of men. The thought brought a measure of discomfort, as though Fiadh looked at her reflection in a pool of water and saw the same flaw in herself. If humans were born into this world with an unceasing craving for more and more, then she must count herself among them. It would simply be a matter of time before the tendency reared its ugly head.

Am I destined to become like those men? she asked herself.

The question left her mind, drifting to Rivya, where it was caught and pondered. *Yours is a different fate.*

How can you be sure? Their blood is my blood.

Rivya growled. *Mankind does not own every vice.* She turned her massive head, pinning Fiadh in her stare. *Had you thought they did?* Fiadh frowned and shrugged, earning her a grumble. *Those traits belong to many peoples. I told you greed was the cause of the evils that came to pass. I did not say who began that dark path.*

Are you saying…? Fiadh paused, struggling to wrap her head around it. *What are you saying?*

That is for Veren and the Great Mother to share.

Fiadh made a face. *Everything is for someone else to share.*

Rivya barked. *You are so impatient!*

She stopped and looked up at Rivya. *I wouldn't say that. I've simply had enough of all this doublespeak you all are so fond of.*

Doublespeak? You talk as though we are children of men whose tongues drip with lies. Rivya snarled.

Fiadh looked shocked at the outburst. *Do not call me a liar, Rivya.*

The Cù-Sìth glanced away, chest rumbling. *I did not call you such.*

Aye, you did.

Rivya shook herself, the action fluffing her thick fur so that it spiked along her shoulders before settling back into place. *I am sorry I offended you. It was not meant.*

That's okay. I'm feeling grumpy, anyway.

Rivya's upper lip lifted in what constituted a Cù-Sìth smile, flashing the white tip of a deadly canine. *Perhaps, I am too.*

Fiadh chuckled. *What a pair we make.*

Dasha landed on her shoulder, making her flinch at his sudden presence, then proceeded to preen her hair. She let him tend to her, cringing when his beak began to sift through her eyebrows. Rivya snorted at the look on her face, and Fiadh clenched her fist, resisting the urge to swat the Cù-Sìth for laughing at her.

When the preening began to feel more like a nuisance than a comfort, Fiadh sighed. "Dasha, you will pluck me bald if you continue riffling through my hair like that."

Mayhap he searches for bugs, Rivya joked.

Her eyes widened, and she giggled. *No doubt, but he'll find none.*

Dasha gave one last tug on her locks and launched into the air, the beat of his wings shifting the loose hair around her face. Fiadh's stomach chose that moment to snarl, and it dawned on her that she couldn't recall when she had last eaten.

Rivya rolled her eye toward her. *Hungry?*

She nodded, cheeks flaming, and clutched her waist as her gut proceeded to let out a string of very noisy gurgles.

You must eat, lest you wake the bodach and they mistake your rumblings for the footfalls of their favorite meal, Rivya told her, keeping her wolf-like face devoid of emotion as Fiadh gasped in fear. At the sound, the Cù-Sìth's expression went through a series of changes, finally ending in barks of laughter that became a yelp as Fiadh smacked her rump and stormed off.

Catching up to her, Rivya tugged at her dress, eyes going wide as the fabric tore. Fiadh's mouth gaped open. "Great Mother, Rivya! This is the only dress I have!"

Dasha chose that moment to join the fray, swooping in and out of the space just before the Cù-Sìth's head. Rivya accepted his antics without complaint, knowing she deserved his chiding. *Ah, Fiadh. I am sorry about the jest. It had become much too serious to my mind.* Glancing at the hole in Fiadh's clothing, she added, *Forgive me for the tear in your dress, as well.*

Fiadh fingered the rip. *You're forgiven, though,* she told her with a frown, *this is the only thing I have to wear. I don't imagine you have a needle and thread with which to repair it?*

Rivya shook her head and moved on, knowing Fiadh would follow.

I thought not. She sighed and looked around, trying to peer through the shadows that surrounded the path they walked. *What's a bodach?*

'Tis a harmless creature. You're not likely to see one of their kind.

She huffed, eyes growing large and hungry as Rivya stopped at a squat tree from which hung massive oblong fruit. Yanking one from a low branch with her mouth, Rivya dropped it in Fiadh's waiting hands.

Peel the skin and eat.

The rind was riddled with bumps, creating grooves in the deep red skin that Fiadh dug her nail into. As her thumb cut through the thickness, a spray of fragrant juices erupted in the air just beyond the opening, its scent a blend of citrus and melon. She ate the entire thing, wiping her sticky hands on her dress when the last of it was gone.

Thank you. I'd never tasted the like. What's it called?

Ahgawi. It is a favorite of the Aos Sí.

Fiadh nodded, looking down at the residue on her hands, spreading her fingers as they stuck together with dried juices.

I will take you to the pool of still waters where you can wash, Rivya said, noting Fiadh's movements.

Thank you. It has been so many days since I bathed. I must smell terrible.

There again was that wolfy laugh. *I will admit you have a powerful scent.* Fiadh blushed. *Follow me. It is not far.*

Fiadh stepped from a line of trees and into a small clearing, at the center of which was a large pool of water. Walking to the edge, she gazed into a dazzling blue expanse that was so clear she could see every rock and plant swaying in its aquatic realm. Looking into the depths and following its sizable curvature, she noted the ground itself opened up, going from sandy bank to cavernous pool with no hint of slow progression. It was as though she could step from the edge of the earth into a kingdom of water. A smile lit up her face as a school of fish swam by just below the surface, their scales a collection of colors she had never seen before.

Turning her head, she found Rivya sitting on her haunches, watching her. "Rivya, it's so beau—"

From out of the water erupted a man who wasn't a man, not in the true sense, cutting her off in shocked silence. Launching himself onto the sandy edge of the pool to perch with his lower body dangling in the water sat what could only be described as a half-man, half-fish. His torso was familiar enough, with padded muscles that rippled under her gaze, but that is where the resemblance ended. Along his sides were blood-red slashes, like the gills of a fish, that slowly puckered, sealing themselves in the air. His arms, though human-looking, ended in hands whose webbing reminded her of the feet of waterfowl. And while his upper body was purely male, his form tapered to a trim waist that blended into the scales and tail of a fish. Her eyes were drawn to the creature's lower extremities, the striking fins that swayed delicately in the water in giant fans of color. Fiadh took a few moments to marvel at the hypnotic movements of a being who had never existed in Fiadh's world until this moment. It wasn't until his upper body shifted, sending a tiny rock splashing into the pool, that her trance was broken.

Fiadh looked into a face devoid of wrinkles or any stamp of time or expression. Smooth, glasslike, and wholly appealing. Eyes, so bright blue they were nearly transparent, regarded her calmly. Rather than feeling self-conscious about her blatantly rude curiosity, he seemed to welcome her scrutiny, accepting it while he himself took in her own form. Pale eyebrows arched above an even brow, crowned with long hair that was so light it was more white than yellow. His face, while masculine, was so breathtaking that the only word she could conjure to describe it was beautiful.

The corners of his mouth lifted, lips parting. "Greetings, Fiadh, daughter of Threa. I am Eradar, guardian of the Merrow."

"Merrow?"

He tilted his head, assessing her. "The people of the still waters, kin to those of the sea."

"Oh... I didn't... I've never heard of your people."

"It is not surprising. Mankind has long relegated many peoples to nothing more than fictions."

Fiadh licked her lips, nervousness making her voice

catch. "You called me something, daughter of… what was it?"

"Threa."

Looking at the Cù-Sìth before her eyes found his, she asked, "Who's Threa?"

Rivya growled a warning.

"Your *keeper* wishes me not to tell you," he said snidely.

Fiadh flushed. "I am no animal. Who is Threa?"

"Your mother."

"M…my mother was Riona," Fiadh stammered.

Eradar tilted his head as he took in her words. "Riona was not your true mother, young one." Rivya snarled low in her throat, to which Eradar shrugged. "It matters not at this moment. You have come, and all of Erabel awaits you. I give you welcome," he swept his hand to encompass the entire expanse of the water, and as it flew outward, more of his people filled the pool, swimming from the depths of a hidden cavern tucked under a submerged ridge. Their bodies flew through the water in graceful twists and turns, heads breaking the surface with little more than a soft ripple. It was breathtaking. Forming a loose circle, they fanned outward, tails undulating in perfect rhythm. From the center of the ring of bodies arose a womanly form with shockingly white hair and a face of exquisite loveliness. Atop her regal head lay a golden crown of twisted metal in the shapes of the water plants that grew in her kingdom.

Eradar leaned forward in a bow. "My queen, may I present Fiadh, daughter of Threa."

Pupils, disturbingly dark against the brightness of her

irises, fixed on Fiadh, pinning her to the ground on which she crouched.

"Fiadh," Eradar began, "Ithraen, Queen of the Merrow."

Fiadh tilted her head in silent genuflection, robbed of words under such a knowing stare. A melodious voice drifted to her ears, spreading through her skull in waves of awareness. "Welcome, Fiadh. Long have we awaited the return of the Aos Sí. Eradar," Ithraen said, turning to him, "you will remain with Fiadh as she swims in my waters."

Eradar bowed, but Fiadh sensed that within Ithraen's command was an underlying message. Sinking beneath the surface in a mesmerizing whirl, Ithraen, and those who had come before her, disappeared into the depths, leaving the surface of the water still as a pane of glass. Moments passed in which she stared at the center of the pool, finally shaking off her stupor as Rivya shifted her weight behind her. Eradar sat, unmoved, on the edge of the water, tail rocking slowly beneath the surface, watching her.

Clearing her throat, Fiadh remarked, "I feel as though the world I knew was but a veil covering what lies within it."

"An apt statement, young Fiadh," Eradar said. "The children of men fear what is different. If it is a veil that has been cast over your life to this point, it has now been lifted, and you shall see all that has been hidden. A new era will dawn." Rivya growled a warning, causing Eradar to chuckle. "But enough of that. Come, swim in our waters and wash away the dirt of your travels."

Stripping her soiled dress from her body, she stood awkwardly in her shift, arms crossing her chest to hide her nakedness beneath the thin fabric. When Eradar showed no interest in her state of undress, she shuffled to the edge of the pool, dipping her toes into water that was surprisingly warm. She shot a surprised glance at Eradar.

He grinned. "My people have an affinity for warmer waters," he told her, breaking the surface and swimming a short distance away, though his head remained above the water. "Can you swim?"

"Aye, Mother taught me," Fiadh replied, stretching her body out and into the water where her shift billowed in the soft current. Clutching the fabric between her legs, she took two long strokes with her arms. It felt delicious. Sinking below the surface, Fiadh opened her eyes and viewed Ithraen's kingdom. There were so many creatures, their tiny noises amplified in the water. They clung to rocks and plants in colorful shells or swam in elegant silence, tails and fins vibrant in the crystalline waters. She spun in a slow circle, taking it all in before her lungs began to ache and she was forced upward to take a breath of air.

"It's beautiful," Fiadh said as Eradar made his way to her, holding out a lump of moss-like plants.

"The realm of the Merrow is unsurpassed in all of Erabel." Rivya snorted at this pronouncement. "The Cù-Sìth have their own opinions on such matters, but they have not the capacity to appreciate true beauty."

Rivya glared at him and rose, walking in a tight circle, and plopping onto the ground with a huff, her back to Eradar.

He laughed and said, "You see? They cannot deny the truth of my words."

Arrogant fish-man, Rivya's mind said to Fiadh with a grumble.

Fiadh laughed, slapping her hand over her mouth when Eradar gave her an odd look.

"Now, young Fiadh, hold out your hand."

She did as she was bid and watched as Eradar dumped the squishy mass he had been holding into her palm. "Ew."

He shook his head. "Patience, young one." Adding what looked like a shredded leaf, Eradar said, "Smell."

A look of distaste washed over her features, but she leaned forward and sniffed. A tart scent wafted into her nose. Clenching her fingers, she watched as foam formed around her digits.

"Soap!" Fiadh announced, blushing as she heard Eradar snicker.

Swimming to the rocky edge, she plopped the slick mass onto a jut of rock and pinched off a chunk to lather in her hands before rubbing it into her hair. It felt so good to wash away the grime that had coated every fiber. Dunking her head, she rinsed, watching as the foam leached into the water, disappearing in moments. Hauling herself up and out, she sat and spent a few minutes scrubbing her skin, seeing it pinken as she worked the mixture over every visible inch. Eradar ignored her ablutions, giving her privacy as he swam to depths she could never manage. One final turn in the water and Fiadh felt infinitely better. It was as though the soap had cleansed more than her worn form, rinsing the sadness and anger from her heart as surely as the dirt from her skin and replacing it with a sense of renewal. For a brief moment, she wondered if there was any truth to the random thought but shook her head, brushing off the possibility as she made her way to the edge of the pool.

Eradar swam after her, taking her arm before she could pull herself out. "You need to not go with the beast, you know."

Rivya rose with a snarl.

He let go of Fiadh's arm and held up his hands. "Peace, Rivya. I meant that only as an invitation. My queen would welcome this one into our realm."

The Cù-Sìth launched herself into the air, landing so close to Fiadh that she felt a smattering of dirt hit her face. Growls, deep and vicious, tore from Rivya's chest. Not wanting to be the cause of a fight, Fiadh hauled herself out of the water.

"Thank you for the invitation Eradar, but I think Rivya has made herself clear, and I have no wish to be the source of a quarrel."

He assessed the Cù-Sìth, then shifted his gaze to Fiadh. "As you wish, but know that you are welcome here."

She nodded and sent a thought to Rivya, sighing with relief as the female backed away.

Standing on the bank, the coolness of the air made Fiadh shiver, but she was loath to put on the soiled clothing that had been tossed on the ground. Rivya looked into a bank of trees just beyond the pool. Fiadh followed her gaze and watched as Krulan walked from the shadows and into the light, carrying a bundle of clothing in his mouth. He dropped it at her feet, and her heart caught for a moment as she looked at a dress, shift, and woolen stockings her mother had once worn.

You went to my hut? she asked.

Aye. I took only what you would need, Krulan told her.

Fiadh let pangs of grief wash over her as she picked up the clothing, but curiously the feeling did not linger, leaving her at peace as she looked for a place to change. Using a natural hedge for privacy, she pulled off her wet shift and hung it on a nearby branch to dry. Dasha poked his head between the small branches of the bush at the worst possible moment and croaked at her.

She gasped. "Shoo, you naughty bird!"

He ducked his head, only to poke it through again.

"Dasha! Leave me be!"

He gave her a few quick chirps, then flew to the ground on the other side of the bushes where she heard his tiny footfalls and pecks at the dirt. She hurriedly slipped into the clean clothes and emerged, giving the raven a look which he found amusing—if the noises he made were any indication. Bidding Eradar farewell, Fiadh followed the two Cù-Sìth into the forest, where they would take her to meet someone whose existence was mysteriously intertwined with hers.

CHAPTER TEN

Fiadh walked between Krulan and Rivya, taking comfort in their presence as they journeyed deeper into Erabel, a place that had survived the Great War, untouched. From the corner of her eyes, she caught glimpses, flashes of movement so quick that by the time she turned her head, there was nothing more than the lush flora that dominated every inch of the landscape. Fiadh shook her head, telling herself there was nothing peculiar. It was only her imagination.

Dasha, never letting her out of his sight, flew from tree to tree overhead, often peppering the quiet with squawks, croaks, and caws, all of which had some meaning as they paraded about her head. Much of what he conveyed was emotion—joy and excitement—but, every now and then, her vision would shift between his and hers, and she saw the world as he saw it. The action kept her off-balance, and she began to feel as though she were floating through the land-scape, adrift among mythical beasts who led her unresisting body to parts unknown. She found herself jerking back to awareness more than once, which only served to prick her temper. She needed to let her mind rest. She needed sleep and from the look of things, that wasn't happening soon enough.

Krulan and Rivya stopped, the abruptness causing Fiadh to bump into Krulan's shoulder, then stumble as her foot snagged on a gnarled root poking up from the ground. "Why'd you stop?" she groused, going quiet as she followed Krulan's heavy stare. Before the trio, within a deep depression of moss-covered earth, stood a man whose existence had resided firmly in stories of the past.

The man. No, he was not a man. The elf was tall and lean with broad shoulders under a rich green tunic that tapered to a trim waist and long muscular legs that seemed to spring from the earth itself in their deep green coverings. His hair, light where hers was dark, was braided for war and fell past his shoulders in fine white strands that caught the slight breeze, curling around the tips of pointed ears that broke through the pale fibers. She fixated on his face, the smooth skin, so like her own, covering a devastatingly handsome visage of prominent cheekbones, straight nose, and squared chin. There was something ethereal about him, and Fiadh felt herself begin to drift, drawn by whatever magnetism he embodied. He oozed power and awareness as though he could read her mind with a glance and understand her very being with an almost frightening intensity. She gaped at him, caught in his violet gaze, losing all sense of time.

Dasha pecked at her foot, bringing her embarrassingly back to the present. "Who are you?" she stammered.

"I am Veren of Oadsera," he told her.

The way he said it made her think it should mean something, but she had never heard of Oadsera. She was about to ask him about its significance when a small movement interrupted her question before it could form.

Just beyond the Aos Sí, a hulking animal waited in shadows too thick to reveal its full form, making this interloper suddenly feel threatening, though it had done nothing to elicit such emotion. Sensing her distress, Veren turned toward the animal and spoke a word in a language she had never heard. His voice matched the beauty of his face, sensual with a timbre that washed through her mind like a slow wave. The creature slowly came into the light, one darkly fettered hoof at a time until it was fully revealed. Fiadh's breath snagged in her chest. A unicorn.

Her legs felt watery as the magnificent animal stepped toward her, its heavy tread reverberating through the ground in muted thumps. Without thinking, she reached toward the creature with her mind, as she did with all wild things, communicating the hand of friendship. Acknowledgment and sentience rocked her thoughts with their earnest clarity, causing her eyes to go wide. The unicorn responded with a message free of words, but of such depth that it flooded her. Without thought, Fiadh reached out her hand, fingers splayed and hovering just beyond the animal's towering frame. Lowering its massive head, the unicorn snuffled her hand, its velvety nose sending tingles through her nerve endings. She marveled at the smoothness as her palm cupped the thick, equine jaw, fingers curling around its ears before tentatively touching the massive horn protruding from the black fur of its forehead. The animal was unlike any story that had traveled to her young ears as a child—tales of elegant horses with gracefully spiraling horns. This was no delicate beast of legend. This was a warhorse of the Aos Sí. Fiadh traced the thick ridges along the horn, the subtle rings so like those of the trunk of a tree, encircling it and adding depth to the dark hues that slowly faded to opaque at the deadly tip.

"Her name is Meara," Veren said in a voice hushed and deep.

Fiadh glanced at him, averting her eyes at the intensity of his stare. "She's beautiful." Turning back to the unicorn, Fiadh stroked the animal's face. "Hello, Meara," she said aloud while in her mind she added, *I'm Fiadh.* Meara bobbed her head, hoof striking the ground to create a deep furrow in the soft earth.

Letting out a faint sigh, Fiadh faced Veren. Meara moved to her side, a stalwart presence as Fiadh looked over the male who Krulan had promised would reveal secrets long buried, laying bare all that had been unsaid throughout the years of her life.

She opened her mouth to speak, snapping it closed when he said, "Fiadh, descendent of Rygeil, daughter of Erabel. Your arrival to these sacred grounds signifies the advent of a long-awaited prophecy when the Aos Sí will once again walk within Danu's shadow. Since the Great War, we have lived outside the warmth of our mother. With you, we will be rejoined. Healed. You are the future of our people."

A long pause followed his pronouncement, during which Fiadh mulled over his words, uncaring of the faces she made. Eradar, too, had made strange claims, her mind flashing back to the name he'd mentioned, Threa, and their supposed relationship, as though what he said were true. Now, here was another whose words jumbled her brain, making her feel as though she had lost her grip on reality.

Dasha, for once, stood still at her feet as though he understood now was not the time for play. Her mind struggled to make any sense of what Veren told her, tried and failed to meld that information with her life, a life utterly devoid of the Aos Sí or prophecies or mythical creatures. It felt like these realities were two planets, alien unto each other, about to collide in some cataclysmic event. It was both unsettling and irritating.

Clearing her throat, Fiadh looked Veren in the eye. "You speak of things that are not part of my reality, as though I am someone known to your people, but I have never seen or heard from anyone like you all the days of my life. How can you say that I am the descendent of someone I've never heard of? That I am somehow linked to this world, *your world*—a world that never existed for me until Krulan brought me into it." The last was said with a sharp glance at the Cù-Sìth who stood watching, his yellow stare free of judgment or rebuke.

Veren cocked his head, his eyes appraising her, taking her measure. "Of your life, I know nothing. I only know that you are awakening, heralding a new beginning long foreseen by those who know such things."

"Do all of you speak in riddles?" she shouted, catching

every eye, including Dasha, who croaked and flew to a low branch. "Even Eradar would tell me nothing but the same nonsense I hear now, and it is driving me mad! Why will you not simply explain things, so they make sense?"

"She met with the Merrow?" Veren asked, censure in his voice as he looked to Rivya and Krulan.

"Is that not allowed?" Fiadh demanded. "Am I not to permitted to speak with other creatures... er... *people* in this place?"

"The Merrow have their own, shall we say, intentions," Veren explained.

Frowning, Fiadh glanced at the Cù-Sìth, then back to Veren. "It seems each of you has your own intentions, and I have yet to see who's I wish to follow," she paused, "if any."

Veren opened his mouth, but she cut him off. "You speak as if I am part of your history, but I know *nothing* of your history. I know nothing of *you*!" She jabbed her finger at him. "What feels like only yesterday, my mother was murdered. I watched her die." She sobbed and angrily wiped her hand across her face. "Her body burned while the people she'd done nothing but care for screamed for the flames to consume her! And you, all of you, did nothing." Krulan looked away upon hearing her words, but not before he caught her glare. "No one saved her. Not even me. *That* is what I know." Fiadh swallowed a few times, collecting herself before whispering, "And I know the man that I loved thinks I betrayed him and would rather see me dead than by his side. And now this..." Fiadh flung her hand weakly, encompassing everything, "I cannot be these things you speak of. I am nothing more than who I am."

Veren strode forward, taking a knee, a handbreadth from her still form. Then, raising his head to look up at her, he proclaimed, "Fiadh, I am sworn to protect you. To see that you reclaim what is yours by birthright, but I see more than the daughter of Erabel standing before me. I see a woman who is unknown, even to herself." He paused, lifting his hand, palm up. "I will show you who you are, Fiadh, if you will but take my hand and let me lead you to the truth."

The pads of his fingers looked soft and inviting, extended in supplication, waiting for her to grasp their strength and surrender the world she had been born into for one that had claimed her. Fiadh clenched her hand as her arm lifted without her will, but she let it go, feeling the tiny trembles radiating through her body at the moment of contact. Veren curled his fingers around hers, and she felt the action went beyond the physical, as though her entire being was embraced, and it was alright. There was nothing to fear. The door to one world closed softly, with little more than a whisper.

A smile lit Veren's face. Fiadh returned the gesture, letting the weight of her palm rest fully in his.

"I am ready to listen."

He nodded. "I will tell you all that I know, and when I have finished, if there is more you wish to hear, I will find the answers. Come," Veren said, tugging on her hand, "let us go to the seat of Erabel and find some comfort for the recounting of your story."

Krulan rose, shaking off the debris that blended with the greenish hues of his pelt—rumbling low in his chest. *Follow, and I will take you to your birthright.*

CHAPTER ELEVEN

The scenery Gideon passed was achingly familiar, heavy with memories of a young woman he had been ready to pledge his life to before he discovered what she really was. Aishling must have sensed his mood because she patted his hand, the action so sweet and innocent that he reluctantly felt it in his heart, a place that had grown guarded.

"Are we almost there?" she asked.

"Aye, we should be there before nightfall."

Her head bumped against his chest as she nodded. "Are the people nice?"

He frowned, not sure how to answer. "I would think so."

Minutes passed as Aishling thought about where they were going and who would be there. She had never left her home until now. Craning her neck to look up at the man behind her, she wondered if he would be her papa now. He certainly looked old enough to be one, but he wasn't happy and silly like her father had been. She missed her family, especially her brother. They would often get into scrapes together, but he had saved her from the people who attacked her home.

"I miss Keiran," she blurted.

"I know," he said quietly. "I miss my brother too."

Twisting her body, she asked, "Did he pull your hair?"

Gideon gave a startled laugh. "Nay, that is a task for older brothers, and he was younger."

"Keiran pulled my hair sometimes, but I pinched him back, so we were even."

"I'm sure he meant no harm."

Facing forward again, she took in the rolling hills and clusters of trees. It looked much like the land around her home, but there was no village, no houses. The place Gideon was taking her felt very far away.

Aishling sighed. "I wish I was home."

"Me too. But we cannot change the past."

She huffed and picked at a loose thread on her tunic. Her bottom was sore from so many days on the horse, though Aridius was the most beautiful animal she'd ever seen. Leaning forward, she pressed her cheek to his mane and kissed him. The animal nickered and tossed his head, making her giggle. Running her hand down his soft neck, she took a few strands of his mane and began to braid them. Gideon watched the swift movements of her fingers before shifting his attention back to their surroundings.

A few minutes later, Aishling announced, "Look, Gideon, he's got braids!"

Glancing down, he saw four clumsy sections of braided mane. "He looks very handsome."

She beamed. "Mama taught me to braid. I'm good at it, but she's better."

"It looks to me like you've got a fair talent," he said, picking up one of the masses and running his fingers along the woven strands.

"Do you gots a lady?" she asked, taking him by surprise.

An image of Fiadh leaped into his mind. "I did once."

"Why isn't she here? Is she dead?"

Gideon shook his head. "She lives, but she lied to me."

"Lying is bad," she said quietly.

"Aye, it is." Not wishing to answer questions about Fiadh, he pulled a woolen blanket from his saddlebag and tucked it around her tiny shoulders. "You should rest now. You'll want to be wide awake when we get to Felmore."

"But I'm not tired," she argued with a yawn.

He snorted. "Aye, you are." Gideon pressed her head against his chest and hummed a tune he hadn't thought of in many years. In time, her body relaxed, and she slumped in his arms, leaving him free to think about things he shouldn't as the ground passed beneath his mount's hooves.

Gideon stopped at the entrance of Felmore Castle. Shifting in his saddle, he looked up at the soldiers who paced the wall-walk in the late afternoon sun as he waited for the raising of the portcullis. Belfirth was opulent compared to this keep, all light and airy. By contrast, the dark stone of Lord Darragh's fortress was stained from the elements and years of neglect, giving the edifice a foreboding look. It occurred to him, as he studied the stronghold, that may have been the intent. He could clearly see that atop the tall walls were well-cared for iron spikes glinting in the waning light, proof that rust and age could be prevented should the lord wish it. As the gate groaned open, he shook Aishling awake.

She looked around, bleary-eyed, and began to struggle.

"Be still, Aishling," he chided. "We have come to Felmore."

"It looks scary," she whimpered.

"It is just a keep, like any other."

Her little face darted from the soldiers along the wall to the massive gate that looked like the mouth of a dragon to her young eyes. "Are the bad people in there?" she asked, anxiety pitching her voice higher than normal.

"Nay, we are far away from them."

He led Aridius through the passageway and into the bailey, wrinkling his nose as the stench of rotted hay and refuse wafted in the air. His home had suffered the stench often enough when the heat of the summer bore down on them, but his father would never allow such squalor to be the norm. A stable boy jogged toward them, taking the reins as he dismounted, and lifted Aishling's trembling body to the ground. "See that my mount gets fresh hay and oats," Gideon said, grabbing the scruff of the child's neck as he turned away. "And put him in a clean stall, boy. I'll not have him come away with thrush."

"Aye, milord."

Gideon watched as Aridius was installed in the dim stable, then scanned his surroundings. Aishling's hands clutched his as though she meant to use all her strength to stay at his side. She would be difficult, he realized, as he looked for a structure in which to leave her while he spoke to Lord Darragh. A few knights were lounging about the courtyard. They eyed him and his charge, laughing and pointing, as though he were some poor country knight, while he brushed off his tunic and strode toward a small alcove at the base of the castle steps.

Wrenching Aishling's hands from his, he pushed her gently onto the stone bench that jutted from the wall. "You must await me here, Aishling."

She shook her head. "I don't like it here. It smells and…" she looked around, eyes wide with fear, "the people look mean."

He couldn't argue with either point. "Never you mind about the smell. No one will bother you if you stay put. I'm going to speak to the lord of this keep, and then I will come and fetch you."

Her bottom lip trembled. "Promise?"

"Aye." She tucked her feet onto the bench, tugging her shift and tunic over the bareness of her legs. "There's a good girl. Wait here, and I will return shortly."

Aishling nodded, tears pooling in her eyes, but said nothing. He studied her for a moment, then stalked to the entrance of the keep.

An older man greeted him just outside the doorway. "Good day, my lord. I am Kean, the steward."

"I am Gideon Hughes of Belfirth."

"This way, my lord," Kean said, leading him into the great hall.

Smoke hung in the air from the massive fireplace.

Gideon noted a thick coating of soot crawling up the wall and wondered briefly why no one had addressed the issue. With Donal at his side, Lord Darragh sat in an oversized chair on the dais, marking his presence but saying nothing. Gideon met his gaze, unimpressed by Darragh's stature and indifferent to the glower emanating from the wiry man.

"Lord Gideon Hughes of Belfirth, my lord," Kean announced as Gideon stood at his side.

Darragh shifted, stretching out his legs like a cat. "Belfirth? You are far from home. What brings you to the western fold?" he asked, noting the man's broad shoulders and warrior stance. It bothered him that an ally of Lord Crommack had arrived unsolicited.

"I have come to warn you of an uprising."

"Oh?"

"The Aos Sí have declared war on men," Gideon said flatly. "They have slaughtered my people and ransacked Lord Crommack's holding, leaving none alive."

Darragh's lips twitched at the news of Eoghan Crommack's death. With the old man gone, none would come for him seeking vengeance for the murder of his daughter and Darragh's young wife. Glancing toward the passage leading to the dungeon, he gave a quick thought for his mother, Haegna, who had once again eluded punishment for her wickedness. He swiped a hand over his mouth to hide his smile and cleared his throat. "It grieves me to hear of your loss. May the Great Mother bless them. But... hm... how am I to say this? Have you proof that it was the Aos Sí?" He watched the young soldier as his words hit their mark, so much like the others who came seeking his aid.

Heat and anger flooded Gideon's features before he could mask them. It further galled him to see Darragh note the emotion and smirk. "Proof? The proof is laying in pools of blood from a thousand corpses!" For a moment, he considered adding what he knew about Fiadh, knowing full-well the man wanted to capture Riona's daughter. But something stayed his tongue, and he had no time to analyze it.

Darragh tsk'd. "You have a temper, young Hughes. Much like your father did."

Gideon's lip curled. "I have my father's skill as well," he said coolly.

"Skill that saw him lead his people to death and destruction," Donal said coldly.

Darragh raised his hand. "Nay, nay, Donal, there is no need for that. Lord Hughes' prowess on the field was well regarded by all." He smiled at Gideon. "*Your* skill in battle is something I am truly interested in." Confusion washed over Gideon's face, but he said nothing, only watched as the lord straightened and rested his hands on the arms of his ornate chair. "You are not the first knight to seek my counsel and support. Others have come from the north and east, claiming what you have said."

Gideon lifted his chin and folded his hands behind his back. "And did *their* words convince you?"

Darragh shrugged. "Let us say that I am open to the possibility that a few Aos Sí may yet live, but…" he said slyly, "I see no need to sound the alarm and raise my banners for crimes that may well be the work of feuding lords or ruffians."

Rage bloomed in Gideon's chest, and he struggled to

contain it, unwilling to give Darragh the satisfaction of seeing him lose control. Was the man a fool, or was there something more sinister at play? If it was a game, one his father had played many times before, he would do well to make subtle moves as he sized up his opponent. "I can assure you that my army and my people were not slaughtered at the hands of men."

"I would like to believe you. Truly I would," he said, casually crossing his ankles, "but you are speaking of a race that my own grandfather, Lord Magnar, ran to ground. His sword was bathed in their blood. So, you will forgive me my skepticism."

Donal crossed his arms. "Have you no army left, my lord?"

"Nay," Gideon said coldly. "I am all that is left of my line."

"That is unfortunate," Darragh said in a tone that implied he didn't view it as unfortunate at all. "We have a dilemma it seems, do we not, Donal?"

His commander nodded. "Aye, my lord."

"If what you say proves true, either by your means or another's, I will raise my banners and strike out to meet the enemy."

Gideon gave him a stiff bow. "Thank you, my lord."

Darragh waved away the gratitude. "I would require fealty, of course."

"My lord?"

"I could use your strong arm if, by some rare chance, the Aos Sí have indeed managed to muster a small force." He paused as though waiting for Gideon to let his anger surface, then added, "In exchange for my support of your cause, you would, of course, pledge yourself to me. Your lands, your holdings, such as they are, to give annual tribute to Felmore, your people, if there are any left, sworn to be my bannermen from now until the end of your line."

Gideon glared at Darragh, whose dark eyes gave away nothing. "I do not make such pledges, but I will lend my strength of arm," he said, earning him a hard stare. "I have much to avenge," he added darkly.

Darragh's mouth curled in a malicious smile. "Well, we can return to such matters at a later date."

"And my answer shall remain the same. You may have my sword and my loyalty for as long as you do battle with the Aos Sí. That much I shall pledge. But no more."

"I like his fire," Darragh said to Donal.

"Aye, he has that," Donal said. "I wonder at his skill with a blade."

Gideon didn't take the bait, only stood silently.

Chuckling, Darragh rose and took measured steps toward Gideon, reaching out his arm to clasp wrists. "You are welcome to stay with the other emissaries who have come seeking my counsel as we consider what you've claimed."

Gideon backed away, intending to leave the hall, when Darragh's voice interrupted his progress.

"I am curious, *Lord Hughes*. Why come to my holding? Why not go south to Taigon and find a place in the king's army?" Gideon began to answer but was cut off abruptly. "Wait... wait," Darragh said, holding out a hand. "Your father and King Stephan have... *had* .... hm... shall we say, bad blood?"

Gideon ground his teeth. "It is no secret."

Darragh sniggered. "I have little use for the king myself. He is a weak man."

Gideon said nothing, only lifted his chin.

"You were wise to come to me in his stead," Darragh said. "*I* rule the western reaches."

Gideon masked his look of distaste, standing stoically as Darragh puffed his chest with imagined greatness and launched into what sounded like a prepared speech of self-importance. When he was finished with his empty monologue, Gideon bowed his head in deference.

"Donal will introduce you to the men who have flocked to me and will give you command over a small band whose skill remains... lacking."

Gideon nodded and followed Donal from the hall.

CHAPTER TWELVE

$\mathcal{M}$eara was at Fiadh's side as Krulan threaded their way through vegetation, whose thick branches were weighted with heavy fruit of every hue. Reaching toward a particularly succulent one the size of an apple and the color of eggplant, she stopped, feeling the smooth skin as she tugged it free. Pressing her thumb into its flesh, Fiadh felt the supple give of the meat inside, hearing the soft tear as her nail pierced the skin, releasing a pungent odor that made her mouth water. It reminded her of the ahgawi she ate earlier, though the scent was less citric. Meara snuffled her shoulder, nudging gently as she eyed Fiadh's hand. Chuckling, Fiadh held it out, watching as the unicorn consumed the fruit in a series of messy smacks from her equine lips.

"Meara has a fondness for jeboa," Veren commented, indicating more of the fruit drooping from the foliage by Fiadh's side. "It's quite safe for you to eat."

Rubbing her sticky, drool-coated palm on her skirts,

Fiadh plucked another with her clean hand and bit into it, feeling the juices drip down her chin as she hummed in pleasure. Grainy sweetness spread across her tongue, dripping down her throat in delicious clots. Swallowing, she took another bite, slurping gently in a bid to devour as much as possible as Dasha hopped on her shoulder and snatched a hunk, flying off with a triumphant caw as Rivya snapped at him.

That bird is overly bold, Rivya growled.

I don't mind his boldness, Fiadh replied, putting an end to her criticism.

The Cù-Sìth grumbled and settled on the ground.

The jeboa was gone in a matter of minutes, leaving only traces of pale orange pulp on her fingertips which she sucked off one at a time. Soft laughter filled the quiet as Veren grabbed a piece himself and neatly ate it with an expertise that left no trace of juicy sweetness on his person. She looked at her messy hands, feeling young and clumsy.

"It appears you like our jeboa fruit," he chuckled.

Fiadh nodded. "It was delicious," she said, reaching for another.

"Perhaps you should wait a bit," Veren told her.

She frowned, plucking one anyway and dropping it into the large pocket of her overskirt. Looking at him, Fiadh said, "For later."

Veren cocked an eyebrow. "As you wish."

"Before we arrive at… wherever Krulan's taking us… I have questions that I'd like answered." He said nothing, and she asked, "Will you tell me of yourself?"

He nodded. "I come from Oadsera, one of the

remaining Aos Sí lands. It lies in the east, in the heart of the Felraine Vale."

The name struck a chord, and Fiadh's heart skipped. That was where Gideon's army was attacked and slaughtered. Fiadh wondered if Veren was among the warriors that cut the army down.

"You would find it different from here," he continued, "though no less beautiful. There are trees as tall as small mountains, their branches spanning distances so great that entire communities rest beneath their shelter. Through the center runs the Naebora River, home of the last of the Enbarr."

Confusion flashed across Fiadh's face. "Enbarr?"

Veren pursed his lips. "I gather you have not heard of them?"

"Nay."

"How shall I describe them?" he said absently, tapping his hand on his leg. "To you, they would look like a horse, pure white with pale pink eyes, but that is where the resemblance ends. The Enbarr cross both land and water, though the remaining few prefer the waters of the Naebora and rarely leave them. They have seen too much of battle, and many lost the will to live in the Great War."

"How awful for them," Fiadh whispered, her natural affinity for wild things unerringly reaching toward that foreign species.

"Aye, many died at the hands of *men*." The last was said with an acid tone that made Fiadh flinch.

"Others," he went on, "went into hiding, carving out a place among our people where they would be protected from that race. You know, it is said the Aos Sí sprang from the place of my birth, from the earth that lies deep within Oadsera—a place warmed by the heart of this world."

"Is it true?" she asked. "Is that where the Aos Sí are from?"

His violet eyes snagged hers, crinkling in the corners. "Perhaps, though there are many legends of our people, many birthplaces, so it is impossible to know from which we truly came."

"Does Erabel have a place among those myths?"

"Nay, though it has its own history, one which rings truer than many I have heard. You see, each kingdom has its histories that seek to carve out a piece of the origin of the Aos Sí, giving each realm prestige or some other desirable trait. But… Erabel is… unique. It is the newest kingdom, birthed in a time of a great resurgence of magic."

"Magic?" Fiadh asked. "I used to think the magic of the Aos Sí was simply a bedtime story parents told their children to frighten them."

Veren cocked an eyebrow, "Is magic evil, then?"

"I…I don't…" Fiadh's mouth ran dry, and she suddenly felt ignorant. A tiny flare of resentment for her mother ignited at having been so sheltered that her view of the world was limited to that of a child's understanding. Just as quickly as it caught, the anger was snuffed out, that odd sense of rightness swallowing it even as she tried to hold onto those bitter feelings.

What was in that water? Fiadh thought for a moment before that too was gone.

The Merrow have ancient power, but they are not a malicious race, Krulan said, his words weaving through her mind.

I meant nothing by it, Fiadh told him.

If they have given you a gift from their sacred waters, accept and do not question it.

You're always telling me not to ask questions, and I'm sick of it, Krulan.

He huffed, the sound loud in the quiet of their surroundings. *Patience, young one. Patience.*

She glanced at Krulan, catching the corner of his eye, and stuck out her tongue. Returning her attention to Veren before Krulan could respond, she said, "In truth, I know nothing of magic or your people. Only fragments of stories meant to foment hatred and fear."

"The children of men would know best how to conjure lies," Veren muttered darkly. "*Our* people," he told her, ignoring the face she made, "have harnessed magic since the beginning of time. It springs from the earth, as we do, and at our birth, it binds itself to us and grows as we age. But," he said, looking deeply into her, "if it is not nurtured, trained, magic can grow twisted and dark."

His words felt like a warning. If she were, by some far stretch of the imagination, part of this strange place, then wouldn't she be warped and twisted?

"You have nothing to fear within yourself, Fiadh," Veren said. "Yours is the magic of Erabel, of Danu herself."

"Do you mean to imply that I am incorruptible?"

He thought for a moment, as though shaping his response. "I would not say that, but it is pure. You need not worry."

Fiadh tucked that away, knowing she'd pull it out later and consider what he meant.

"Do they all look like you?" she blurted. "The Aos Sí."

"Don't you mean like us?" he teased.

She rolled her eyes. "I have yet to embrace those claims."

Veren laughed, the sound bouncing off the trees in a resonant melody. "Ah, Fiadh, I have longed to meet you, and I find that my anticipation has been richly rewarded." She made a face but bit her tongue, and he continued, "Each tribe is different. Those of us from Oadsera look much like me, with pale hair and violet eyes, while you and your grandfather are blessed with your darker coloring and green eyes. Many of those from other kingdoms are much like us, light-skinned and lanky bodies, but the peoples of the north and south have features as varied as the lands they dwell in."

Veren reached toward her, brushing her hair away from her face, and let out a gasp as he tucked it behind her ear. "Who mutilated your ears?" he demanded, anger flushing his face.

"What do you mean?" Fiadh asked, feeling the tips of her ears where thick scar tissue left them somewhat blunted. "When I was a babe, I was attacked by a neighbor's dog. Mother did the best she could, but the damage was great."

Pity washed over Veren's features. "Ah, Fiadh, that is just a story your mother told you, to keep you hidden, safe, from mankind."

"Wha… what do you mean?"

"Your ears," Veren said softly, "were once like mine. I

would guess that she cut them when you were but a few weeks old."

Fiadh spun away from him, her hands pressed to her mangled ears, feeling the scars that she had long since regarded as nothing more than an unfortunate accident she could never recall. Had her ears truly been pointed? It seemed impossible, but as she ran her fingers over the ugly edges, doubt took root and, within it, came images of her brother, Calum. His hair, dark like hers, had always been long, hadn't it? Was it to hide something, or was it simply the result of a mother who could not bear to cut her son's beautiful hair?

Uncomfortable with how he had shifted her focus, she straightened her shoulders and turned to Veren. "The scars on my ears are long since healed and their origins unimportant. Let us speak more of this place."

His eyes danced for a moment, but he gave in. "What would you like to know?"

"Why Erabel? Why not do—whatever it is you are aiming to do—in your own homeland?"

The muscles in his jaw ticked before he smoothed his features. "Erabel has a rare place in our history. Like all peoples, the Aos Sí inhabited pockets across the world, at times nomadic as they sought new lands, and it was a small band, those with a rare link to Danu, who settled in a place of power within Dorcha Wood. As they established a permanent settlement, Erabel was born and from those beginnings grew a tribe with unique powers."

Fiadh's brow creased. "Do you share that bloodline?"

"My grandmother was of Erabel and wed my grandfather during the festival of Ré. Erabel is in my blood, though thinned with that of another tribe." Veren looked away for a moment, fixed his eyes on a low-hanging branch on which sat a large owl whose yellow gaze watched the interlopers. "In the Great War, when so many of our people were slaughtered, those of us who remained... struggled. There were so many gone. It was a dark time." He paused, throat bobbing as he swallowed around a lump of old grief. "For some of us, there was no recovery, and madness took them, or they simply withered until Danu came, embracing them as she ferried their lifeforce to the shores of Varellaen." Veren looked at Fiadh. "But, others were riddled with so much rage that they welcomed the darkness within themselves. Rygeil is one who began to seek it. " He looked meaningfully at her when he added, "Erabel is the light."

"And me? What is it you claim me to be?"

He smiled wryly. "Claim?"

She tilted her head and stared up at him. "Aye, claim. I've seen no proof of the fanciful tales you and Eradar are so fond of telling me."

"Proof?"

She nodded curtly.

"The proof is all around you, Fiadh. Look at your raven!"

She turned to Dasha, who spread his wings, positively gloating at the attention. He let out a shrill cry and bobbed his head. Fiadh couldn't help but smile, which only served to encourage the bird to louder, more flagrant displays until Veren quietly said, "That will do, Dasha."

If birds could make a face, he gave Veren one worthy of

eyebrow-raising, but he did quiet, feathers settling with only a couple of garbled croaks.

"Did you have a connection such as that before you crossed the boundaries of Erabel?"

She shook her head. "Nay," she whispered.

"Erabel is in your blood. You are the child of Threa, and she was the daughter of Rygeil. Your mother was strong, powerful, but she could not survive the darkness that consumed her world. You are what is left of her. You, Fiadh, are the beacon that calls to the true children of Danu." He took her hand and stroked her fingertips, titling them backward until their palms pressed against each other. "Close your eyes. Trust me," he said at her uncertainty. "Now, reach out with your mind, and you will feel me there."

Sweeping her lashes down, she shut her eyes and focused her senses on the texture of his skin beneath her hand, the smoothness, so at odds with the warrior who stood before her. Fiadh cocked her head as tingles of awareness began at her fingertips and traveled through her blood and into her mind. Her mouth gaped in the moment of their connection, and her mind went blank, coming to blinding life as a deep awareness of him swelled until it became a palpable thing, so strong she could feel the tether that bound her to him— an iron cable that nothing, save death, could sunder. Veren pulled his hand from hers, and though she felt the loss of the contact, the sensations of him with her consciousness did not wane.

Fiadh opened her eyes, and Veren took a step back, an expression of wonder engulfing his face. "What?" she asked, rubbing her hands together to rekindle the sensations from moments ago.

A huge grin split his face, making his already striking visage positively breathtaking. "Your eyes are glowing with her light."

"Huh?"

"Danu's blood is within you, Fiadh. It is unmistakable. I think our connection amplified it, or perhaps it is simply your return to the home of your people, but I can see the change, and it is exquisite."

Fiadh touched her face as if she could feel what Veren saw. She looked at Dasha, who met her stare, cocking his head so that his purple iris snagged hers. Without effort, Fiadh slipped from her perspective to his and looked upon herself. It was there, just as Veren said. A luminance, so much like the other creatures of this strange place. She let go of Dasha, then felt Krulan tapping at her mind.

Look there, Fiadh. It is the seat of your kingdom.

CHAPTER THIRTEEN

It wasn't what she had anticipated, and, yet, it was everything she imagined. The heart of Erabel was a wildly overgrown collection of ancient buildings with breathtaking spires and arched entries. The white of the stone aged over time until its starkness had become a muted grey that blended among the dappled shadows of massive trees. A myriad of complex masonry, with creatures and peoples of every type, was carved into the rocky facades so deeply that time could only blunt the artistry, not erase it.

Fiadh looked up, noting that over everything were vines twined with flowers and waterfalls of moss that bathed the extraordinary world in every greenish hue Fiadh could conceive.

Veren and the Cù-Sìth stood at Fiadh's sides as her gaze consumed what remained of the most beautiful civilization she had ever seen. Despite the absence of the Aos Sí, the settlement thrived, its inhabitants feathered and furred, darting in and out of openings or scurrying along overrun cobbled pathways. It was haunting. It was beautiful.

Dasha flew to the top of a stone pillar, cawing at her with wings splayed, inviting her to play. *Aye!* she told him, opening herself to his playful excitement, feeling the weight she carried fall away as Dasha's joy filled her mind. Meara nickered and ambled to a bush hanging with fruit, snatching a piece with her velvety lips. Fiadh smiled at the unicorn, then glanced at Veren and jerked her head, indicating the raven. He nodded and went to sit on a bench, Krulan and Rivya following.

Dasha leaned forward, head down, and watched her enter the large, overgrown courtyard. She put her hands on her hips and looked up at him. He croaked, then tucked his head beneath a wing, turning slightly to completely cover his sharp eyes. Fiadh ran, shutting her mind to him lest he sensed her thoughts, and hid among a thick patch of bushes. The flap of his wings indicated his flight to find her. Clamping her hand over her mouth to keep from giggling, she listened as he swept through the courtyard or hopped from branches and stone, looking for her. When he came particularly close, she held her breath, muscles bunching. Dasha cawed triumphantly, and she erupted from her hiding place with a screech as he chased her.

Fiadh's laughter filled the air.

Veren spoke softly to Krulan and Rivya, his face reflecting contentment as he watched the girl dance among the flowers and ruins. Whether she had accepted it or not, Erabel had taken hold of her, filling her body with a power she had yet to fully realize and test. She looked so like her mother, Threa, he mused. Her smile. The carefree spirit that shone in her face. And, though she knew it not, Fiadh exuded Threa's strength. She would need it in the days to come.

Panting, face flushed, Fiadh trudged to where the trio sat, collapsing on the bench beside Veren. "Dasha would test anyone's stamina," she said, watching the bird sail through the sky with no sign of weariness.

It is his rapscallion heart that makes him tireless, Rivya said wryly.

Fiadh snorted. *I doubt it not.*

"It's beautiful here," Fiadh said to no one in particular.

"Aye, it is. You should have seen it when all the tribes gathered for the festival of Ré. There was food and music, talk and song. The candlelight mirrored the stars…" he said wistfully, drifting off in thought before turning to face her. "Mayhap, these halls will fill with celebration again someday."

She ducked her head. "That would be something I would like to see."

"Come, let me show you more," Veren said, indicating the most prominent structure.

Fiadh nodded and reached for Krulan's shoulder, sinking her hand into his fur to give her ballast. Everywhere she looked, she caught sight of new and familiar creatures, some like Darrow, who crept to the edges of the walkways and watched her with dark, penetrating eyes. Unlike the people of the Coll, whose reddish skin blended with the darkness of the Hazel trees they called home, these beings had skin so pale it appeared pink, creating a stark contrast to the darkness of their knowing stare. She nodded to them as the group passed, feeling the weight of their perusal as they sized her up. Fiadh held her head high, and Veren glanced at her, thinking how regal she looked.

Krulan, with Rivya at his side—rulers in their own right—took the small party into the hallowed halls of Erabel while Dasha flew ahead of his mistress. A delicately arched entry, easily twice the height of a man, opened into a wide hall that branched in three directions. Krulan led her along a straight path and into an enormous room lined with benches and tables caked in years of dust. Fiadh gazed in wonder, drawn to the murals that covered the walls in exquisite depictions of the history of this sacred place. Despite decades of neglect, the great hall smelled sweet, bedecked in cascades of flowers that hung from drooping branches or vines that erupted from cracks and crevices throughout the derelict interior. Birds flitted about, trilling welcome as Fiadh stepped slowly through the hall, her footfalls crunching dried petals and leaves that covered the floor in a dazzling mosaic of color and texture. It was beautiful. And melancholy. The room felt bereft though it was filled with life, as though the heart of it had been torn out, leaving a shell of what it had been.

Fiadh gave Krulan a look, waiting until he bobbed his head slowly, communicating his permission to wander about alone before they got down to serious business. The whisper of her gown as it brushed the floor followed her as she strolled the quiet space. Hidden under the ravages of time were artifacts of a people Fiadh knew little about yet was connected with in a way she could not fully accept. She swept a finger through a layer of dust to see the patterns on an ornate plate that sat forlornly on the edge of a table and turned her head, noting a vase on its side next to an overturned chair. It dawned on her that the room was filled with the leavings of people who had fled in haste. The realization made the scene feel ominous, though Fiadh knew the threat which had forced the residents from these exquisite halls was long gone.

Settling her gaze on Veren, Fiadh asked, "What happened here?"

A shadow fell over Veren's features as he extended a hand, beckoning her. She walked toward him, eyeing his fingers, their length and pale perfection, before placing hers in his grasp, feeling the tickle of awareness that washed over her skin. "Come, there is a place I want to show you."

Krulan and Rivya stayed behind as Veren led Fiadh through a small archway and into what must have once been a breathtaking garden. It was the heart of the structure, surrounded as though to keep it safe. In the center grew an enormous oak, so tall that its uppermost branches spilled up and over the edifice, casting a play of shadows upon the floor. Fiadh craned her neck as she took it in. Its impossible height and girth, as though the halls of the Aos Sí had grown around it, cradling its magnificence. Dasha flew in circles around the tree, the beating of his wings sending leaves fluttering. Angling toward the earth, he landed at her feet and looked at her.

She reached down and stroked his head, watching his feathers puff forward. Hopping away, he led her to the massive oak, jerking his head to the trunk of the tree with a series of quick motions. Glancing from him to the oak, she let her feet take her the remainder of the way, cocking her head as a tugging sensation bloomed in her chest, like that of a fisherman whose line has caught. Fiadh was being reeled in, pulled by a force that wrapped itself around her mind and body. When she was little more than a finger-length from the oak, she stopped and pressed her hand against the rough bark, running her fingers along the rises and dips.

From within the tree came a voice, clear as though its owner stood at her side, motherly in its warmth and entreaty. *Fiadh, my daughter. You have come.*

Her eyes went wide, and she pressed her palms flatter, needing to feel and hear more, her mouth slipping open in a small moue. Power radiated from the oak, slowly at first, a nearly imperceptible tremor that grew until it bordered on pain. Fiadh's arms locked, body going rigid. She clenched her jaw so tightly her face ached as currents of energy poured over and into her, racing through her blood and into every organ, surging through every vessel until heat bloomed with such intensity that a whimper escaped her lips. She stood, immobile, ensnared by a being whose essence sank so deep she felt it in her core. Fiadh's body began to shake, fingers gripping the bark so fiercely they curled into claws.

She called to Krulan in her mind, begging him to help her, free her before her heart raced in such a frantic tempo it tore through her chest. Fiadh felt him catch her thought and respond.

Open yourself. Ask what you will, and Danu will show you. Through her, you will discover who you are.

Fiadh gritted her teeth, willing her mind to let go, empty of all thought. Flares of warning washed over her in waves of red, and she beat them back, forcing herself to abandon her mental defenses. Suddenly, she stood beneath the mighty oak no more. A piece of her was ripped from her body and flung into the air, propelled through space and time, pulled past decades of dizzying scenes before coming to rest in a time not her own.

CHAPTER FOURTEEN

*D*onal led Gideon as far as the inner bailey, motioning to the outbuilding where various men had claimed space for themselves and their retinue. Thanking the commander, Gideon took off to the alcove where he had left Aishling, coming to an abrupt halt when he saw that she was missing. He spun in a slow circle, marking every face, every shadowed recess, and finding nothing. Thinking she may have gone to the stables to see Aridius, he strode into the building, barking at the stable boy to show him where his mount had been housed. The boy led him to a stall, but aside from his horse, she was gone. Panic sent his heart racing. Had she wandered off?

Patting Aridius absently, he turned to the stable boy who watched him warily from a few paces away, hands twisting in his worn tunic. "Boy," Gideon said, motioning for the child to come closer.

He moved two steps and stopped, fear in his face as he darted a glance at Gideon's hands. "Aye, milord?"

"I arrived with a young girl." The boy nodded. "Did you see where she went?"

"Nay, milord."

Gideon ground his teeth, anger and worry flashing in his eyes as he looked toward the stable opening. Giving the boy a curt nod, he left, his feet eating up the distance in his haste to find his charge. Just before his stride took him out of the stable, he heard a noise.

"What?" he asked, turning around to face the child who had come after him.

The boy fingered the edge of his tunic where a hole in the woolen fabric grew wider. "I… know not where she went, but…" he paused, eyes wide as they scanned the bailey. Stepping closer and motioning for Gideon to lean in, he whispered, "the witch may have taken her. Children go missing here, milord."

"Witch?"

"Aye, I've seen her. She takes young ones. They don't come back. Not ever."

Straightening, Gideon looked around, trying to make sense of the boy's warning. Of witches, he knew naught but the foul ravings of suspicious people. Riona had suffered for that ignorance in this very village, and by the man he had just met with. He was not one to see evil where there was none, but mayhap the boy had spoken, not of witchery, but of some other wicked vice.

"Where might this witch be found?"

The child's face scrunched as he recalled where he'd seen the woman. "I've seen her around the cellar often enough."

"Where is that?"

Motioning to an alcove, he said, "Just through there, milord." He scampered off into the safety of the smells and sounds of the stable.

Gideon's hands clenched as he stalked to the alcove the boy had indicated. It was a dark passageway, lit only by the sunlight that pierced the murder holes along one wall. There were three doorways branching off from the passage, and he stood for a moment, eyes flicking from one to the other, indecision rooting his feet to the stone. A muffled noise drifted to his ears, and he zeroed in on the door from which it came, cocking his head to listen. There it was again, a whimper, then a plea that ripped through his body like a rage-tipped arrow. He burst through the entry, a roar tearing from his chest as he saw Aishling being dragged through a tiny doorway not much taller than herself by a wizened maidservant.

He ran to the child, wrenching her away from hands that held her arm in a vise-like grip. Gideon hissed and spat at the old woman, reigning curses at her as she scuttled away in fear. He swept Aishling into his arms and fled, not stopping until he had burst into the stables and yelled for the boy to ready his mount.

Aishling shook and twined her arms around his neck. "Are you hurt?" he asked, running his hands along her back in search of injury.

She shook her head. "I told her I didn't want to go, but she made me."

"It's not your fault," he told her, patting her head as she

began to sob. "Hush, now. We are leaving this place. Hush, Aishling."

From the dimness of the stable came Aridius, led by the boy who looked at Aishling and blanched. His frightened eyes found Gideon's, and he gulped. "Y… your horse, milord."

Gideon took the reins, dropping two silver coins in the boy's hand. "For your aid and your silence."

His small fingers curled around the money, an amount he'd never possessed until that moment. "Aye, milord. None shall hear of it."

Swinging up behind Aishling, he rode sedately through the bailey, not wishing to attract unwanted attention, and left the castle, kicking the horse into a gallop as soon as he deemed it safe.

They didn't stop for hours, not until the sun sank below the horizon. Aishling had fallen asleep, her ordeal and the hard ride having taken their toll. Gideon spread a blanket on the ground and gently placed her within its folds, crouching at her side when she was settled. He should never have taken her to Felmore. Even if that crazed woman hadn't snatched her, she would not have been safe. Witch or no, a castle full of bloodthirsty men on the cusp of war was no place for a child. He sighed and dropped his head, hands clutching his skull. The souls of his family, of all of Belfirth, called to him for vengeance and he could not ignore their pleas. But, this girl also called to him in some indefinable way. He could turn his back on war, on the blood and screams that had dogged him for so long. They could leave this place, go into the wilds of the north, into the peaks of the Scarlet Mountains, where no lord or king held sway, and carve out a life together. He could be a father, a role he had tasted on Fiadh's lips before she'd betrayed him.

Here now was a second chance for a different life. He had enough money to build a small manor, buy a plot of land, tend it and raise the girl to a life of peace and ease and plenty far away from the troubles and wars of men and elves. And as Darragh's lickspittle had pointed out, what difference would his blade alone make in the coming war? He brought no armies to the fray. And yet… he had sworn an oath, sworn it over the broken bodies of his family. He would avenge them—those who murdered them, who murdered his people, who murdered Aishling's family. They would pay.

Rubbing down and tethering his mount, Gideon thought it over, feeling the pull of both futures. He fetched a crust of bread and the wineskin from his saddlebag and sat on a rock not far from where Aishling slept, mind churning as he ate. Looking up at the stars blanketing the sky, he spoke to the Great Mother. At first, the words were stilted, coming in fits and starts as he acknowledged she held sway over all people, even the Aos Sí. Which race the goddess preferred and protected was a mystery, but if she heard him, if she still resided in the realms of *his* people, perhaps she would guide his hand.

He spoke of many things as he muttered into the soft breeze blowing through the landscape, in the end, admitting his wish to leave the life of a soldier and find peace some-where. When he'd finished, he listened, hoping for a reply, something, some nudge to go this way or that. But all was silent save for a gentle wind that lifted his hair, almost pulling it. He looked toward the direction it blew—the Scarlet Mountains.

He had made a promise to Aishling, that fragile, innocent thing who had nobody in the world but him. He had promised he would not leave her. And what was worth more, a promise to the living or a promise to the dead? All he knew was he could fight and die and, mayhap, take a few Aos Sí with him. But what would it achieve? It would not bring his brother back to life, nor his father or mother or any of them. But for this child, this girl who was the last of his people, the last of the people he was sworn to serve and protect. Aye, he could make a difference there. He could see her safe and happy, at least.

They began their journey early the following day, heading in a northeasterly direction. If he were to keep them alive in the remote peaks of the Scarlet Mountains, he'd need more than the dwindling foodstuffs in his saddlebag. Aishling was quiet for much of the morning as they rode, perking up when they stopped at midday.

"Where will we go now?" she asked, stuffing a small hunk of cheese in her mouth.

"First, we'll stop at Dungraven for food and supplies, and then we'll head north."

She tilted her head and squinted into the horizon. "I'm tired of riding," Aishling sighed, then looked over at Aridius. "Sorry, Aridius. I didn't mean to hurt your feelings." The animal lifted his head and nickered. She looked at Gideon and said, "He forgives me."

Arching an eyebrow, Gideon asked, "Aye? And how would you be knowing that?"

"He told me!" She grinned.

He laughed. "I suppose he did."

It took some doing to get Aishling up and back on his mount, including the promise of sweets when they arrived at Dungraven, but they eventually resumed their trek, eating up the distance in long stretches of hours. As the sun began its slow descent, Gideon caught the scent of smoke in the air and yanked on the reins. Dungraven would be just beyond the rise, he figured, looking toward the crest of the hill they traveled. There was an unnatural quiet amidst the acrid scent of smoke, a quiet he knew the meaning of.

"Why did we—"

He clamped a hand over Aishling's mouth. "Sssh." She nodded, and he let go.

Sharp eyes scanned their surroundings, struggling to peer into copses of trees that could hide a contingent of elves who would cut them down in minutes. Gideon guided Aridius backward, ears trained to the slightest noise. When he deemed it safe, he leaned forward, low on the horse's neck, pressing Aishling's body tight against him, and sent the animal into a gallop. They rode in the dark, a dangerous gamble as he would be unable to see obstacles that could lame his horse and send them walking in search of safety. The child had long since fallen asleep, her body having flopped at an odd angle in the cradle of his arms.

Gideon stopped at the top of a small ridge, indecision

beating against his brain. If he went to Dungraven, he knew what he would find. Blood and death. The Aos Sí would not stop. They would come and keep coming until mankind was wiped from the land as surely as their kind had been thought to be. Aye, he could take the girl and run from them for a time, build their manor, live their lives, but unless they were defeated, then one day the Aos Sí would come for them too. It might be a year, two years, or ten. But Rygeil would find them. Anger coursed through his veins, vengeance coating his mouth like venom. He would not let more people fall under the blades of those wretched beings. Not if he were a man. As the son of Ross Hughes, sole heir of Belfirth, he had to pick up his sword and fight. And if the war to come took his life, so be it. It would be a soldier's death that took him, not old age, as he kept hidden like a deserter.

He would not be a traitor to his race.

Inhaling deeply, Gideon steeled himself from what he would have to do. Not far from where they stood was a small farmstead he had visited as he and Fiadh had fled to Belfirth. He recalled the man and woman they had met, a kind couple who would surely take on a small child. Glancing at Aishling's face, her mouth parted in slumber, he accepted the truth that the dream of starting anew in the wilds of the Scarlet Mountains was just that. A dream.

CHAPTER FIFTEEN

S he had no voice. No body. No anchor to the world that spilled before her as she hung suspended in a courtyard she had run through with Dasha in flight behind her. Only it looked different now. Gone were the overgrown vines and flowers, the hallmarks of neglect. Fiadh looked upon the seat of Erabel as it had been long ago, and in the center of the scene, pulling her incorporeal form like a tether, was a child.

She had pale skin and black hair, her pointed ears poking through strands that had grown tangled as she hunched over a young bird whose wing was clearly broken. Fiadh saw her brilliant green eyes flash to the Cù-Sìth, who lounged a short distance from her, watching as the two communicated, though no words were spoken. She recognized Krulan's face and form, unchanged by the years since this time. The child flashed him a look of worry, then looked back at the raven. She listened to the girl's small voice chanting, her little hands moving over the bird in slow passes. The raven's wing stretched, and Fiadh heard a tiny snap as the bones shifted and began to mend. The bird croaked painfully but remained still as another series of strange words and phrases washed over it. Finally, the child sat back and grinned at Krulan. The Cù-Sìth passed a message of some sort, earning him a nod from the child.

"Oh, Dasha, I am so sorry I had hurt you. But you are healed now," she said to the raven, the sound like tiny bells ringing through the scenery.

Fiadh's mouth dropped open. Dasha? Her Dasha? How was that possible?

Fiadh's eyes widened as she watched the child cup the bird in her hands and whisper, "I gave you a special gift."

The bird cocked his head and pinned her with a violet stare.

"When I fixed your wing," she said, casting a glance at Krulan. "I bound you to my blood, gave you long life, like mine. We can be friends forever now."

She scrunched her shoulders as the bird began to preen her hair with soft gurgles of understanding. Fiadh watched it all, overwhelmed by it, her mind struggling to accept what had been made so clear.

The raven began to dance in circles at the child's feet, eliciting giggles and making Fiadh smile. He has not changed, Fiadh mused.

Dasha bobbed his head and croaked at the child. "Alright, but no flying, it's not fair! You hide first," she said and covered her eyes.

The raven hopped away, making a racket as he pretended to hide among a flowering bush before stealthily walking into a dark recess under a bench. Krulan looked on as the child jumped up and began searching the courtyard, crowing with delight when she found the bird. It was like watching the game she had played with Dasha, and she wondered what Krulan had thought of it as he looked on, like he was doing now.

Another child ran into the scene. He was older than the girl but still young. Fiadh studied him as he called out, "Threa! Where have you been? Your father was asking for you."

Hearing the girl-child's name made Fiadh's eyes go wide. Threa? Fiadh looked at her with renewed interest.

"Krulan wanted to play in the garden," she told him, earning her a rumble of disagreement from the Cù-Sìth.

"I doubt your father will believe that."

She stuck her tongue out and whispered to Dasha, who cawed shrilly and began to circle the children. Threa laughed when the raven swooped down and plucked strands of hair from her friend's head.

"Ouch! Dasha, leave me be!" he yelled, rubbing the spot that throbbed.

"Come, Dasha," Threa called, "Aeson does not wish to play."

The boy grumbled, eyed Threa, then ran at her, knocking her into a soft patch of grass and bolting away. She gave chase, and soon the laughter of children and cawing of a raven filled the air. Krulan watched the pair at play, but Fiadh noticed how his gaze never quite left Threa.

When their energy was spent, they stretched out on the grass, Dasha perched on a branch nearby, preening. Fiadh studied the raven, admiring his feathers. *You haven't changed a bit, have you?*

For many minutes, the children talked of simple things, but eventually, Aeson, chest puffed, said, "I heard your father talking about an uprising among the men who live nearby."

Threa made a face. "He always talks of war."

"Aye, but I think it's different this time."

She shook her head. "I don't want to hear it."

"Threa," Aeson said, sitting up, "war will happen whether you talk about it or not."

"Sometimes you talk like you want a war," she grumbled.

He thought for a moment. "I want the men who hurt our people to stop. If that means war, then…" He shrugged, not bothering to finish.

"I don't want you to go into battle," Threa whispered.

He laughed. "You need not worry. If war comes, it will have ended long before I am old enough to fight. The weapons of men are no match for our warriors. It will be over before the festival of Ré, if it even starts."

She nodded and settled back into the grass, but worry remained a stamp upon her face, not easing its mark until Aeson lured her into another game, and exhaustion took them. Krulan rose, shaking off debris, and made his way to Threa, bumping her shoulder when she refused to get up.

Aeson rose and held out his hand. "You had best mind Krulan."

"He likes to boss me around," Threa complained. "But I let him most of the time."

"As if you could stop him!"

"I could too!" she cried. "Dasha would help me."

Krulan let out a low growl and butted her, sending her sprawling.

"Hey! That wasn't fair!" she yelled, glowering at Aeson, who burst into laughter. Dasha cried shrilly and dive-bombed the Cù-Sìth, which only served to send both children into hysterics. Krulan snapped at the bird, snatching his tail feather and let him dangle from his mouth, squawking.

"Don't hurt him, Krulan!" Threa shouted, scooping the raven into her arms. She cooed to the bird, stroking his feathers while shooting daggers at Krulan. But her anger didn't last, and soon she was hugging the Cù-Sìth as she let him lead her from the courtyard and to her father.

Fiadh wanted to stay and follow Threa, but Danu took her from that time, dropping her seamlessly into another.

CHAPTER SIXTEEN

Threa strolled through a lush garden, plucking a jeboa fruit from a low branch and biting into it. She was no longer a child. Looking closely at Threa's features, Fiadh's eyes went wide. That was her own face upon the water, only older and, somehow, more experienced.

The truth of it sank its teeth into her. It pierced the last shred of resistance she had held onto, rupturing it as she accepted what had been true all along. Threa was her mother. Reaching a ghostly hand to her ears, those mutilated things Veren had been repelled by, she ran her fingers over them, feeling a moment of shock as the disfigured flesh was nothing more than a smooth point so like Threa's. This was her true self, as she would have been had Riona not taken a blade to the tips of her ears and cut them, thereby hiding her among a people who would have known what she was had they remained whole.

She remembered hints of sadness, hints of guilt in

Riona's eyes whenever Fiadh noticed her glance at her ears. Now she understood, and with that understanding came gratitude and forgiveness. Riona had sacrificed so much to keep her safe. It must have been hard. It must have broken her heart to cut her child.

It's alright, Mother, Fiadh sent into the void. *You don't need to feel bad about it. You don't need to feel guilty. I understand why you did it, why you had to do it. I love you.*

Fiadh felt a measure of peace and shifted her attention back to the scene that played out, a new awareness and knowledge tickling her mind.

Finishing off the fruit, Threa rubbed her hands on her gown and turned her head, eyes lighting up when a handsome male stalked toward her. She ran to him, launching herself into his arms. They kissed passionately, and Fiadh looked away, uncomfortable witnessing their intimacy and only returning her watchful eyes when she heard their voices.

"I have missed you, Aeson," Threa whispered, twining her fingers into the hair at the nape of his neck.

"And I, you," he said, running his hand along her spine. "But I cannot stay."

She pulled back. "What?"

He sighed and pulled her to a bench, taking her hand as they sat. "Laenfar has fallen."

Threa gasped. "How?"

"The mages betrayed us. They have aligned themselves with men and are making war on every kingdom. Soon, they will set their eyes on Erabel."

Fiadh was as shocked as Threa. They both looked at the

beauty of their surroundings. It was as though, at that moment, she and her mother were of one mind.

"That cannot be," Threa whispered. "They have been allies for centuries."

"Those days are gone."

Threa stood and began to pace. "Is my father sending you into battle?"

Aeson nodded.

Tears filled her eyes as Threa ran toward him, falling to her knees at his feet. "Please don't go!"

"I must, Threa. Your father commands. He needs all of his warriors to fight against mankind's armies, especially now that there is a greater threat aiding them."

"But *I* need you."

"Erabel needs me." He looked around. "All of this needs me. And yes, you need me. You need me to fight for you, even though you don't want it."

"I don't need you to fight, Aeson. I need you to live."

He glanced away, saying nothing.

She clutched his hands, kneading them as her mind raced. The war with men had not been over quickly. It had gone on, and on and on and on. What should have been quelled in days had spanned years, slowly taking its toll on every clan. To hear that mages had turned their backs on her people made her stomach twist. Elven armies could withstand many things, their magic was a powerful weapon in battle, but the armies of men had something her people never would: numbers. Their soldiers came in waves, their numbers so great that magic had ceased to tilt the confrontations in her peoples' favor. For every man that fell, a hundred more took his place. But when one of *her* people fell, all that was left was another empty chair at the festival of Ré.

It was the mages who had saved the day in many skirmishes. But, what now? What would become of her people? Her Aeson?

Threa looked up at him, tears pooling and spilling from her eyes. He captured one, brought it to his mouth, and tasted her grief.

"I must look awful." She glanced up, eyes puffy.

"You've never been more beautiful than you are now." Wrapping her body in a fierce hug, he lifted her, sweeping her legs over his so that she rested in his lap like a child.

"We could run away," she said quietly.

Aeson gave a pained smile. "And leave our people to die?"

She twined her arms around his neck. "I fear that if you go off to war, you won't come back."

"I'll always come back to you," he whispered.

Threa cried quietly as Aeson murmured in her ear, things too muffled for Fiadh to hear. Her heart broke a little as she watched her mother cry in the arms of the man she loved. She realized as she looked at the pair that she and Gideon had only experienced the first blush of love. This, what she was witnessing, was the depth of it, the bond that, even she, saw and felt. Perhaps, one day, she would experience something that pure.

"Shall we talk of other things?" Threa asked.

Aeson raised a brow. "I would rather do things that do not require words."

She swatted him. "Have you nothing else on your mind?"

"With you in my arms? Nay."

Threa laughed as he began to nuzzle her neck, the mirth becoming sighs of pleasure as he trailed kisses down her long neck.

"Shall we find a quiet corner away from prying eyes?" she asked, nipping the tip of his ear and taking his hand.

The pair ducked into a darkened area enclosed by thick patches of bushes. They gasped, bodies writhing in the shadows. Fiadh looked away, embarrassed, and drifted toward a tree where Dasha slept, beak tucked between his wings. It was many minutes before she heard talking from where they lay.

"The gathering has begun," Threa said in a breathy voice, their passions spent. "We should be present."

Aeson hummed and sprinkled her face with kisses, finally pulling away, though the fire in his eyes had not dimmed. "I suppose you are right. Let us join them."

They rose and dressed, the gravity of what the gathering had been called for weighing on their minds.

"Kaelari believes Carmun may have a part in this," Aeson said, pulling Fiadh from her thoughts.

"Carmun?" Threa questioned. "I thought she was dead."

"Many believed her to be, but Zaeleria has had visions."

Threa frowned. "What visions?"

"Nothing distinct. Kaelari says something is obscuring Zaeleria's sight."

"That could be anything," Threa argued. "Kaelari is rash to summon the name of one so evil."

"What if she is right? What if Carmun has returned?" he countered.

Worry marred the perfection of Threa's face. Carmun was an evil being. Evil and powerful. If she had returned and set her eyes on the Aos Sí when her people had already begun to lose ground in their war with men… Threa shook her head. It did not bear thinking.

"We should seek peace with mankind," she offered.

He shook his head. "Maybe in the first years of the war, a treaty may have been possible, but it is well past that now. There has been too much blood, too much hate, too much death. Men speak of us like we are monsters, evil things. They will never offer us peace now, especially not when they see they are winning."

"But we didn't start this war."

"It doesn't matter who started it. Only who ends it," he said grimly.

Threa snuggled into his chest, wrapping her arms around his waist, seeking comfort. "Let us hope Kaelari is wrong."

"Aye."

Leaving their secret hideaway hand in hand, they made their way to the great hall.

Fiadh hung, suspended, above the gathering as Threa and Aeson found their place among the crowd. Her eyes swung from one person to another, noting how many wore faces whose features had become familiar, while others were very different. She saw those whose pale hair and skin mirrored Veren's, each flashing eyes as violet as his. But around them, in small pockets, were Aos Sí whose faces and forms were as varied as the wild things in her beloved Dorcha Wood.

There were people with skin so dark it seemed to absorb the light, made all the more striking by eyes of intense blue, while others looked as though they were kissed by the sun or the moon—earthy brown and pale white. Their forms were all graceful limbs, at odds with the muscles that rippled beneath the skin of northerners or the small statures of those from the south. One common trait was eyes of limpid brilliance that marked them as fae, even if their pointed ears had not.

And all were arguing, voices raised in fierce debate, while one man sat upon a dais, watching and listening but offering no words to calm their rising tempers. Fiadh drifted toward him, the pull of his presence blocking out the din until all she saw was him. Like her, he had pale skin and dark hair with eyes a shade of green so light they appeared nearly translucent. At a signal she had missed, a hush fell over the hall, as though sound itself was swallowed in a sudden intake of breath.

He raised his hand, and all eyes fixed on him. "You have all come for one purpose," he said in a voice that reverberated throughout the enormous space, reaching every ear tuned to his voice. "Our war with the children of men has taken a shocking toll. But that is not the sole reason for our gathering. Rumor has come that Carmun has risen, her sons by her side."

"Aye," a womanly voice called out. "She threatens us all."

"Has she crossed your borders? Have her sons?"

The female, whose dark skin swallowed the light streaming from an array of carved openings along the ceiling, frowned. "It matters not if she or her progeny have set foot in our sacred land. Her very presence is a threat and should be dealt with. Our histories have taught us such, and we must heed their warnings."

"Ah, Kaelari," he said, "you are wise to seek knowledge from the past."

The female nodded solemnly but remained quiet.

"But…" he began, glancing across the crowd, "are we bound by those events? Doomed to repeat them?"

"Nay, Rygeil, there is no path set before us that we cannot alter, but I see great danger in her coming. Our ancestors saw the power her kind wields. She is a threat to us all." Kaelari said the last with a sweep of an intense, blue stare that encompassed those around her. "With her sons at her side, Carmun could turn her foul gaze on us and finish what her forefathers began."

Rygeil? Is that what she called him? Was this who Gideon had spoken of when his memory had returned? The brutal king who had slaughtered his army. Fiadh scrutinized him. He did not look very old, though she knew little of how Aos Sí aged. One person said they lived for hundreds of years, while another claimed they were blessed with eternal life. She scowled, remembering how Veren had fobbed off the question of his age when she had asked.

A deep voice filled the hall with quiet authority,

tempering the air around him. "Your words are important for all to hear, Kaelari." Rygeil paused and looked about the hall. "Carmun is of a line with a long, bloody history, and you are wise to remind us of the past."

Kaelari nodded, then raised her head proudly.

"Yet, to seek her out when she has done naught is folly."

Kaelari opened her mouth, blue eyes flashing, only to snap it shut when Rygeil arched his brow.

"This war has drawn on too long. Our armies are flagging. You have all come here," he said, his voice booming through the hall. "To seek counsel as we press forward to beat back the children of men and the mages who aid them. We do not have warriors to spare to go hunting after a rumor when real men with real swords and real spears are at our very gates."

His eyes fell on the gathering. "The greatest battles of this terrible war are approaching. What comes will decide the outcome one way or the other. If we can stop them here, maybe we can turn the tide. I need every warrior that can carry a sword, spear, or bow to face them. If they break through our lines, then the war is truly lost."

He turned to Kaelari. "You are to take your warriors and lead them against Lord Magnar and the men of Felmore. You are *not* to turn tail and run from the fight to go chasing rumors and whispers of Carmun while the fate of Erabel hangs in the balance."

Murmurs filled the hall, quieting as Rygeil continued. "We shall be watchful of this threat, but you will not hunt them down." He looked hard at Kaelari, who lifted her chin with defiance. "We will not bring the wrath of that foul being upon our people."

Kaelari cleared her throat. "I hear your words, Rygeil, but I beg you to reconsider. Even if our warriors fall, Danu's protection won't. Our people can seek refuge behind the protective barriers no enemy of Danu can cross. We may lose the war, yes, we may lose all our lands beyond those barriers, true enough, but our people will live on."

Rygeil glared at her defiance.

"But, if Carmun works her magic and breaks through the barriers that protect us, then *all* could be slain." She paused and darted her eyes about the room before landing back on Rygeil's. "I need but a few warriors. A dozen will make a scant difference to the battle but could be enough to stop Carmun. She has passed within a few leagues of the realms of each one of us here." Kaelari flung her arm toward the gathering. "She is plotting. I feel it. If we strike now, she will be taken by surprise."

"If Carmun and her children have truly awakened, you'd need twice a hundred warriors and mayhap more to stop her, all while tens of thousands of men are approaching. We cannot spare the swords. We need them here. I'll hear no more on this. We will break the armies of men. They grow overbold and fix their eyes on our sacred realms, where we are strongest. This is our chance. Carmun can wait."

Rising, Rygeil released the crowd and signaled to a waiting servant to bring food and drink before drifting toward those who held his view and would support his declaration.

Kaelari stalked away, a small group of Aos Sí trailing behind her. Fiadh followed, drawn by the strong woman, as the group traveled through corridors and into a lush garden dripping with flowers and fruit. It looked vaguely familiar, and Fiadh realized with a start that she had walked through it as it was now, overgrown and ruined.

"He is blind to the truth!" Kaelari shouted to a chorus of agreement. "Carmun will be the death of us all. I sense it, as does Zaeleria." Those around her muttered, fear reflected in their faces at the mention of the most powerful seer known to their kind. "Aye, she has seen it."

"Does Rygeil know of this?" an Aos Sí male asked.

Flinging her hand in the direction of the great hall, Kaelari sneered, "He sees nothing but the comfort of his hall and the fullness of his belly."

"You risk much with those words," he muttered. "He sees all the warriors of men marching on our gates, and he is not wrong in that."

"I care not. Let him hear me. He risks letting the one creature, who could bring down our barriers so those the armies of men can enter the heart of Danu and slaughter us all, walk freely up to them and cast her dark spells." She stalked away. "All will pay the price of his indifference."

At that moment, Threa strolled into the garden. "Kaelari," she said. "When will you ever learn to mind your tongue and school your face?"

Kaelari cocked an eyebrow. "I see no need to hide behind a facade for the sake of your father's pride."

Threa chuckled. "Aye, he does have enough pride to fill that entire hall and then some."

Her snide comment released the tension in the air, and the females embraced.

"Saw you that display, Threa?" Kaelari asked.

"Saw and marked his stubbornness, but I find that I am not disappointed in his words. I have no taste for war, as well you know."

"Aye, you never did."

The mood of the small gathering lifted as individuals broke off into pairs or alone to other parts of their surroundings, leaving the old friends to talk quietly. Threa and Kaelari found a seat in the shade and sat side-by-side in silence for a few minutes. Dasha landed at Threa's feet and pecked her soft leather boot.

"Dasha still haunts your steps, I see," Kaelari remarked. "It's remarkable how long he's lived."

Threa ignored the latter comment and said, "He certainly gets me into trouble more often than naught." She stroked the raven's head, then sent the bird off and looked at Kaelari. "Do you truly think Carmun is a threat to us?"

She sighed and nodded. "I do. I cannot explain how I know, but… darkness is coming. We should act, but your father shackles us."

"You were always the fighter, Kaelari. Do you recall how often I would land on my back at your feet?"

"It doesn't have to be a memory, Threa. I would be happy to have you there again should you like to spar."

Threa laughed. "Nay, I prefer my current view. Besides," she gave a furtive glance at a dim passage, "I have another I wish to… hm… what did you say? Spar with?"

"Oh, aye? And who would that be?"

"Never you mind," Threa said, kissing her friend on the cheek. "I will leave you now, but I ask that you let your heart cool before you make any decisions."

"Still playing the intercessor, I see. I hear you, my friend." She looked at Threa and smiled. "Be easy. I will not leap rashly into another battle."

"So, there are times you are not rash?" Threa asked, cocking an eye.

Kaelari swatted her. "Off with you! Enjoy your tryst."

Fiadh followed Threa as she sedately made her way from Kaelari's company, noting how she glanced back at her friend to see if she was being watched before breaking into a run. Wanting nothing more than to be pulled along in Threa's wake, Fiadh found herself reaching toward the female, hands passing through the folds of her tunic, reminding her it was only a memory.

CHAPTER SEVENTEEN

hrea flung herself into the arms of Aeson, who lifted her up and swung her around in a full circle before setting her on her feet. They kissed passionately, clinging to one another as hands found their way to familiar places and words of love were spoken in harsh whispers.

Fiadh watched the pair, a smile lighting her face as she noted the joy in her mother's eyes, for there could be no doubt of it now. She was looking at the Aos Sí who had given birth to her, as impossible as that felt. And the male, in whose arms her mother basked, could that be her father? Fiadh studied him, noting the same dark hair, pale skin, and vibrant eyes, the color of spring's first leaves. They were her features too. She was a blend of them both with Threa's heart-shaped face and her father's long lashes and straight nose.

"Aeson," Threa said. "How I want you!"

"Aye, I can see that you do," he laughed, releasing her from his arms as she pinched him.

"Knave! How dare you poke fun at me. Shall I find solace with another?"

He growled and nipped her chin. "You are mine."

She squealed. "Pearal does have a fine face and form."

Aeson growled and grabbed Threa, lifting her into his arms, where he cradled her. "I could drop you on your backside."

"You wouldn't!"

He released his arms for a moment, grabbing onto her again as she gasped. "Nay, I wouldn't, for you are too precious to me."

Threa smiled and nuzzled his chest, sighing with contentment as he took her to a small bench. The scene was so intimate that Fiadh had the urge to look away, but she was drawn to the pair and couldn't. They spoke quietly as she watched, leaving her to observe every feature and expression. Her attention was pulled back to their words when Aeson stood and began to pace.

"What did you think of my father's words?"

Aeson huffed. "He likes to hear himself talk. And he has an astonishing ego," Aeson said, frowning.

"It even surpasses yours," Threa told him blandly.

His eyes widened, and he burst into laughter, the sound bouncing off the walls. "And I am the knave?"

"I learned my skill from you, my love. You were ever my teacher when we were young."

"It's a pity I was not a poor one!" He laughed and sat next to her, taking her hand in his, tracing his fingers along the smooth skin of her palm. "Kaelari had strong words."

Threa nodded. "She always does."

"True enough, but I find truth in what she says."

"Oh?"

Aeson took a deep breath, letting it out slowly. "She is right to fear Carmun's movements. I, too, feel something is coming."

Threa looked away and bit her lip. "I do not want to hear this."

"Not hearing it doesn't make it go away," Aeson said quietly. "For all his arrogance, your father at least has a strategy… for good or ill. He wishes to deal with the enemy we can see before the one we cannot." He pursed his lips. "But if the choice were mine, I'd have given Kaelari her dozen warriors to seek out Carmun. The risk is… well… he risks all. I fear for the future."

She reached up and traced his features, her fingertip trailing over the smoothness of his brow. The action sent a pang through Fiadh as she recalled Gideon touching her the same way. It felt so long ago, suddenly—another life in another time.

"I love you," Threa said.

Aeson pressed his lips to hers.

"I do not wish to see you riding off to war."

"I will always come back to you," he told her, lifting her hand to kiss her palm.

She curled her fingers around his kiss as though to keep it as a child does with a pretty stone. "Let us talk of other things," she pleaded softly.

"As you wish. What shall I tell you? How I will long for your touch when we are parted?"

"That's a start," she said, smiling.

Their talk grew quiet, and Fiadh drifted among the words, sometimes hearing them and other times simply listening to their meaningless hum. Contentment made her close her eyes, the blackness swallowing her.

When she woke, the room was gone, as were Aeson and Threa, and she was lying on the grass at the base of the giant oak, Dasha standing over her, worriedly croaking, tugging at her hair.

She rolled to her side, telling the raven she was well. He eyed her and pecked the ground twice, unconvinced, thrusting his head into her loose hand. Fiadh soothed his worry and soon had him puffing his feathers and twisting this way and that so she could reach all the itchy spots. When he was appeased, he took to the air and perched on a branch. She watched him for a moment, marveling at the knowledge that he had been Threa's long before he had become hers. There would be much he could share when she learned the way of it.

Veren walked toward her as she sat up on the moss-covered ground, crouching when he was an arm's length away. "I sense you went on a journey."

"Aye, I suppose that is one way to put it."

From a distance, Fiadh heard Meara whinny. Veren turned toward the sound, smiling ruefully.

"What is it?"

"She grows bored and fat," Veren said, chuckling. "She is not meant for idleness. I will send her into the forest tomorrow where she can roam until I have need of her."

"I know what it feels like to be confined," Fiadh muttered.

Veren heard her, but ignored the comment. His attention was fixed on something more important. "Care to talk about what you were shown?" he asked and reached for her hands to pull her up.

They found a seat, and Fiadh stared at the huge oak for a few moments, her mind reeling with all she had been shown. It had felt surreal, hovering in space as she had been, watching the past unfold. Seeing Threa and Aeson had a profound impact, one she would need to sort out when she had time alone. The experience had left its mark. She felt it, carved into her mind, the certainty that though Riona was the mother of her heart, she was not the one who had birthed her. Somehow, and she meant to learn the details, Threa had left her in Riona's care. She and her brother. Why remained a mystery, but one she now understood Danu would show her.

Shifting to meet Veren's patient gaze, Fiadh told him what she saw, all of it, wishing for there to be no secrets. Just as she was honest with him, he would be honest with her. He listened, nodding or smiling every now and then. Fiadh was in the midst of telling him pieces of what she'd witnessed with Aeson and Threa when she stopped and pinned him with a look.

"How old are you?"

Surprise, followed by chagrin, flooded his face. He laughed softly. "I had wondered if you would ask again."

"Well? I'm asking now."

"We do not mark time as you do. Our calendars, such as they are, follow the ebb and flow of the moon and seasons, and are therefore, changeable. But, if I were to put a number to it, I would say that I have seen approximately one hundred twenty winters."

She gaped. One hundred twenty? He looked only a few years older than she. Eyeing him, she said, "You look very young… for your age."

He laughed. "I am but a babe among our kind."

"If you are considered a babe, then what will they say of me?" she asked.

Veren tried to mask the pleasure that crossed his face, but she saw it. "So, you believe now."

"Believe what?" she asked, playing dumb.

"That you are one of us. That you are… of Erabel."

Fiadh jerked her head in a quick nod. "Aye, seeing her… Threa… changed things."

"I understand, and I am glad of it. Erabel," he started, then glanced at the oak, "Nay, Danu herself, has long awaited your return. Your arrival marks a beginning, and I am honored to stand with you at the dawn of it."

CHAPTER EIGHTEEN

Gideon guided his mount around an expanse of trees that opened to rolling green hills and spied Owen and Marion's small farm on the rise. He let out a shrill whistle as they approached, causing Aishling to clamp her hands over her ears and alerting Owen of their presence, lest he think they were marauders.

"Are we getting some food before we go to the mountains?" Aishling asked.

"Aye, we'll have a nice meal." His eyes skittered from hers.

The farmer came to the door. "Who comes?" he called out, brandishing a knife.

"'Tis Gideon of Belfirth. I passed through not long ago."

"Milord," Owen said, rushing out the door to grab the horse's reins. "Marion!" The woman poked her head out. "Prepare a meal for his lordship and his guest."

"Aye, husband," she said, bustling back into their small home.

"Milady is not with you?"

Gideon's jaw ticked, and he shook his head. "She returned to her home."

Owen cocked an eyebrow but said nothing, only watched as Gideon dragged himself off the horse's back with the weariness of a man who had traveled too long in the saddle and lifted the child before setting her on her feet. "This is Aishling. She is from Belfirth."

The man nodded, eyeing the girl for a moment. "You are both welcome. Come inside and sit by the fire. I'll tend to your mount."

"Thank you, Owen," he said, limping toward the light pouring from the doorway, the girl's hand clutched in his.

Marion fussed over the child as they settled themselves by the hearth, giving her a hearty serving of dark bread filled with nuts and seeds and covered with a thick layer of blackberry jam from last season's crop. When Aishling had finished a second helping, Marion took her to a corner of the single-room home and gave her hands and face a bath with a dampened cloth before slipping off her travel-worn clothes and giving her a clean shift. It hung on her like a sack, trailing on the floor, before Marion took a length of twine and fashioned a belt to hold it up. Clucking her tongue, she looked the girl over, noting the way the child's eyes had grown droopy with the fullness of her belly. The men watched as Aishling was tucked into the single bed.

"She shows weariness of hard travel, poor wee one," Marion said as she stood next to her husband.

Sadness filled Gideon's face for a moment as he glanced at the small lump under the bedding. "Aye, we have been journeying for days."

"How came you by her, may I ask? It is clear she's not your own," Owen said.

Gideon explained what he had found as he came upon what was left of Belfirth's army and lands. He told them of Aishling and her family, of his trek to Felmore to seek aid, though he left out what had made him leave that place. Owen and his wife looked stricken as he spoke, having known many souls who had lived within those boundaries.

"Being so remote," Gideon said, "I don't imagine an elven army would pass this way, but you should keep a close watch and decide on a refuge should you need to flee." They nodded, eyes wide. "And..." he said, looking toward the sleeping child, "I would ask a boon. I cannot take the child with me. War is no place for children."

"We will take her," Owen said, earning him a nod of approval from his wife. "Marion and I were not blessed with children of our own, and we would care for her as though she were our daughter."

Relief made Gideon's shoulders relax, though his heart felt strangely heavy. "I thank you both. She has... been through much."

Marion looked fondly at Gideon. It was a look he had seen on his mother's face, and it made his grief surface before he swallowed it down.

The woman leaned toward him and took his hand. "I can see that you've grown fond of the girl."

"Aye."

"You need not worry, milord," she said, glancing toward the bed. "She'll want for nothing. I promise you that."

"Thank you, Marion. Aishling needs a mother and father and I… I cannot be those things. I will leave at midday after she has rested."

They nodded and began gathering foodstuffs and a few meager supplies for his journey back to Felmore. He would join Lord Darragh's army and wait for events that were sure to come, and when they did, he would see his family, all his people, avenged. And when it was over, when the cursed Aos Sí were gone for once and all, then, perhaps, he would return here and fetch Aishling, taking her to Belfirth where he would rebuild in peace.

The noon hour came, and he knew he must be on his way. Sitting on the edge of the bed, Gideon nudged Aishling awake, wincing at the brilliant smile she gave him.

"I had a good dream," she said, fiddling with the cuff of his sleeve.

"I am glad of it." He looked away for a moment, swallowing hard. "It is time to go."

She sat up, brushing back the lock of hair that fell into her face. "Could we not stay a bit longer? Miss Marion has yummy jam and bread."

Gideon smiled. "Aye, she does at that, and you may have as much as you'd like."

Aishling clapped her hands and flung her arms around his neck.

He reached up and pried them loose, standing slowly, before taking a step away. His throat bobbed as he said,

"You can't come with me, Aishling." Her brow wrinkled. "You must stay here with Marion and Owen."

Her face crumpled, and she got to her knees, reaching for him. "I don't want to stay here. I want to go with you."

"I'm sorry, Aishling. It's not safe. You must stay."

"But you promised," she cried. "You promised you wouldn't leave me!"

The girl sobbed, and Marion swooped in, taking the child in her arms and whispering words of comfort.

"I would give her a safe world," he said, throat bobbing. "She… she will be my heir."

"Milord?" Marion asked, glancing at the girl in her arms.

Gideon knelt. "Aye, she will be the heir of Belfirth. Should I not come back, you are witness."

Gideon reached up and took Aishling's hand. She snatched it away and buried her face in Marion's chest.

"Please, Aishling. I wish to give you all that I have. My name. My title."

"I don't want it," she sobbed. "You said you'd never leave me."

He looked stricken. "Marion, you are witness."

The woman nodded, eyes pooling.

"I decree that Aishling… Hughes is the sole heir of Belfirth. Upon my death, she will inherit the fiefdom."

"Aye, milord. Should the need arise, we will see it done."

He nodded, his hand reaching for Aishling before curling and falling to his side. Gideon turned and left the house, finding Owen waiting for him with his mount freshly groomed and fed.

"She'll come 'round, milord. Have no fear of it."

He nodded and took the reins, looking back as Marion stood in the doorway with Aishling in her arms. "Goodbye, Aishling. Be a good girl, now."

She wrenched herself out of Marion's arms and ran to him. Dropping the reins, he caught her, feeling his body rock as she launched herself into him. Through her sobbing, he heard pleas to stay with him, but hardened himself to them, knowing she could not go where he was heading. Stroking her back, he whispered to her of the many things her life with her new family held in store for her.

"I don't want a new family. I want you," she cried.

"And I, you, but we do not always get what we want, Aishling."

"You promised you wouldn't leave me."

He held her in his arms, and he wasn't sure why he said it, but when he did, he knew only death would break this vow. "And I also promised I would come back."

She looked at him and sniffed, her eyes puffy and red. He rubbed the tears from her soft cheeks with hard calloused thumbs. He pulled her away from his chest, feeling her resistance. "I will come back for you one day."

She whimpered and tried to take hold of him again, but Owen, seeing what needed to be done, wrapped his arms around her small torso and pulled her away.

Digging out a small pouch from within his tunic, he took six gold coins and held them out to the farmer and his wife. They balked and tried to refuse, but he insisted. "I would help with her care. Please..." he gulped, looking at the struggling child, "please... take it."

They relented and Marion clutched the money in her fist. "The Great Mother bless you and keep you safe," she said.

He nodded and mounted Aridius, hearing Aishling scream his name and knowing the sound would haunt him forever.

CHAPTER NINETEEN

Fiadh strolled through the decrepit halls of the keep with Veren at her side. Dasha, in his usual form, tried to engage her in play, but she shooed him away, needing to gain a complete picture of what Danu had shown her.

"I saw my mother," she began. "Did you know Threa?"

Veren nodded. "I knew her, but not as well as some."

"She was deeply in love."

"Aye."

Fiadh looked up, his words confirming what she already felt. It had been a priceless gift, being taken to a time where she could see, almost meet, the one who had given her life. Of course, what Danu had shown her was not the sum of all that Fiadh wanted, needed, to know, but it was a start. Through those memories, Threa had become real.

She knew she would return to the oak—that magnificent tree that held Danu in its massive form—for more of that past, those things which she did not want to voice just yet. In the meantime, there were questions that Veren could likely answer. A name that had been digging into her brain as though it were a living thing.

"Who is Carmun?" Fiadh asked.

Veren's lips mashed together in an unhappy line. "It is said she was of the Fomorian line," Veren said.

"What are Fomorians?"

"Giants, monsters, and all things evil. However, she and her sons bore no resemblance to those foul beings. There are those who believe she is the offspring of an Aos Sí, captured and imprisoned for breeding with an ancient evil, Balor, until the aberration we know as Carmun was birthed. In truth, her origin was either never known or had been lost through time, long before the Great War."

Veren settled on an ornate bench covered in thick layers of vines. "Hundreds of years ago, the Aos Sí warred with the Fomorians and eradicated them from these lands, but Carmun remained, hidden. Many believed her dead. A young woman at the time of that war, she bided her time in secrecy as, unbeknownst even to the wisest of our people, she carried triplets, having been impregnated before the fall of Fomori. When Carmun gave birth to Dian, Dub, and Dothur, we felt their arrival as a sickness in the very earth itself. But Rygeil wanted none of the bloodshed of the previous war. He had known the cost of pitting Aos Sí against Fomorians, and the Great War had already cost too many lives. Sadly, that resistance was his downfall as surely as it was the downfall of us all."

He paused, remembering. "Following the Great War, a small contingent of the fiercest warriors from every tribe, led by Kaelari actually, banded together to hunt down Carmun and her sons. They found them, killing all but one who escaped into the sea, where he was consumed by the creatures that live there."

Veren grew pensive. "We lost so many in that war, thousands. Before she was killed, Carmun, with the aid of armies of men, had breached every realm, and our people fled, abandoning what was left of their homes and gathering at a place of power deep in the Felraine Vale. It was there that I saw Rygeil… change."

"What do you mean?"

He looked away for a moment, eyes shuttered. "When the people of Erabel were… slaughtered," he paused, throat bobbing past a lump of grief. "Rygeil grew ruthless, and as the years passed, he became more powerful, feeding on hatred until it eclipsed the man you saw through Danu's memories."

"That's horrible."

He closed his eyes briefly and let out a long breath. "All he saw was vengeance. It is not our way, but so many were lost. So many. And those that remained… not all survived the grief."

He looked away, his gaze seeing things beyond the vine-covered walls. "In truth, Rygeil's hate was born many years before the battle at Erabel. Pritha, his wife and your grandmother, was killed by a roving band of soldiers as she and a small group of envoys traveled to our northern realms. Bitterness consumed him following her death, and the outcome of the Great War fed that rage until it became monstrous. Rygeil nursed his anger, plotting, eventually settling on the bloody path he has chosen to carve into this world. He bled Oadsera of its power in pursuit of that vengeance, feeding on it until it became a barren thing, leeched utterly. It is no longer the home of my youth. He declared himself king of all the tribes, and there were none who dared challenge him."

He looked at her, pained. "I do not know what power he had harnessed before he entered Oadsera, for what he wielded I had never seen until he crossed into those borders, but whatever the source, he coveted greater powers beyond it and, in the end, commanded more than the elements of the earth. It was as though he became a life-giver, though unnatural. Twisted." He paused, frowning. "Rygeil turned that power on his people and commanded those who were left to breed." He stopped and looked at her. "We do not age as men do. Our lives span dozens of theirs. As such, a couple may have only one or two children over their lifetime. Rygeil changed this, calling on whatever ancient magic he had culled, twisting it to his whim and breathing it into the very air of that place with words of power unlike any we had seen. The wombs of Aos Sí females quickened."

"Is… is that how my brother and I came to be? Through his awful power?" Fiadh asked, aghast at the possibility.

"Nay, you are not tainted with that darkness. But Rygeil's thoughts never left Threa. Her blood was of Erabel, and Rygeil coveted it. To what end, I do not know."

Fiadh's shoulders slumped with the weight of what he had shared. She looked at her lap, where her hand now rested, entwined with his, then up at the huge oak. Veren studied her. She felt his gaze but kept her mind fixed on the tree and the past that had unfolded before her.

"And now I am here."

"It is your birthright, Fiadh."

Though some truths had been lifted from their veils of secrecy, pieces were yet missing. She gazed at him for a few moments. "Why are you here? There must be a reason that you have come and no other."

Veren smiled. "Lyri, my mother, was very close with Threa. The two had become friends at a gathering of the clans when they were very young. And, though they lived in different realms, they kept in constant contact through messengers. They were like sisters."

Fiadh's eyes softened as she imagined such a bond.

"She would've sent me long ago to find you, but we knew nothing of your existence until the day Rygeil brought your brother to Oadsera."

"What?" Fiadh yelled, coming to her feet.

The action sent Dasha to her side, his eyes boring into Veren, the one who must be the source of her distress. Lunging forward, the raven pecked at Veren's hand, tearing his skin as he angrily croaked and hissed, wings flapping as he made to strike again. Veren yelped and clutched the appendage, scooting away.

"Dasha, cease!" Fiadh said harshly, earning her gurgles of reluctant obedience.

Fire sparked in her eyes, and the wind began to stir around her, though she appeared unaware of it. "Are you saying my brother lives?"

He nodded, keeping the angry raven in his sights.

"That's not… possible. Mother said… she said he was killed during a storm. Calum and Father. They were killed."

"And she may have believed such. But he did not die in a storm. Rygeil took him."

"Why didn't he take me as well?" she asked, unable to keep the hurt from her voice.

"He hadn't known you existed."

"I don't understand." She paced, muttering before spinning around and pinning him with a glare. "I want to see him."

"That is not possible."

"Why?" she screeched. "He's my brother! You need to take me to him. Now!"

Veren shook his head. "If I were to do that, you would be in Rygeil's hands, and he wants nothing more than to absorb your powers for his own dark purpose."

"I don't care!" she cried. "He's all I have left of my family. Can't you understand that?"

Rising, Veren strode to her, grabbing her arms to keep her still. She tried to fight him, cursing his secrets, hating the ignorance she had lived in all these years. He let her rage, telling her that he had not known she thought Calum dead and, yes, he would tell her all that she asked if it was within his power. Eventually, she calmed, as did the wind, which had begun to funnel, whipping up debris. Veren marked it but said nothing.

"Fiadh, I would not put you in the hands of your grandfather, no matter how much you pleaded. The light of Erabel is gone from him. Do you understand what I'm telling you?"

She nodded numbly.

"He would bleed you of your power, and you would be nothing but a weapon for him to wield. No will of your own. No strength to fight his darkness. Would Riona have wanted that for you? Would Threa?"

Turning tear-filled eyes to him, she replied, "Nay."

"I understand your heartache. Believe me, I do. But I will not deliver what Rygeil seeks. I will not forsake your mother. Neither of them."

Fiadh looked up at him. "Do you think she knew of Rygeil?"

"Who? Riona?"

She nodded.

He looked away, considering. "It is possible. I know not what words, if any, passed between her and Threa. I believe she kept you hidden in Dorcha Wood to keep you from Lord Darragh."

Fiadh swallowed hard as the horrible day her mother had been killed bubbled to the surface with awful clarity. "Aye, she did keep me safe, for as long as she could."

Veren led her back to the bench, leaving her to her thoughts for a few minutes while he contented himself watching Dasha comfort her. The bird was very protective, and he was glad to see it. From the passageway behind him, he heard Krulan coming and craned his neck to see the powerful Cù-Sìth. He, too, acted as a shield for Fiadh, having followed her beyond the borders of Dorcha Wood, risking much to keep her safe.

Krulan walked past the pair, settling himself closer to Fiadh, Veren noted. He gave the Cù-Sìth a wry grin and was rewarded with a low rumble. Fiadh glanced at Krulan, then returned her attention to Dasha, who twisted his head at such an angle under her gentle fingers it was a wonder his neck didn't snap.

"Dasha was bonded to Threa," she said to no one in particular, though she had already told Veren when she recounted her journey into the past.

Aye, I remember, Krulan said.

Why didn't you tell me? she asked.

It was not for me to tell. There are some things the Great Mother wishes you to see, not hear, and her will binds me.

Fiadh sighed and patted Dasha's head, indicating he had monopolized enough of her time. He flew to a nearby stone pedestal. She studied him for a moment then looked at Krulan. *Did you know Calum lived?*

There was a long pause before he responded. *Aye.*

I see.

Nay, you do not. What you assume is only part of the story.

She glared at him. *Then tell me the rest of it!*

I cannot.

Cannot? Or will not?

He growled. *Ask Veren what you wish to know. He is not bound as I am.*

Fiadh shifted and caught Veren staring at her, knowing he had likely heard every thought that passed between Krulan and her. She needed to work on guarding her thoughts. "How did Rygeil know of Calum?"

"Calum told me the story once, as he knows it, though, what is truth and what are falsehoods, I cannot say." He took a deep breath. "Lord Darragh tried to steal your brother."

"Darragh tried to take him?" she whispered.

Veren looked at her. "Aye, Darragh, grandson of Magnar, spawn of the blood witch, Haegna."

She frowned. "Who is Haegna?"

He looked surprised by the question. "She is Darragh's mother. Have you never heard of her?"

"Nay. Perhaps, she died when I was young?"

Veren shook his head. "Would that she had. Her dark presence squats in the castle still. She coveted your brother, or so I am told. Our seers felt it, an evil that mirrored Carmun's, and when that witch's eye fell on Calum, Rygeil sent a small contingent to take your brother and bring him here. They were going to come in the night and steal him away under cover of darkness, but Darragh had already put his plans in motion. Your father was slain."

She flinched.

"Rygeil's scouts were almost too late when they called on the wind and rain while earthmovers shook the ground, creating a powerful storm that killed Darragh's soldiers, narrowly missing him. I am told Krulan felt their presence and attempted to protect Calum, but Rygeil's scouts drove them off," he said, eyeing the Cù-Sìth.

Is that true? Fiadh asked, tapping Krulan's mind.

It is the great shame of my life. Two of my own were killed. I did not protect them. Nor did I protect your brother. Krulan got up and walked away stiffly.

She followed him and placed a hand on his back, feeling his muscles twitch. *It wasn't your fault.*

Krulan growled and shrugged her off. *I will not fail a second time, little one.*

Veren watched the exchange and waited for Fiadh's attention to return to him. "Krulan went to your mother that night, and she left, understanding that Darragh would come for you too."

She cocked her head and turned to Krulan. "Is this true?"

It is.

"But… are you saying that you could speak to my mother as you do me?" Fiadh asked, looking at the Cù-Sìth.

I spoke to you, as I have always done, and you told my words to your mother, though it was clear from her frightened eyes that she thought I would eat her.

That's not funny, Krulan.

He grumbled in his chest and looked away.

"I have no memory of what you're saying," she said quietly. "The first time I saw Krulan and his pack, I was older. I…" she pinned the Cù-Sìth with a stare. "How long have you been watching over me?"

Krulan stared back. *Since your birth, though from a distance when you lived outside the protection of Dorcha Wood.*

Thank you, Krulan. You know I value your strength and friendship. Addressing them both she said, "I wish… I wish I hadn't been kept from the truth. It seems unnecessary."

"I do not know why Riona did not tell you who you are," Veren told her, "though I understand her keeping you hidden as you grew up in the realm of men. If the people in your village had known you were Aos Sí, they would've burned you for it."

You should ask the Great Mother, Krulan rumbled.

Fiadh nodded. "Is Calum well?" she asked, grief tinging her words.

"He is well enough."

"Is there something more you wish to tell me, Veren?"

He closed his eyes and looked away before meeting hers again. "When Rygeil had your brother in his grasp, he... used him."

"I don't understand."

"You have a wealth of power running in your veins. It is even more than others of Erabel, and I cannot explain it. But Rygeil sensed it the moment your brother arrived in Oadsera."

"If that's true, that Calum and I have such power, why did he not come for me too?" Fiadh asked.

Veren glanced at the Cù-Sìth. "Rygeil did learn of you through your brother and tried to fetch you, but... let us simply say... Krulan would not allow it. Two of Rygeil's most revered fighters were slain in an attempt, having tangled with the Cù-Sìth as they remained within the power of Dorcha Wood. In Erabel, they are even stronger."

Krulan growled low in his chest.

"Krulan," Fiadh said with shock, "are you more powerful than Rygeil?"

Veren chuckled, earning a flash of teeth from the Cù-Sìth. "He would like to think so, but that is not so. The Cù-Sìth are formidable fighters and can kill our kind, but their power is not limitless. However, what he can do is call upon the power of Dorcha Wood, an energy imbued with Danu. I am sure you have felt the awareness of the forest. How it speaks to you."

She nodded.

"Rygeil has sent scouts to find and take you over the years, but the wood awakens, alerting Krulan to their presence, and they are not willing to tangle with him and his pack. Rygeil… is a patient man. He will not sacrifice more of his warriors when he is confident you will come to him eventually."

Her eyebrows rose. "He believes I will come to him?"

"Aye," he told her. "And I fear he may use Calum to do it."

Fiadh strolled away, mulling over his words, thinking about her brother. Alive. He was alive. She knew, as she tried to picture his face as a child, that she would fight for him. Her twin. Her other half. The how of it was a mystery, but if Rygeil thought to use Calum as a weapon against her, he had sorely underestimated her.

CHAPTER TWENTY

Haegna met Darragh with maniacal laughter as he unlocked the door to her cell and ushered her maid, Emer, out. "Cease your caterwauling, woman!" he snapped.

She giggled, looking up at him from her down-turned face. "Another visit? My sweet boy has missed his mother."

Grabbing a stool, he sat with a sigh, shaking his head as she sniggered. "You try my patience, old woman. I should wring your neck."

"Then get on with it!" she snapped, her mood shifting like her fractured mind. "I birthed a weakling who could not even keep a mage within his frail grasp!"

Darragh jumped to his feet and grabbed her neck, smiling darkly as her face began to purple. She didn't fight, taking away the pleasure of the act, and he let her go.

She began to laugh between fits of coughing as her wrinkled face went from hues of blue to red to its normal pallid color.

He scowled. "The mage is no use to me anymore, so it matters not," he told her, snarling at her look of disdain. "He told me all I need to know."

"He was of use to me!" she raged. "His blood…" she licked her lips, "would have lent me such power I could have made you king, and you let him escape."

"I did no such thing!" he thundered. "That creature killed my men, and I will see him repaid at my leisure."

Haegna gave an ugly laugh. "You would have to catch him first, and I don't think he would let you a second time."

Darragh cut the air with his hand, shushing her. She let him and waited, folding her withered hands in her lap. In those moments, she looked harmless, just an old hag who begged for scraps of food on the muddy roads of Felmore. How little her features showed of her true nature.

Haegna watched her son, mulling over if the time had come to tell him whose blood coursed through her veins, his as well as he was of her womb, though she had made sure never to birth another. He had leeched too much of her power as she grew him inside her body. Another babe would have sucked her dry.

Darragh stood up and began to pace. "News has come of the Aos Sí wiping out entire fiefdoms. King Stephan must know of this, but he does not respond, nor have my messengers returned."

"Your messengers are likely dead," she said simply. "As for the king, he is obsessed with riches and women to slake his lust. You do not need his support." She leaned forward. "Crush the Aos Sí, and you will rule the western reaches and beyond. Men will flock to you, so many that you will take the crown without a drop of blood spilled."

He snorted. "So you say, old woman, but your sight has failed you before."

She hissed at him, but said nothing.

"I have already begun amassing troops, though I will let the lords of the north and east spend their blood before I send my soldiers. Of course," he said, shrugging, "the young and old I have pressed into service will be no loss if they die under the sword."

Haegna looked at him, pleased. "You impress me, my son."

Darragh eyed her, feeling out her words for deceit and finding none. "You did not raise a dolt, Mother."

"Perhaps not," she said quietly, her face shifting to mirror the terrible thoughts that entered her mind. "Did you bring me a gift? My Emer had a young girl in her clutches, and the tasty morsel got away."

Darragh's lip curled. "A gift?" he asked. "I have no time to entertain your appetite."

"I grow weak," she whined.

He laughed harshly. "Your bones are so brittle I could break your neck with a flick of my wrist, old woman. No amount of blood will make them stronger."

She pouted and turned away from him like a child. "Then you get nothing from me. Not even the warning on the tip of my tongue."

Darragh spat and cursed at her, growing more incensed when she wiped the spittle from her cheek and licked off her fingers, one digit at a time. "You would withhold information from me?" he raged. "I could have you thrown in the street outside these walls and watch you burn when Felmore folk accuse you of the witch you are!"

Haegna pressed her lips in a firm line.

He threw a vase, narrowly missing her head. "If I promise to bring you a *gift*, will you tell me?"

Her demeanor changed in an instant. "Of course, my love. I would do anything for you," she cajoled.

Darragh let out a sigh, composed his face, and picked up the stool he had knocked over, sitting on it with measured calm. "Very well. I will bring you a fresh-faced youth."

She patted his cheek. "Such a loving boy. You take good care of me."

Leaning into her rocker, she folded her hands, lacing her fingers together and resting them on her stomach. "You had a visitor."

"I have had many, as you well know."

"But this one," she said, "came alone. No retinue. Of course, how could he have one when all his people had been slain?"

A look of surprise lit his face. "You mean the man from the east? Lord Hughes' son and heir?"

She nodded slowly. "He has been on your lands once before."

He shook his head. "Nay, I have not seen him until this day."

Haegna laughed, the sound riddled with condescension.

Darragh rose and launched himself at her, his face so close to hers their noses almost touched. "Do not mock me!"

She tsk'd. "Such a temper, my love. You will send your-self into apoplexy."

"Do not toy with me, mother," he said darkly. "I have but to turn the key in that lock," he growled, stabbing his finger toward the doorway, "and leave you to rot."

A lunatic smile played about her mouth.

He ignored it and settled back onto the stool. "Now," he began in a measured tone, "stop speaking in riddles and tell me what you mean."

"How little you see, my son."

He gave an exasperated sigh. "Have you anything to tell me to earn your gift?"

Haegna's eyes grew cold as she mashed her lips together, remaining silent.

Darragh snarled and paced the room. "Sightless, am I? Weak? Do not forget that it is I who lets you live."

"You have too little sight to see that you have brought the enemy into your house!" she spat.

"Explain."

"Lord Hughes' son *has* been here before," she told him.

Darragh shook his head, but Haegna merely smiled.

"Aye," she said, "when he arrived the first time, he was accosted by three of your men. Sadly, they did not survive the encounter."

The vein in Darragh's temples began to throb beneath his pale skin. "My men?"

"They must have thought him an easy mark," Haegna said, grinning. "I should like to have seen that fight."

Darragh stood, grinding his teeth as anger sang in his veins. "I'll kill him."

"Nay," she interrupted. "You will not."

"You think to stop me?"

"Sit down and listen!" she barked at him. He made a face, but did as she said. "Let him live. Make him think he has earned your trust. He will lead you to the witch's daughter. I want her. I need her blood. Her power. He is her weakness. Allow him in your confidence, and the reward will be worth ten of your men. And when we have her…" she licked her lips. "Then, you shall slit his throat."

Let the man live and gain his trust she had said, as though the man were still on his lands. Donal had informed him that Gideon had fled with a young girl following their meeting. He need only look to his mother to ascertain the likelihood of why the man had left in such haste. But he would return, of that Darragh was certain. There was rage in the young warrior, a trait he knew well. Regardless, it galled him to consider letting the man who had slain his guardsmen go on unpunished.

"I do not like this."

"You do not have to!" Haegna snapped. "You will do it!"

For a moment, Darragh looked like the small boy. But, just as quickly as it came, it was gone, replaced by simmering wrath. "There will come a time when you will cease to be of use to me. Pray that time does not come too quickly."

With that, he stalked away from her, stopping at the threshold as she called out, "Do not forget my gift."

He spat on the floor, sending her a glare. But he would reward her, as he always did. Before he locked her in, he added softly, "What if I took the witch's daughter to wife?

Imagine the blood of her child on your tongue. A babe. Hers and mine… to whet your appetite."

Haegna moaned with pleasure and hissed as he shut her in.

CHAPTER TWENTY-ONE

Fiadh slept fitfully, finally giving up and throwing off the worn blankets, another gift from Krulan from her former home in Dorcha Wood. It was dark, the blackness of the night making her room so dim she used her hands to find her way to the door. Dasha grumbled from somewhere in the corner, part of his consciousness alerted to her movements, but too tired to full awaken. Slipping out of her room, she made her way to the oak, to Danu. She wanted to see Threa.

The moon was a sliver of light in the sky when she came to the tree. Craning her neck, she looked up at the massive branches and whispered into the night, greeting Danu, asking the Great Mother to take her back into the past. To her mother. She needed to know what happened to her. A gentle breeze washed over Fiadh's cheeks as though in answer. She stepped to the trunk of the tree and, as before, pressed her palms firmly to the bark. A bolt of energy passed through her, locking her muscles and making her grit her teeth. In moments, she was untethered, floating, free.

Danu tugged Fiadh's incorporeal form through the ether and deposited her in a room filled with tears.

Threa hunched over Aeson, her hands slick with blood, hovering above a gaping wound in his chest. She chanted, eyes clenched, though tears escaped them in tiny rivers. Her words of power came in wet syllables, garbled things, fragmented by the force of her sobbing. She had healed before, Fiadh had seen it when Threa mended Dasha's broken wing, but Aeson's dreadful injury was sapping Threa's strength. It was a mortal wound.

His mangled chest rose and fell in a shallow rhythm, eyes staring at the ceiling while his mouth worked to pull air into his beleaguered lungs. Aeson shifted his gaze and stared at Threa. Fiadh could tell it was hopeless. The wound was clearly fatal, but Threa refused to stop trying.

"Threa," his thready voice rasped.

"I am here, my love." Her hands never left their position as healing power struggled to mend what could not be mended.

Aeson blinked slowly. "I love you."

"And I, you." A sob broke through her lips. Shoulders quaking, she continued working over him, desperate. "Stay with me, my love. I beg you."

Kaelari melted from the shadows, having silently passed through the open door, to stand at Threa's side. Her face was stricken as she looked at Aeson. "He was ambushed in an open field, no trees to protect him."

"Why weren't you at his side?" Threa cried. "How could you leave him to fight alone?"

"I didn't," she pleaded. "He was not alone. The others… almost all were slain by a horde of Magnar's men who were aided by a powerful mage. Xander cast a shadow with dark magic, concealing the soldiers from our warriors until it was too late. Aeson fought them off, but there were so many. Too many."

"Where were *you*? I begged you to stay with him." Threa looked down, her mouth dragging in grief for what she knew she could not heal. "You should have been there."

Kaelari's face was lined with guilt, having been hunting Carmun with a small band of warriors when Aeson was overrun. "I… I love him like a brother."

Threa's face crumpled. "Leave us. Please."

"I'm so sorry, Threa." She turned away and shut the door behind her.

Aeson's eyes were unfocused orbs as Threa lifted her hands from his body, finally accepting that the Great Mother would ferry him to Varellaen, and none could stop her. She stroked Aeson's face, wiping away a sheen of sweat, then leaned over, snagging his attention. His pupils dilated as they tried to fix on her, settling in their normal state as she whispered his name. He smiled wearily and tried to lift his hand to touch her face. It rose slightly, only to fall to the pallet with a soft thump.

Threa pressed her mouth to his pale lips. "I had hoped you would meet your son, my love."

His eyes flickered open, her words, for the briefest moment, doing what her spells could not.

"Aye, he grows in my womb. I will tell him of his father," she gulped, unable to continue.

Aeson tried to smile. "Tell… tell him… his father… love —" His body went slack, breath leaving him in a gentle gush.

Clutching his lifeless form, Threa broke, her wails of anguish carrying beyond the door where a single tear trailed down Kaelari's cheek.

Fiadh felt his leaving as a dagger to her heart. Her father, a man she had never known, was gone. Aching, she watched her mother collapse over Aeson's body. She reached out her hand, wanting to touch her, to comfort her, crying out when her fingers passed through Threa's shoulder as though she were nothing. She hung above the scene, watching Aeson's body grow cold as Threa clung to him.

Eventually, two individuals Fiadh had not seen before entered the room. With Threa watching through bloodshot eyes, they bathed Aeson, singing softly of Danu and Varel-laen. When their ministrations were finished, his body was covered in a thin sheet with strange markings.

Kaelari hung in the doorway until they bowed to Threa and left. She said nothing, only reached over, and taking Threa's hand, gripped it tightly.

Threa gulped. "I… I didn't mean."

"I know, my friend. I know."

Nothing was spoken, and yet, so much was said as Fiadh watched the two females turn and cling to each other and walk from the room, closing the door gently behind them.

Fiadh trailed after the pair, her insubstantial form

weighed down with heartache. It was a familiar agony. Terrible in its power.

Kaelari tucked Threa into her bed and sat on the edge, her voice rising in a song so familiar and strange that it made Fiadh's heart stutter. The lyrics sang of love and loss, of hope and sorrow, of renewal following death. Threa kept her hand in Kaelari's, their fingers entwined, finally succumbing to sleep as the song drifted to silence.

CHAPTER TWENTY-TWO

Threa sat numbly as Rygeil spoke to the council. Her grief was too raw, and she had no wish to be there.

Fiadh glanced about the room, recognizing Kaelari and two other Aos Sí, whose names she had forgotten. The others present at the meeting were strangers. Unsure how many days had passed since the scene of her father's death, Fiadh kept her attention fixed on Threa, wishing she could lend the female strength, but knowing all of this had come and gone long ago.

"We have lost this war, Rygeil. Many of our fiercest warriors have fallen, and we have none to take their place," an intimidating female said, darting her eyes to Threa, whose face was a mask of pain. "Even now, Magnar is pressing his advantage. Soon his armies will be at these very borders."

"Impossible!" Rygeil thundered. "He cannot break the spells that protect Erabel. No man can!"

Kaelari swung her eyes to him. They were cold, unflinching. "He can, and he will. Magnar is aided by the power I warned you of. Carmun aids him. She and her foul offspring. Erabel will fall." Beneath her rage, guilt flickered. She had not been at the battle that took Aeson's life, not that it would have made a difference, and she had failed to defeat Carmun. Though, she had found her and been driven off by the vile creature's offspring.

Rygeil stood up, knocking his chair to the floor. Threa's eyes flicked to it, but she said nothing.

"I should have you hanged for abandoning my army, leaving them to fight alone while you chased a ghost!" he yelled. "And what good did it do you? You didn't bring me Carmun, and my warriors are dead." Rygeil began to pace. "How did it come to this? Men have naught but steel."

"They have numbers, Rygeil," said a male whose face was vaguely familiar. "The sheer size of their armies has dwarfed our own. And when those battles draw us into open fields, we are lost. They have bled us dry and brought us to our knees. They are like a hive of ants swarming a mound." He paused, the muscles in his jaw ticking. "Had the mages who fight beside Magnar not used their vile shadows to hide his men, perhaps Aeson and the others would have gained the upper hand. But, if what Kaelari says is true and men are also aligned with Carmun…" He let his implication hang in the air.

Dark clouds rolled across the sky, their shape and color unnatural and ominous. Bodies shifted, eyes darting upward to track their movements, the sounds of chairs creaking under their weight the only noise.

Rygeil stood in disbelief. "The war is lost," he whispered.

Kaelari flashed him a look, thinly veiling her anger. "Aye, and we must flee. Carmun will drain the barriers and bring them down if she stands with them. Her power may not be able to keep them down for long, but long enough for the children of men to slaughter us all."

The sound of thunder rolled through the gathering, though it came not from the sky but from the tread of Magnar's army as the drums of war beat beyond the barrier protecting Erabel.

Looking at his daughter, Rygeil tried to come to terms with Kaelari's words. An idea lit his face, darkening it as it took root. "Threa, inform our people that we are abandoning Erabel. Fenean. Arryn. Come with me." He stalked from the room, the male and female at his heels.

Threa emotionlessly watched them go. She looked like a shell of who Fiadh had come to know, her movements slow and pained. Kaelari rose and sat at her side, shooing the others from the room.

"You must do as your father says."

Awareness sparked a tiny movement in Threa's features. "Aye," she said listlessly.

"Threa." Kaelari shook the female's arm. "You must go. There is no time to waste. Even now, Magnar is maneuvering his army. We are out of time."

Threa looked at her friend, and Fiadh gasped at what she saw in her mother's face. It was… empty.

"I will not leave him," she said.

Kaelari's brow wrinkled. "Who?"

"Aeson."

Opening and closing her mouth for a moment, Kaelari grasped Threa's chin and turned her face toward hers. "He's gone, Threa."

"I know, but he lies here." Her eyes slanted to an arched window in the stone wall where Fiadh could see an expanse of greenery where the bodies of all who had fallen rested, encased in earth and stone.

"I will not let you whither next to his burial mound!" Shoving her chair back, Kaelari rose and dragged Threa from her seat, shaking the female who stood limply. "You will leave this place, if not for Aeson, then for the sake of his son!"

Fiadh saw the moment Kaelari's words hit their mark. Threa's face constricted, melting into a mask of anguish. She flung her arms around Kaelari and sobbed. Watching, unable to lend her voice to the grief, Fiadh floated through their storm of torment, feeling the moment when the two had spent themselves and looking up to see them standing face to face.

Kaelari had her palms pressed to Threa's, whispering words that Fiadh could not make out. They spun in the air around the females, almost tangible in their purpose, before sinking into Threa's body, where they rooted themselves. Threa's shoulders slumped as Kaelari's voice grew silent. She let out a sigh and stared into the vibrant eyes that glowed from within the female's dark features. Nodding, she let Kaelari lead her out of the room. By the time the pair had made it to the end of the passage, Threa had undergone a shift and stood tall, wearing the mantle she had been born into.

Commanding a small group of her people, the flight from Erabel was set in motion. A foul wind blew through the air, thick with dark magic, as the protective spells around Erabel flinched like living things.

"It grows weak," Kaelari said, looking in the direction of the war drums that ripped through the air. "Do you feel that?"

Threa nodded. "It feels like sickness. Fever."

Grasping Threa's hands, Kaelari said, "The barrier may hold, or Carmun may bring it down, and if she does, it will not last. Danu's power is greater than hers and will drive her evil out in the end, but…" She glanced toward the rising din. "Think what that horde could do in that time."

"Go, Kaelari."

Kaelari nodded firmly and called for her fiercest warriors, a group of males and females from many clans. The halls of Erabel were a hum of activity as Threa went to her room, morosely packing a small bag of belongings.

She touched her stomach, hands splayed over her womb. "Your son grows strong, Aeson. So strong. I can feel his power, and it is greater than my own." Threa's voice bounced gently off the walls. "But I am weary. Not only in my body. I don't know if I have the strength…" Her throat bobbed, and she looked down at her hand, leaving her thought unfinished.

From outside her open door came the sound of feet. Threa looked up and saw Rygeil, two of his closest advisors at his side, Kaelari dogging his steps.

"You cannot mean to do this!" Kaelari said. "It is a violation!"

"The spells will lend Danu's strength to my arm, turn my skin to oak," he said, eyes blazing. "I will march out and meet their armies myself. I will slay their king and set them to flight!"

"Fool!" Kaelari screamed. "The only thing that protects our people is that barrier! If you drain her power, it will fall, and Danu will be unable to rebuild it!"

Rygeil glared at her coldly and jerked his head to his guards, who shoved her aside. Glancing at Threa, who stood gaping, he strode past without a word. She looked at Kaelari and saw the fear and rage in her eyes. The female shook her head and continued begging Rygeil to cease whatever he had fixed his mind to. Poking her head out of her doorway, Threa watched the group disappear, worry creasing her features.

Dasha, who had been unusually quiet since Aeson's death, hopped to the floor and walked toward his mistress, taking the hem of her gown in his beak and tugging.

Threa glanced at him. "Aye, I hear you." She walked back to her satchel and resumed packing her things, often stopping to stare at nothing, her thoughts fractured, only to have Dasha bring her back to the present.

A violent surge of power rent the air, throwing Threa to her knees as Carmun's voice echoed through the madness that encompassed Erabel. Fiadh watched in horror as her mother's body writhed, flailing, her mouth gaping like a fish.

What's happening? Fiadh screamed though there was no sound as she had no true voice in this place and time.

Threa went rigid, her face a mask of agony. Chest arching painfully, she gasped, sucking in air with ragged pants. "Great Mother!" she yelled, lips contorting in a grimace of pain. "What is this? Dasha," she called out, "what does my father do?

The raven swept through Erabel, wings beating against storms that had filled the sky. His sharp eyes found Rygeil standing before the massive oak with a ritual blade in his hand. Muttering spells, he stabbed the tree, the physical embodiment of Danu, digging his dagger deep into the trunk. Power spilled from the wound in flashes of light where Rygeil consumed them.

"Father, no!" Threa screamed.

Fiadh felt helpless watching her mother writhe, under an assault she could not see the source of, coming to sudden awareness as a voice echoed through the chamber.

He has betrayed me! Danu roared.

Threa thrashed, feeling Rygeil's mind dispassionately thrust his will into Danu, ravaging the goddess' power and taking that strength for his own. Danu wept, and for a brief moment, Fiadh saw her ghostly form huddled in the corner of the room before it disappeared, carried away like leaves on the wind. Silence, ominous, followed her leaving. Threa could hear nothing of the lifeforms that had filled her mind since she was a girl. They were gone. She reached for them in panic, calling out to Danu, but there was no response.

A thunderous crack rippled through the air as bolts of lightning flashed in the sky. Frightened screams followed, filling the halls. Fiadh cast her eyes about seeing Dasha cry shrilly as he tried to rouse Threa, who now lay prone on the cold stone floor.

Shouts erupted from outside the room, followed by

Rygeil's booming voice. "Let him come to me now! I will lay waste to his army and rid the world of that vile witch who feeds him." He stalked past the doorway, his form somehow larger and his eyes blazing red with heat and violence.

Threa whimpered at the sight of him and clutched at her womb. Sharp pains stole her breath. *Too soon! It's too soon!* But she felt so weak.

Father! she called out, though the words never left her mouth.

Barely glancing at his daughter's form, Rygeil barked an order for someone to rouse his daughter and take her to safety.

Dasha grew frantic as two males swept into the room and lifted Threa onto the bed. She reached out to him, sensing his panic, but the bond was weak.

After many moments, her eyes began to blink, and she pushed their hands away. "I am well. Leave me."

They looked unsure.

"Go. I will be along shortly."

They left, and she rose slowly, her movements sluggish. Dasha hopped onto her satchel, pecking at it in desperation. With arms that felt like lead, Threa swung the strap over her shoulder and held out her arm for the raven. He raced up the limb and preened her hair frantically. She batted him away but left him on her shoulder, where he continued to prod her to make haste.

Kaelari rounded the corner, nearly colliding with Threa. Grabbing her arms, she said, "Thank the Great Mother, you are leaving. Rygeil has lost his mind. There is no time! Krulan!"

The Cù-Sìth raced toward them, stopping and spinning in a cloud of dirt as two riders bore down on him. Threa gaped, having never seen men like these. They came to kill. Snarling viciously, Krulan leaped at them, knocking the first rider to the ground, where he ripped out his throat. His companion screamed and tried to bolt, but the Cù-Sìth was on him in moments, his massive claws tearing the man from his saddle in ribbons of blood.

Kaelari hefted Threa against her and ran for the Cù-Sìth, swinging her friend onto his back. "Run!" she commanded, watching the pair for a moment before sprinting into the melee.

They made their way through the keep as all around them bodies streaked past, children crying, soldiers shouting. Dasha flew above, cawing in fear. Taking fistfuls of his fur, Threa pressed herself between Krulan's shoulder blades. At the contact, a low buzz reverberated through her head. She followed its source with her mind, sagging in relief when a connection was made. She could hear Krulan and he, her. In the background of her thoughts, others, though dimmed, began to spark within her mind. But Danu herself was absent. Krulan reassured Threa as his massive strides ate up the ground, racing past others who ran, their possessions clutched in her arms.

At the border of Erabel, Fiadh saw Rygeil standing defiantly against the swarm of Magnar's men, who loosed arrows and filled the air with battle cries. He raised his hands, and she could feel the power emanating from him. Stolen power. Warped and twisted. Snarling, Rygeil unleashed it at the men, searing dozens in a single strike.

They fell to the ground, dead or screaming. But others, hundreds of others, so many she could not see where the army ended, took the place of their fallen comrades, and within the chaos, Fiadh felt a sickness in the air. It was a fog of dark magic that crept over the land, stabbing into and through the protections that had kept Erabel safe for centuries.

Mages, interspersed among Magnar's soldiers, unleashed spells to weaken the elves, robbing them of their magic. Kaelari darted among the men, taking down half a dozen before she was flung into the air by a powerful blast. Rolling to her side, she staggered to her knees and glared at the one who'd felled her.

"Traitor!" she screamed.

The mage grinned and raised his arms, a ball of flame lighting the sky above his head. With a flick of his wrist, he sent it into a small group of Aos Sí mothers and their young, killing them instantly.

"Xander, have you no mercy?" Kaelari cried.

He looked at her coldly. "None."

Roaring with fury, she launched herself at him, but he was gone in a billow of smoke, the sound of his laughter echoing behind him.

Fiadh didn't see the end of the battle, tethered to Threa as though by a chain of iron. She drifted, the landscape blurring, following in Krulan's wake as he tore through Dorcha Wood.

They must have been close to the eastern border, the same place she had found Gideon, when a palpable current of energy washed over the woods, blasting outward then reeling back, leaching the power from the earth with greedy hunger. Fiadh sensed where it coalesced, feeling Rygeil draw it in as though she had become her mother for a brief moment.

Threa's thoughts fluttered weakly. *Father, no!*

He shut her out, his ravenous gaze falling on the mages who stood among Magnar's army. They fell or fled, their magic no match for the power Rygeil had stolen. In the shadows of the battle, Carmun watched, her face and form hidden, but Fiadh could feel it, slick like oil. Sinister. And she felt the moment those hungry eyes fell on Rygeil.

Sensing Carmun's presence, Rygeil unleashed the full force of his power on her, wounding her so gravely that she fled, her sons at her side. He grinned at her retreating form, ignorant of the curses she spat into the wind as she turned her gaze toward other Aos Sí realms whose borders were no match for her. Instead, drunk on power that was already waning, Rygeil advanced as Erabel was engulfed.

Threa slid from Krulan's body, tumbling to the ground in a blur of twisting limbs. She came to rest on her side, eyes closed, though Fiadh could see the subtle movement of her chest.

Dasha screamed, swooping from the sky in a black tornado to land at her head. She didn't stir, though he cawed and pecked.

Krulan nudged him aside and snuffled at Threa, licking her cheek with such force that he jostled her head. Panic filled the Cù-Sìth's eyes. From a distance, he could hear what sounded like thunder, though it was unnatural, filling the air with a metallic stench.

Dasha croaked and riffled his beak through Threa's hair, but there was no movement beyond the shallow rise and fall of her breathing. The raven looked at the Cù-Sìth, his violet eyes haunted by awful understanding.

As if born of the mists that blanketed Dorcha Wood, an Aos Sí female Fiadh had never seen before materialized, walking sedately through the undergrowth as trees gave her welcome, bending their branches to stroke her cheeks and arms. Kneeling at Threa's head, she cupped her face and looked deeply into her mother's mind.

Fiadh watched, wishing she could know what words the female sent to Threa. Without warning, the Aos Sí female glanced up, finding Fiadh, as impossible as that was.

Daughter of Erabel, I am Zaeleria.

The name triggered a brief memory of Kaelari speaking to Threa of a female who had visions.

We will meet again in your own time, Zaeleria told her. *Fear not, young one, for I am with you.*

She shifted her attention back to Threa as though nothing had passed between them, leaving Fiadh at odds with what she had heard in her mind. It was not possible. This was a memory, and yet… Her mind couldn't grasp it, and she let it go, caught, once again, in the scene that played out before her.

Zaeleria looked at Krulan. *You will bear her to a quiet glen, and there she will sleep as her mind and body heal.*

Helping Krulan lift the limp body of her mother onto his back, they walked deep into the forest, stopping at a small glen tucked beneath the bowers of a circle of oak trees. Threa was laid upon the ground, her hands placed lovingly atop her womb in which Fiadh, and her brother, lived and grew.

Lifting her arms, palms up, Zaeleria spun a web of spells that pulled quartz from the ground, gathering the mineral into clusters that wove together, forming a thin wall on all sides of Threa's form. Fiadh watched as it grew, arching to form a burial mound, though, within its translucent barriers, she saw her mother sleep.

When Zaeleria had finished, she looked at Krulan and Dasha. "I have done all I can."

Dasha gave a broken croak and darted his eye to the mound.

"I hear thee, but she cannot."

Dasha's feathers flattened, and he hung his head, his beak coming to rest against his breast.

"Threa will awaken or succumb. I can do nothing more. Protect her, and one day she may rise and reclaim her place with Danu."

Zaeleria stroked Krulan's face, and he turned his head into her touch. She did the same with Dasha, then looked at Fiadh once again and melted into the forest.

CHAPTER TWENTY-THREE

Threa did not wake. Her body, though alive, lay suspended, untouched by the ravages of time as years turned to decades. Fiadh watched Dorcha Wood shift and change with the seasons and years. Again, and again, the snows rose and melted, the leaves fell and grew as Danu took her through time. But what remained was her mother's living tomb, guarded by Krulan.

The soft hum of a woman's voice interrupted the quiet, and Fiadh shifted, seeking the source, and found herself looking at Riona.

Mother.

Her eyes latched onto the woman and would not leave. She looked so young, so full of life. Fiadh reached toward her, aching to beg Riona to wrap her in her arms as she had when she was a child. *I miss you so much*, Fiadh mouthed, her heart aching, knowing Riona could not hear the words.

A low growl penetrated her mind, and she reluctantly looked away from the woman who had raised her.

Krulan, lying next to the quartz mound that sheltered Threa, stood, hackles rising. He seemed to grow in size with each passing moment until his form was the stuff of nightmares.

Fiadh looked from him to Riona in terror. *No, Krulan!* But he could not hear her. What she watched with horror had already passed.

Snarling, Krulan tore through the trees, his eyes fixed on Riona, who heard the noise and stood paralyzed. Launching himself at the undefended woman, he pinned her to the ground, his lips curling in fury, revealing the deadly points of his serrated teeth. Riona's eyes bugged, but the breath had been knocked out of her at the impact, and she could only stare into the face of death.

Beyond the fierce snarling came a noise, a cracking sound like that of a rock splitting and falling to the earth. Krulan looked up, his massive paws still pinning Riona to the ground, and craned his neck to look behind him. He gave a soft woof of disbelief and bolted, leaving the woman on the ground.

Fiadh hovered over her mother, watching as she gulped huge pulls of air, color returning to her face. Riona staggered to her knees and looked at where Krulan had gone, fear making her eyes wild. Bunching her dress, she made to run, but halted the moment she lifted her foot by the melodious sound of a woman's voice. Turning slowly, Riona watched as Threa stepped through the trees, Krulan at her side. A raven swept by as Riona stood transfixed, ruffling the hair on her head with his passing.

She need not have looked for the female's pointed ears to see that the voice she had heard did not belong to a woman. No, it was evident in the blazing eyes and ethereal beauty that who Riona saw coming toward her was Aos Sí.

Threa stumbled, leaning heavily on Krulan's shoulder. At the movement, Riona reached toward the female to help, pulling her hands away when Krulan sent her a warning growl.

"Hush, Krulan," Threa said. "She means no harm."

Riona's mouth worked, but no sound came out. The ghosts of the Aos Sí had long haunted Dorcha Wood. Those people had gone, driven from their home years before she was born, though the stain of their existence still shadowed the forest. It was not possible to see one of their kind standing before her, but here she was. Riona studied the female, noting her frailness, the sickly pallor of her skin. She was not well.

Swallowing past her fear, while casting glances at the menacing beast at the female's side, Riona said, "You are hurt. I can help."

How like Mother, Fiadh thought. Even in the face of terrible fear, she would give aid to one who needed it.

Threa smiled sadly. "Nay, I fear you cannot heal my body."

"I am a healer," Riona argued, "let me help you."

Krulan looked up at Threa, a soft rumbling traveling through his chest. "Aye, I hear you, my friend. I have slept through lifetimes of men, but I am tired beyond measure. I have not the strength."

Riona watched the exchange in awe, some of her fear leaving her body as her limbs ceased to tremor.

Threa walked toward the woman, holding out her hand to stop Krulan's progress as they came face to face. Lifting her hands so that they hovered on either side of Riona's head, she asked, "May I?"

Eyeing the female's shaking hands, Riona nodded, unsure why she stood so passive but unable to do anything more.

Threa pressed her hands to her skull and closed her eyes. Minutes passed as she delved into Riona's mind, getting a sense of the woman without the need for words. There were no falsehoods that would not be revealed, no ugliness that would not be laid bare as Threa sifted through Riona's mind. Having seen all she needed, she let go, arms sagging with unnatural exhaustion.

"I do need your aid, Riona."

Her mother's eyes grew wide. "How?"

"It matters not. My time is short."

Confusion spread over Riona's face, and she reached into her satchel. "I have a tonic that may help you."

Threa smiled wanly. "You are a good woman, but that is not the aid I seek." She reached for Riona's arms and pulled, tugging the woman to the ground, so the two kneeled knee to knee.

"You… you must help me," Threa begged.

Riona nodded.

Clutching Riona's head with hands that were weaker than moments before, Threa leaned forward and pressed her lips to her mouth, breathing into them, the force of it parting Riona's mouth. Power, from so deep in Threa's body that it shook every muscle, rippled and came splashing out into the immobile woman. The ground shook, trees bending in the undulations, as Threa pulled away and began chanting in some beautiful and forgotten tongue. Riona remained motionless, unable to move under a spell that kept her anchored.

Threa called to the Great Mother. But it was no ordinary plea or prayer. Intertwined in each utterance was power, laced with a life-giving force that even Fiadh's ethereal form could sense. Light bloomed between the two as Danu herself coalesced into something tangible. At first, she was an indistinguishable blob, though corporeal to some degree. The particles of her form shifted, clustered and bonded, forming a distinctly feminine being whose skin and flowing hair were silver as the face of the moon. Danu looked from one to the other, lifting her hand to stroke Threa's face.

In a thready voice, Threa whispered, "Please."

The goddess nodded, though sadness shone from eyes so pale a blue they rivaled the color of the sky on a spring day. Danu positioned herself between them and reached out a hand to both their wombs, pressing her palms to each, joining them through her own delicate body. Riona and Threa went rigid. Inner light bloomed from Danu, exploding, making Fiadh flinch at its shocking brightness. Wonder filled Threa's face as Danu made known that she carried not one but two babes. Twins. The joy quickly faded as the warmth and light that had joined them dimmed. Riona fell to her side while Threa withered, curling in on herself and clutching her middle. Tears streamed down her face as she choked out a blessing of thanks.

Danu looked at her, love spilling from her unearthly face. With a moan, Riona came to, a flash of fear marring her features as she looked at Threa and the being who all but cradled her.

Threa, her voice reedy, said, "I have given you my children."

Riona clutched her stomach.

"I could not..." She breathed heavily, lips growing pale and blue. "My time has ended. I beg you, keep them secret, raise them as your own, as a... human. None can know. None. I beg you."

Agony filled Riona's face as she watched the female weaken. "I don't understand."

"My life is spent, but my children must live on. They must... live."

Threa slumped over, and Riona crawled to her, lifting her head into her lap and gently patting her cheeks.

Blinking slowly, Threa came to, tears leaking from her eyes and trailing into the dark hair framing her face. "Long have our kind fought each other, but we are not evil. You are not evil. Perhaps... my children... will bring peace... maybe they..." She panted, unable to form the words.

Danu watched, sending wind whispering through the trees to lift Riona's hair. She closed her eyes and breathed deeply, a smile touching her lips. "I hear you, Great Mother."

Relief made Threa's shoulders sag as a sob broke through her lips.

Riona reached for her hand, taking it in hers, cupping the cold fingers in the warmth of her palms. "My husband and I could not have children. You have blessed us."

Threa nodded. "Tell them… someday… tell them… when they are ready." She sagged, a sigh escaping her mouth as her heart beat its last.

Dasha landed next to Threa's body, a stem hanging from his beak. He looked at Riona with knowing eyes and laid the flower next to Threa's form, the petals touching her still fingers. Croaking softly, he preened a few strands of her hair and pressed his head against hers before turning away and launching into the sky.

From the trees, a hulking form separated itself. Riona looked at the Cù-Sìth, rising as he nudged her aside. Krulan gently took Threa's body into his mouth and bore her away. Danu kept her knowing gaze on Riona, waiting for the woman to turn to her. When she did, the Great Mother pressed her insubstantial lips to her forehead and began to dim, becoming nothing more than a rustle of leaves.

Fiadh came to at the base of the oak, heaving, her face a mess of tears. Krulan, like a shadow, drifted to her side.

I will take you to her.

Fiadh followed him as he led her to Threa's burial mound. It looked so familiar, sending a pang of sadness through her as she saw the shadowy body of her mother tucked within its heart. Laying her hands on the surface, she whispered to Threa, the words pouring from her heart as Krulan looked on.

When she was finished, she turned to the Cù-Sìth. *Thank you.*

CHAPTER TWENTY-FOUR

Gideon rode hard for Felmore, shutting his mind to the sadness that tried to claim it. Aishling was safe. That is all he could ask for and, if he survived the coming war, he *would* return for her. Aridius' hooves beat upon the earth, covering lands that had grown more poignant with each journey he'd taken.

Fiadh.

Aishling.

The two had become entwined somehow, the trauma of his partings with each of them threading them together, no matter how hard his mind struggled to rip them apart. Feeling a need to harden himself as he did before any battle, Gideon focused on his rage, dredging up the images of his family, willing the fury and grief they elicited to form into the wrath he would unleash on the Aos Sí. Anger bloomed in his mind and heart, staining everything red like the blood that had blackened the earth under the bodies of Belfirth's people.

He was so distracted by his dark thoughts, it was many minutes before he heard the shouts behind him. Craning his neck, he saw a small band of men on the rise he had descended earlier before stopping midday to rest his horse and ease the cramping in his legs. Pulling on the reins, Aridius danced in a circle, blowing hard, hooves stomping. Gideon waited for the party to come closer, noting the banner from the north in the hand of a squire.

"Greetings," he yelled when the men were in hearing distance.

They nodded and kicked their mounts into a canter, quickly closing the distance. "From where do you hail?" one of the soldiers asked.

"Belfirth in the east. And you?"

"Haerford in the north."

Gideon nodded. "Where are you bound?"

"We go to Felmore to request aid from Lord Darragh on behalf of Lord Glaison. Word has spread of the return of the Aos Sí." The man paused and spat on the ground, hands a blur of movement to ward off evil. "It is said he has command over the western fold."

Gideon couldn't argue with Darragh's grip on those who dwelled in the western reaches, but the man himself left much to be desired. He was conniving, and there was something else, but Gideon was hard-pressed to pin down what it was that bothered him. "Aye, he is a formidable lord. I, too, ride to Felmore."

The knight slapped Gideon on the back. "Then let us travel together. The wilds are no place for a man alone."

Riding next to them, Gideon listened as they shared

their travels, but it became clear that the route they had taken from their distant holding in the north had not led them through the devastation Gideon had witnessed. It gave him no pleasure to share what he had seen, but the telling of it bolstered his anger and thirst for revenge. By the time the band reached Felmore the following day, every man among them was ready to go to war.

Their horses wove their way through clusters of soldiers that had grown in number since his last visit, the men at Gideon's side remarking on the sheer size of the army dwarfing any threat. Tents dotted the muddy fields as men practiced their swordplay or strolled about, trying to coax local girls and women to join them for a bit of bed play. Passing beneath the portcullis, the crowds thinned, but even here, Gideon took note of the many faces he had not seen before.

Gideon left Aridius in the care of the stable boy, walking with the child into the dimness along the rows of stalls until he found a suitably clean one. It would be temporary shelter for his mount due to overcrowding, but he was glad to have it. Giving the lad a coin for his troubles, he left and made his way to the great hall. The men from the north were wrapping up a brief audience with Darragh when he entered, and he stood back, waiting, noting how the commander, Donal, marked his arrival. The northerners clapped him on the back as they passed, and Gideon strode to the dais, bowing low at Darragh's feet.

"The heir of Belfirth returns!" Darragh said in greeting.

"My lord."

"And where did you scamper off to after last we met?"

Gideon schooled his face. "I had some unfinished Belfirth business."

Darragh's eyebrows rose minutely. "I see... well, it is good to see that you have returned. Have you given thought to my proposal?"

He eyed the man as he sat, as though he were the king himself. If Darragh thought his empty congeniality would push Gideon to bend the knee, he was mistaken. Darragh was a means to an end. Nothing more. He had a feeling the lord saw him in the same light.

"I have. I will lend you my sword in battle as I have much to avenge, but that is all that I offer."

Donal cleared his throat. "You ask our lord to rally his forces against an enemy who is little more than a fairy tale, and you refuse to pay him homage?"

Gideon clenched his jaw, unsure why Donal continued to push this line when the rise of the Aos Si was beyond denying now. "I assure you the Aos Sí are no creatures from children's stories. They are attacking holdings in the east and north. In time, their eyes will fix on the west, on Dorcha Wood and whatever power they believe that accursed forest holds."

"Ah, Dorcha Wood. Fear you that forest?" Darragh leaned forward.

"I fear nothing." Gideon's eyes bore into the lord.

"You, and others, say the Aos Sí have declared war on mankind. Yet, I have seen nothing of these supposed attacks." Darragh smirked. "Is Felmore so great that the Aos Si fear to venture here?"

Gideon seethed, not bothering to mask his emotion.

"But, that is not to say that I do not find some merit in your telling." Darragh shifted in his chair. "Since you fled my hall when last we met, a score of others have knelt before me, all with similar stories."

Lifting his chin, Gideon glanced from one man to the other as Darragh leaned toward Donal and whispered something.

"Nay, my lord, he has yet to kneel. One could think he has no honor," Donal said coldly.

Darragh tsk'd. "Donal, sheathe your tongue lest you rouse Lord Hughes' ire, and he finds your neck at the tip of his sword."

Gideon released his grip from the hilt he'd grasped.

Darragh let his hands drape on the arms of the chair, fingers tapping the polished wood. "So, Lord Gideon Hughes, the man who does not make pledges. The lord who commands no swords but his own. You tell me Belfirth was overrun. Its people slaughtered?"

Gideon nodded.

"Its castle? There is no one to defend it? No men, no Aos Sí? Its fields barren, unguarded, and untended. All dead? All gone?"

Gideon tensed.

"It seems to me that you are lord of, well, lord of nothing at all, really." He turned to Donal. "Donal here, now he is a man who does make pledges. Isn't that so, Donal?"

"My life and my sword are yours, my lord."

"And those of your sons and their sons?" Darragh asked.

"Now and forever, my lord."

"Then away with you to Belfirth, with twice a hundred men, *Lord Donal Leith*. Make the keep safe and send for some peasants from Felmore to work your fields."

Donal's eyes glowed with gratitude while Gideon looked on with disbelief that quickly turned to fury.

"You dare?!" Gideon shouted. "Belfirth is *my* birthright, *my* land, only the king may raise a lord and only the king may take it from me, and even the king would never—"

"Then away with you to the king if you wish to protest it. See how far that gets you. Or lend your sword to my armies as it pleases you. I care not. But do not come before me without bending your knee."

Indecision and powerless anger suffused Gideon's face. He was trapped, needing the army, which had grown three-fold since he'd last met with Darragh, but reluctant to align himself to a man whom he did not trust. He glared at the Lord of Felmore as he sat waiting patiently, his hands now still on the rounded edges of the arms of his chair. Dredging up the visceral images of the slain bodies of his family and folk, he let rage take hold, welcoming its simplicity. If kneeling before Darragh was the means by which he took his vengeance, so be it.

Without a flicker of surprise, Darragh watched Gideon sink to one knee and lower his head, listening with grim pleasure as he pledged his fealty. "There now, that's a good lad. I welcome you into my service, *Lord Gideon Hughes*."

Donal's eyes flashed hatred, but to which man they were aimed, one could not tell by looking.

Darragh lifted his hands. "You'll have to wait a while before you come into a lordship, Donal." He looked back to

Gideon. "Now that you have pledged yourself to me, Lord Hughes, perhaps you will join my war council when we convene this evening. And tomorrow, you shall have your contingent of men."

Nodding stiffly, Gideon offered a quick bow. "I would be honored."

"Very good. Ah, here comes refreshment." His hand waved to a young maid who bore a large mug in her hand. "You must be thirsty from your travels."

Gideon took the drink with thanks, gulping it down in huge pulls, as much to rid himself of the sour taste of fealty that lined his throat as to finish it quickly so he could leave the hall.

The smile that split Darragh's face as he watched Gideon's throat work was not a pretty one. Within the folds of his lips was something dark and cruel that traveled to the man's cold stare. Unflinching under his gaze, Gideon wiped his mouth and met Darragh's eyes, holding them, unaware of the moment an oily will slipped into his mind, ferreting out what he kept hidden from the Lord of Felmore.

Haegna pinned Gideon's feet to the ground with awful power, acknowledging the moment her son felt her presence within the young lord, and discarding it, intent on learning what she sought. She would pass along what she deemed Darragh worthy of hearing, hoarding the rest. She took her time, taking pleasure as the man's mind flinched and writhed under her assault. Memories revealed themselves, some sweet, others dripping with blood. Haegna took them all. With a final thrust into events he had buried deep in his brain, she tore the last of what she sought from him, leaving him stumbling as awareness returned.

Gideon jerked his head as soon as she released her hold, shaking off the odd cloudiness that muffled his mind, and took his leave, never seeing the feral grin that filled Darragh's face.

CHAPTER TWENTY-FIVE

Veren woke Fiadh as the sun broke through the trees, its rays finding their way through a narrow slit in her bedroom wall. Dasha squawked loudly as he nudged her with his beak, prodding at her back until she groaned and rolled over. She felt wrung out, depleted. Seeing what had occurred in these very halls made her heart hurt.

With bleary eyes, she looked up at Veren.

He took in her pallid face and the dark circles under her eyes. "Did you not sleep?"

Shaking her head, Fiadh sat up, bunching the blankets in her lap. "Not well." Groaning, Fiadh set her feet on the ground and hobbled toward him, her feet curling as the cold floor sank into her tender flesh.

He bowed as she stood before him, shaking off her tiredness.

Fiadh's eyes went wide, and she reached out. "Veren, please, don't."

Dasha, not to be outdone, mimicked Veren, splaying his wings behind him and tilting his head toward the ground. She rolled her eyes.

Ignoring the raven, Veren looked at her. "Should I not pledge myself to you?" He grinned and composed himself like that of a knight. "My sword in your defense. My council when you wish it. My..." He smiled. "My friendship."

Her eyes wrinkled with pleasure. "It is the latter I need the most."

"Then it is yours." He grabbed her hand and pressed his lips to her knuckles.

She felt the warmth of his breath and the energy that coursed through the point of contact in the gentle buzzing in her head.

Veren spun on his feet. "I will leave you to dress, and then we will break our fast. I think you will be pleased by the changes about the hall," he added cryptically.

Her brow creased, but he darted from the room before she could determine his meaning. Soon enough, Fiadh saw what Veren had implied. All about her was a hum of energy. Creatures of all kinds scurried about, trimming, cleaning, readying the keep as though company would arrive any day. Fiadh smiled at all who passed, offering her gratitude for their hard work. Most nodded and returned to their labors, but some gazed at her with awe, welcoming her home.

And Erabel *had* begun to feel like home.

Much to Fiadh's surprise, there were warm sweet rolls and jugs of water set upon a freshly scrubbed table in the great hall. Veren sat on a bench while Krulan and Rivya lounged on the stone. Fiadh stopped as she met Krulan's eyes, suddenly taken back to the heartbreaking scene when Krulan had fled Erabel with Threa.

Krulan, she began, *I never thanked you for trying to save her. I am more grateful than you can know.*

The Cù-Sìth nodded, dissecting her meaning in moments, as yellow eyes bore into her. *I would do the same for you, young one.*

She flashed him a smile tinged with sadness and found a seat next to Veren. "It appears we have kitchen staff," she said, grabbing a roll and tearing off a chunk of the soft bread.

"They have been waiting all this time, never having left Erabel, though your people did."

Fiadh chewed thoughtfully, admiring all that had been done since her arrival.

Dasha landed on the table and sauntered to the plate of rolls, snatching one before Veren could stop him. The raven gave a muffled crow, bread hanging from his beak.

"You would do well to teach him some manners," Veren said, watching as the bird found a place to land far out of reach.

Fiadh glanced at Dasha, seeing him for the marvel that he truly was. "I would not change a feather on his head."

Veren harrumphed. "Spoiled bird."

"Aye, he is that." Fiadh laughed and popped the last of her roll into her mouth.

They rose and left the hall, winding their way through passages that had been unkempt only days before and now were clear and lovely. Dasha flew ahead, loudly belting out a raucous song of croaks and caws. The group rounded a corner that led into a large orchard. Birds and insects of every color flew from tree to tree, filling the air with the hum of wings. Dasha joined them, his wingspan eclipsing all others, casting shadows where he flew against the sun.

Veren took her through the field of trees, pointing out every variety and its uses. She tried to concentrate and remember all he said, but her head was swimming with the heady scents and sounds around her. In the end, she could only recall two varieties but not their uses. She knew what he was doing as he led her about. Veren wanted her to feel at home, to get a sense of Erabel in a way that was not tinged with its sad history. As the hours passed and he showed her more, she admitted that it was working.

At midday meal, as she bit into grapes whose sweetness rivaled any she had eaten before, she asked what had been churning in her mind since they had last spoken. "How do you think Rygeil plans to use Calum to get to me?"

He sighed. "The whole story?"

"Aye."

"Very well." Veren got up and strode a few paces away. Fiadh watched as his long, slender fingers traced the edges of a species of lily she had never seen before. Fragrance bloomed under his touch, sweet and strong, traveling through the air to her nose. Dropping his hand, he stared, seeing nothing. "As I told you, when Calum was brought before Rygeil, he was very young." Veren glanced at her.

"We were three years old when Father died."

He nodded. "I was a grown man when Calum came to Oadsera and took little notice of him. But, long had I watched Rygeil and knew the child would come to no good under your grandfather's care. From that young age, he began to shape your brother into a weapon of war, siphoning his power in small doses while feeding him fear and hatred. Since he could not have you, he took all he could from Calum, leaving whatever gifts Danu had passed to him as nothing more than shadows of what they had been. Or could've become."

"Calum—" he studied Fiadh for a moment before continuing, "has become what Rygeil molded him into. Vengeful. Angry. Fixated on erasing mankind from this world, reclaiming what he sees as his birthright. And to do that, he needs you."

"I see," Fiadh whispered.

"Danu blessed you both, Fiadh. Rygeil has used those blessings since Calum was brought to him, spinning those powers into dark magic. Our numbers have grown, far surpassing any in our history." He faced her, trying to explain. "We… our people do not bear but one or two children in our lifetimes. Those natural cycles have been warped and twisted by Rygeil's dark power."

"I understand what you're saying," she told him.

"Those born under Rygeil's eye," he continued, "are taken at a tender age to be molded into a legion with one mind and one purpose. And they will come for you. Rygeil feels that with your strength and gifts, he will be as a god, and the realms of men will crumble, and while I would not mourn the loss of their kind, I do not support his vision."

Fiadh winced at his blunt statement of the slaughter of an entire race but let it go for the moment. "Why now?"

"He has honed a fighting force for decades, unlike any in

our histories. They are ready and have been unleashed in pockets in the east. It is a test of sorts to see how strong his armies are, how stealthy. But, your strength is yet to be tested. I would imagine he wants to tap into your raw potential, hone it to his will before you become too powerful." He pursed his lips with distaste at the thought. "But you cannot be touched when in the safety of Dorcha Wood or Erabel itself. Unwilling to sacrifice his trusted warriors, Rygeil considered other ways to pull you from Dorcha Wood. He used the heir of Belfirth to lure you out."

Fiadh gasped. "What?"

He looked at her askance. "I wasn't sure how much you knew, if Gideon told you."

"His memory was lost for much of the time we were together," she whispered.

"The minds of men have become… pliable… in Rygeil's hands, though Ross' son was the first to be tested with such a far-reaching purpose. Had Krulan not followed, you would have been taken and the man with you, killed." Veren paused. "But… his plan was thwarted, and while his armies continue to attack various holdings, he plots in the shadows, seeking a way to infiltrate Erabel or coax you out again. Calum is the perfect weapon."

"He cannot defeat mankind without me?"

"That is a question even Rygeil himself does not know the answer to. For all his power, he still fears all-out war with men. He remembers what happened the last time our people fought. But if he combines your strength with his, well…" he shrugged. "Then the age of men will soon be at an end."

"How do you know all of this?"

He clenched his jaw as though bracing himself. "I was one of his commanders."

"What?" she shouted, the reality of what he was saying sinking into her with ugly clarity. "Were you… did you lead the attack on Gideon's army?"

"I did."

The revelation felt like a punch in the gut, and she stood and backed away from him. "You murdered them. It was… it was butchery!"

Veren read the betrayal in her face and the accusation in her voice. "It was war."

She shook her head. "No. It was murder."

"Fiadh, please, you have to understand. I had to get close to him," he pleaded. "I needed him to trust me. So, I led his army in order to get close enough to learn his plans so that when the time came, when he made his move for you, I would know."

She stared at him, the warmth gone from her face. "I saw what you did to those men, hundreds of them. Slaughtered and left to rot."

"And you have also seen what they did to *us*!"

"No, it wasn't like that, this… what you did… was… monstrous."

Veren's face shifted from entreaty to harshness. "If you believe that, then you have never seen war. It is an ugly, brutal thing that cares nothing for fathers and sons, wives and daughters. It is merciless, and so must we be in the face of it."

"You killed his father and brother," she said brokenly.

"They would have done the same to me." There was no give in his expression. "Men hunted us down, picking off those who fled, killing entire families. They showed no mercy! None! Why would we give them quarter?"

"You can't know they wouldn't have." Heat bloomed in her limbs, and the earth shifted at her feet, but she felt nothing, saw nothing but hurt and anger.

Dasha came sailing through the air, screeching, and aimed himself at Veren. Fiadh reached out to him before he attacked and forcefully bade him to stop. Unable to fight the strength of her command, he banked to the side and landed on the ground, stalking toward Veren with wings splayed in a threatening display.

Fiadh kept Dasha in her sights and came back at Veren, fire thrumming through her veins. "You walk around here acting as though you are in the right when you never gave them a chance at peace! Did you cut them down? Lord Ross and his son? Was it your hand that killed them?"

He shook his head. "No. I was not in the thick of it."

She made a face and stalked away, leaving the raven to menace him.

Krulan! she called out, sensing him hear her thought.

The Cù-Sìth materialized from the shadows. *I am here.*

I want to leave this place. I need to go. Now.

You cannot. He told her plainly.

You can't keep me here!

Aye, I can, and I will should you leave me no choice.

Fiadh threw back her head and screamed, the sound ripping through the sky as surely as the gust of wind that followed it tore through the trees, shredding leaves and twigs. Her hands turned into fists, sending currents of energy in crackles of electricity into the ground where they churned, rippling through the soil in small waves. Heart beating so rapidly, she felt it thrum against the confines of her chest. She turned, her eyes glowing with a fierce light, and faced Veren.

He took a step back, seeing her fury and fearing it.

"I will not be a tool of war!" she roared, her voice doubling and trebling until every living thing within its hearing cowered.

Veren held up his hands. "Fiadh, please, you are pushing yourself too far! The power you're using will drain you, maybe even kill you. Please, stop!"

She glared at him, part of her mind registering what he said and knowing it was the truth. Her limbs trembled. Numbness that began at the tips of her fingers spread up her arm and wrapped around her skull. The world grew dim, gray and colorless. From outside herself, she heard Dasha caw in distress while Veren shouted and Krulan growled. She tried to open her mouth, but her breath was gone. As darkness came, she welcomed it.

CHAPTER TWENTY-SIX

Fiadh's eyes cracked open to find Dasha standing on her chest, his beak a finger length from her nose. She made a face and reached up to stroke his head. He clacked at her, closing his eyes as she dug the tips of her fingers between the quills where the casings had become itchy masses. After a few minutes, Dasha stepped away and fluttered to the floor, walking awkwardly to the doorway where Veren stood waiting.

As their eyes met, the events of the previous day came flooding back. She stiffened and tried to rise.

"Fiadh, wait, please. Just hear me out. I have been walking and thinking after you... after you... fell." He walked slowly toward her, hands open at his sides. "I know you think I've betrayed you, that I am something monstrous."

She clenched her jaw, girding herself.

"What I did... the battle I waged with Lord Hughes' army..." He mashed his lips. "I have no love for mankind.

The evils they have done to our people fomented such a hatred that, at times, I cannot see beyond it. In the Great War, I saw such agony. The children of our people slain. Males and females abused and murdered. There was so much blood. So much death."

She sank into her pallet and watched him warily.

"I am glad you have never seen war. It… changes you. It makes you hard, and I believe—*I know*—it weakens our connection with the Great Mother. She is life itself. How could she want so much death? I am ashamed that I had not given that contradiction much thought, if any." He shook his head. "Long have I hated the children of men." He put his head in his hands. "I still hate them. To tell you differently would be a lie. But, seeing you, being in your presence… how can they all be evil, mindless machines of war?"

She studied him with a guarded expression, but said nothing.

"Riona, your mother, is of their world. Somehow, she took you and Calum in, kept you safe for as long as she could. She… she loved you, as the Great Mother loves all life within her landscape. Even man." His voice choked out the last part as though it was ash in his mouth. "Riona is proof that mankind is not inherently evil. Krulan showed me that, though I have little doubt that to put mankind in a positive light was *not* his intent. He shared his memories so that I could understand you better and, in understanding you, I have come to understand *her*. She tried to save Threa, an Aos Sí she had been taught to hate and despise, but who she saw only as a person, a person in need of help. She could not save her body, none could, but with her goodness,

her kindness, she saved her soul, saved you, and perhaps…
perhaps even saved our people. In all the hate and death, it
was not one of our people, not an Aos Sí, but your mother,
Riona, a human, who offered the first outstretched hand,
the first act of kindness between our peoples. Mayhap that
one kindness will save us all before this story is done."

Fiadh felt a reluctant softening of her heart.

"I will not ask your forgiveness." He glanced at Dasha,
who gurgled as he settled on the blankets at Fiadh's feet.
"But I need you to know that I took no joy in the battle
against Lord Ross' people. I knew it was an ill-fated attack."
His fingers picked at a loose thread on the edge of his tunic.
"Rygeil wanted to test the strength of his army but had yet
to make a decision about his future moves that he was
willing to share. I couldn't leave, not until I knew his mind.
When that battle was over, and we had made camp far from
those killing fields, he came to me, filled with such pride and
malice that I could hardly stomach it, but as he had tested
his army, he believed too that he had tested me. He believed
me loyal to him now. And so he laid out his plans to use
Gideon to lure you from the protection of Dorcha Wood.
He sent me, and a small band of warriors, back to Oadsera
just after that battle to replenish those who had been
wounded or slain. I fulfilled that role, but I did not return to
his ranks. Instead, I prepared to leave my home, knowing I
could never come back." Veren snagged her eyes and held
her. "I am not a monster, Fiadh."

She held his stare, looking beyond his words and into
that wealth of emotion he kept locked away. How she
tapped into him, she couldn't say, but he was laid bare

before her. Fiadh felt his hatred, grief, and longing. Somewhere in his rage was the name of a sibling, slain in the Great War but not spoken of in their conversations. She left the stolen memory where it lay hidden.

"If you say it, I will go." He looked pained. "But, I beg you to let me stay by your side."

Fiadh studied him. Should she tell him to leave? To take his hate and go? In the end, she said nothing, and Veren visibly relaxed.

Dasha crept to her side and tugged at her shift. Fiadh glanced at him, intending to brush him away, but he would not have it. He yanked at the fabric, pulling so hard the tip of his beak pierced the linen.

"Dasha!"

He had the decency to look abashed, but only for a moment. Pigeon-walking to her other side, he snapped his beak and tugged at the fabric again.

Shaking her head, she said, "You are a knave, but I see what you're doing."

Petting him lovingly, she dug into her memories and pulled up images of Riona, holding them in her mind. What would Mother tell her if she were here? Would she forgive? Fiadh looked away, seeing nothing, but feeling the weight of Veren's stare.

Riona suddenly felt like a paragon. She had such *goodness*, and as her silence grew more damning, Fiadh began to fear she may never measure up to that woman. There was nothing of her old life waiting for her. That had been taken as surely as her innocent view of the world had been stolen. She was here. This was home. And, if what Veren said was true, others would come, all with similar hatred for a people who had shown her so much ugliness and so much love. Fiadh was torn between the past and the future.

With vibrant clarity, another memory settled in her mind. The village of Felmore laid out before her, at the center of which hung the charred remains of her mother still lashed to the pole on which they'd burned her. There was rage, so much rage as Fiadh watched villagers go about their lives as if nothing had happened, as though the world had not ended as she felt it had. She had wanted to kill them, to unleash an awful vengeance, and she had subconsciously called to beasts with fangs and claws and talons to do her bidding. In those moments, she had become a monster.

Letting the memory sink back into her mind, she turned to Veren. "I do not know what the future holds nor my part in it. But I am not immune to the hatred you feel. I have felt it too." She shifted on the pallet. "I accept what you did to Gideon's army. To do otherwise would be pretending it did not happen, and I was there, I saw the bloody remains. And, in the end, I know that his army had marched into that valley for two purposes." She paused, recalling Gideon's recounting of Lord Ross' intent to find the Aos Sí and destroy them. "They sought to face a looming threat, yes, but also to kill for the sake of the hatred they felt toward a people they too had no interest in bargaining peace with."

Veren opened his mouth to speak, but she held up her hand.

"I cannot see what is coming. I can only learn from the past and what I think—what I *feel*—is that we cannot live in a world absent of an entire people. There must be a balance, as there had been so many lifetimes ago. I think… I think that is what Danu wants of me. Perhaps, that is why I am here. The question now is whether you would stand by my side as I fight for that future."

Going to his knees, Veren bowed his head and made a vow, knowing what may come would test his loyalty in the face of the hatred that still burned in his heart, but acknowledging that her words, her purpose, rang with truth.

CHAPTER TWENTY-SEVEN

That afternoon Veren found Fiadh in the great hall, two swords in his fists.

She grimaced. "Why are you looking at me with those in your hands?"

He sat next to her, leaning the blades against the table. "Because you are to learn how to use one."

Fiadh muttered darkly about the male species and their fascination with weaponry.

Veren chuckled. "You could show a little enthusiasm."

She stuck her tongue out at him and folded her arms across her chest like a spoiled child. "I will not learn to kill people with a sword."

He cocked an eye. "Oh, not even if our people's fiercest warrior taught you?"

Fiadh smirked. "Oh? Who would that be?" She looked around as though whomever he spoke of would appear.

"You jest but nay, I am not talking about myself." Rising, Veren held out his hand. "Come, I will take you to her."

Grasping his fingers, Fiadh let him pull her to her feet. They walked through the keep and into what must have been a vibrant arena in Threa's youth. Fiadh looked around, noting the rows of benches that lined the circular area.

"What was this used for?"

Veren scanned the structure, remembering. "Many things. I have been here for the Tailteann festival. All the tribes gathered for a fortnight of games and celebration."

"It must have been very grand."

"Aye." He looked down at her. "Perhaps, we will see those days again."

She smiled, but it turned out crooked as she imagined so many of her people here, wanting to meet her, wishing to talk. That future felt intimidating. Veren laughed and hauled her into the open expanse. Out of the corner of her eye, Fiadh saw Krulan walk onto the edge of the field where he lay down, resting his head on his front paws.

"He watches over you closely," Veren remarked.

She nodded. "Aye, he has become my shadow."

Dasha screeched and clacked his beak at her as he paced at her feet before flying into a tree and plucking an acorn. She watched, confused, as he carried it in his beak and flew toward Krulan. The raven hovered above the Cù-Sìth for a moment, then dropped the seed. It landed on Krulan's head.

Fiadh exploded into a fit of giggles as Krulan leaped to his feet, snarling, while the bird taunted him from the branches above.

"I would tell Dasha to remain in those trees lest he seeks to feel the bite of Krulan's teeth," Veren said with laughter.

"Aye, that is sound advice."

Veren suddenly jerked his head as someone stepped onto the field.

Fiadh stood rooted, mouth parted, as she watched the female's progress, in awe of the grace and beauty in every movement. Like Veren, she wore a long green tunic and leggings, her feet encased in pliable boots laced around her slim calves. Kaelari was even more striking in person than when she had witnessed events of the past, her skin a lustrous black like a moving shadow. Adding to her imposing appearance was a scar that bisected her left brow and traveled down her cheek, the pale pink of the tissues covering the old wound contrasting with her dark skin. How the blade responsible for it missed her eye was a mystery. The last time Fiadh had seen Kaelari, she was whole, the memory of the warrior charging into battle seared into her mind. She could only assume the wound was inflicted when Erabel was attacked.

Kaelari studied Fiadh when they were a few paces from each other, her vibrant blue eyes missing nothing. Fiadh shifted under her scrutiny, causing Kaelari to flash a smile of bright white teeth, followed by a throaty chuckle.

"The daughter of Erabel," she said, her voice rich and sensual. "It is an honor to stand in your presence."

Fiadh blushed and spluttered, tongue-tied.

Kaelari grinned broadly and reached out to clasp Fiadh's wrist. Strength poured from her fingers as she took Fiadh's arm, warmth radiating from the points of contact.

Fiadh looked down at their linked limbs, marveling that she was in the company of someone so familiar, while also a stranger.

"I am Kaelari."

"I know," she managed to get out.

Kaelari looked at Veren with surprise.

"Fiadh communed with Danu, who shared some of our history," he explained.

A knowing look filled her face. "Ah, I see. That is well as she should know her past in order to shape our future."

Fiadh looked from one to the other. It was clear that they had a deep camaraderie. The thought must have been stamped on her face because Kaelari turned to her and said, "Veren and I have fought and trained side by side for many years. He and I..." she smiled slyly. "Let us say that we have our history."

Veren laughed. "That is one way to put it. What Kaelari is not telling you is that I longed to be her mate for many years and did all that I could to capture her attention, but she had eyes for another."

"You have a strong arm, Veren, but you could never match my appetites."

Heat flooded Fiadh's face.

Kaelari marked it and laughed. "Oh, young one. You have much to learn about your people."

"I do not doubt that," she said wryly, having regained her composure.

"I like her," Kaelari declared.

What followed was a recounting of many of the things Danu had shown her, though each was given a fresh perspective, and not all of what Fiadh had been shown was shared.

When it grew quiet, Kaelari's mouth turned down, and she looked at Veren. "Rygeil is sending Calum and a dozen of his best fighters. Among them is an earthmover."

Veren frowned. "When?"

"A sennight at best."

"Does Rygeil know of your leaving?"

She shook her head. "He believes I am scouting lands in the south where he plans another round of attacks, one of which will be at the seat of the king in Taigon."

"If he attacks and kills King Stephan, there will be an uprising to surpass any before it. He will unite all mankind against us. Outlanders from north and south, far beyond the borders of Stephen's realm. Does Rygeil not understand just how numerous the armies of men have become? Victory over such numbers—it is impossible. This war will be the end of us all."

"He knows it," Kaelari said grimly, "but he cares not. He believes he has the power to overcome all, and mayhap he does." She glanced at Fiadh. "Especially once he brings the daughter of Erabel to heel."

"That he will never do," Veren said darkly.

"Think you so?"

He nodded, glancing at Fiadh, who had set her lips in a thin line.

"It is what he wants, Veren. Already, he has decimated entire fiefdoms in the east, killing everyone. It is madness. Rulers of the north and south have begun to gather their forces, while here in the west, Rygeil remains blind to their movements. It will only be a matter of time before men amass armies that dwarf our numbers. Just like last time." Kaelari ground her teeth, eyes flashing, as she jerked her head toward Fiadh. "But this time, he has prepared. For a hundred years, he has delved deep into the dark arts, mastered magic lost since the time of the giants. I know not what evils he has yet to reveal, but I do know that he means to steal this one from her place of power and use her as he has done his grandson. Rygeil is unhinged. Even now, the land begins to wither from his taint. If he gets ahold of her, there will be no stopping him. He will kill us all in his quest for power, though I believe he would win a war if one were waged."

"He has grown so powerful?"

She darted a glance at Fiadh, who lifted her chin.

Returning her attention to Veren, she said, "After you left, he sent ravens who marked your direction. He knows where you went and why."

Fiadh drifted away as the two continued to talk, her head buzzing with the knowledge that, like Veren, Kaelari had been part of the slaughter of Gideon's army. She didn't know how to feel about that. There was anger and sadness, but a small part of her also understood where those murderous acts stemmed from. But, to hear whole communities had also been sacked filled her with dread and grief. The people of those villages were not soldiers. They were innocent, like Riona. Tragic casualties of unmitigated vengeance.

Would Kaelari put aside her hatred of mankind as Veren said he would? Could she ever forgive their acts?

Fiadh sighed, weary of the past that haunted her, too tired to face things that felt insurmountable. The future was a murky thing, clouded in so much prejudice and hate. How could *she* do anything to stop the tide of war?

Meandering to a low wall, she leaned her elbows on it. The voices of Kaelari and Veren nothing but faint noises in the background. She looked at her hands, turning them palm up as she flexed her fingers. Though she had not spoken of it to Veren, she had felt frightening power spill from them and wondered at it. In truth, what she felt radiating from her palms was not the only thing she'd become aware of. The Aos Sí had magic running through their veins, or so the stories went. If true, she held that magic within herself. It could be a weapon if she chose it to be.

"You have come at a dire time, Fiadh," Kaelari said quietly as she came to stand at her side. "We need your strength. You are the future of our people."

"I am just a girl who stumbled into a world I do not recognize. I don't know how to be what you need."

Kaelari reached over and stroked her cheek, the sensation so like Riona's motherly hands that tears pricked her eyes. "Did Veren tell you that your coming was foreseen?"

"He said something of it."

"Zaeleria, the most gifted of our seers, saw your return to Erabel. She spoke of one who would be imbued with the power of Danu, who could wield it as no Aos Sí before her. Your brother could've have fulfilled that prophecy, but—" She shook her head.

Fiadh looked stricken. "Is there no hope for him?"

"I do not believe so, but I have not the sight to see it."

She paused. "Veren told me that you struggle with the knowledge that he attacked Lord Hughes' army." Kaelari stared at Fiadh. "I was there as well. My blade took many lives that day. Anger burned in my heart as I slew those men. But even in the heat of that fury, I knew the wrong of it. Men had not begun that battle. We had."

Fiadh nodded. "Thank you. I… I had never seen the carnage of battle on such a scale. It was terrible." She fiddled with her hands, darting her eyes to Kaelari. "You told Veren that Rygeil attacked villages. Did you… were you part of that?"

Shame flickered in Kaelari's face. "Nay, but I regret that I was not."

Fiadh's eyes widened.

Holding up her hand, Kaelari said, "Do not misinterpret my meaning. I do not make war on the innocent. Those who fight alongside me are of the same mind." She glanced at Veren, who nodded. "Rygeil knows this. I believe that is why he ordered me to take my warriors and scout out any bands of soldiers who had escaped during battle." She sighed. "Had I known of his intentions, I would have confronted him and done whatever was within my power to stop him."

Relief caused Fiadh's chest to loosen. Had Kaelari said she had slaughtered women and children, she was unsure how she would've reacted. To do something so monstrous… she shook her head.

"Aye, it was, but I cannot undo the past. I can only look forward." She took Fiadh's hand. "There is more power in you than all of us combined. Danu has blessed you with it for a purpose, and I mean to help you draw it out."

Kaelari began to explore Fiadh's strengths, testing her, feeling out ways to elicit that power and turn it into something she could command. Anger was an obvious trigger and what Fiadh had used without realizing it. But Kaelari needed her to be able to call upon the magic in her blood without that rage.

"You must feel it in your gut," Kaelari said, pressing her hands to Fiadh's middle. "Focus on it, let it fill you, but keep it tight, centered."

Fiadh frowned and closed her eyes, thinking only of the air around her, willing it to move. She was rewarded with a breeze that grew stronger as her body hummed with power. Soon, the wind became a funnel, pulling dirt and grass from the field.

Kaelari clapped, breaking Fiadh's concentration. "Well done! Now, take that same energy and channel it into the earth."

She nodded, holding her arms to her sides and slightly away from her body, fingers splayed. It took more effort than the air, and her head began to ache. Without the anger she had fed off when she'd confronted Veren, her reservoir of strength felt harder to pull from. Gritting her teeth, Fiadh visualized the ground itself, the dirt and rock, letting out a whoosh of air when something clicked, and the ground beneath her feet shifted. She followed the movement with her mind, bending it to her will so that it rose and fell in shallow waves.

Dasha cawed as the tree on which he was perched

shook. Her connection severed, and she looked at him in consternation.

Kaelari laughed. "I see that one has not changed. Again!"

Fiadh cried peace after another hour and lurched toward Krulan, who lay in the shade. He gave her a wolfy chuckle as she sagged to her knees and crawled toward him, flopping onto her back to rest her head against his side, her weary arms dropping to the ground like lifeless things.

"I am glad my exhaustion amuses you," she muttered.

A rumble from his chest sent tremors through her body.

They lay beneath the shade. Fiadh's weary body relaxing as tension and fatigue slowly left her.

She is a strong fighter, Krulan remarked, observing Kaelari as she sparred with Veren. *You would do well to learn what she has to teach you. I may not always be by your side, protecting you.*

You would leave me? she asked, lacing the question with mock offense.

Only if you stop training.

She huffed and poked his side, a pleased smile lifting her mouth when he flinched involuntarily. *And to think I once feared for my life when you stepped from the shadows.*

You would have been wise to fear me.

Fiadh snorted. *Those days are in the past. I know better now.*

What do you know?

You are naught but a ball of fur—a comfortable place to rest my head.

Rivya, who had just joined them, barked a laugh. *Aye, I can attest to that!*

See, even your mate says it is so. Fiadh settled her head more firmly into his side.

You females are all alike. Think you know everything, Krulan grumbled.

We don't think we do, we know we do. Rivya stretched, eyeing her mate with humor.

Fiadh gave a startled laugh, which turned into a very vocal complaint as Krulan rose, robbing her of her pillow.

Shaking the debris off his fur, he said, *Rest is over, young one.*

Veren strolled over, swords in his hands. She made a face and slowly got to her knees, using Rivya's strong back to push herself up the rest of the way. With arms that hung limply, she trudged to him, looking at the weapons with distaste.

"I do not see why I must train with those if I can knock them from an enemy's hand with a gust of wind."

He smirked. "Oh? Try it."

She focused, centering herself, and called on the wind. Reaching out a hand, she propelled a gust toward his sword arm, grinning when the blade wavered. With a flick of his wrist, he wrested it from the air that circled the metal, swinging it in a series of slashes that appeared to cut the pockets of air until they were little more than a gentle breeze. She gaped and squinted, taking a deep breath and gritting her teeth before unleashing another blast, only to see it dealt with the same precision.

Dropping her arm, she asked, "Are you going to do that every time?"

"Until you realize you cannot take the sword from my hand."

She gave the blade on the ground a black look, then stalked over and grabbed it. "You win. Teach."

By the time they finished, the sun had begun its descent, and her arms were no better than lumps of abused flesh. He slapped her back, Kaelari falling into step beside them, as they made their way inside where a small feast was laid out in the great hall. Krulan and Rivya joined them a few minutes later.

Fiadh looked at them, noting how they licked their muzzles as they made themselves comfortable in the corner of the large room.

Krulan, she said.

He looked up. *What do you eat?*

We hunt in Dorcha Wood.

Is there a law that you are not to hunt within Erabel?

We do not eat our protected, he said flatly. *There is plenty to sustain us beyond Erabel, though we hunt only what we need to fill our bellies.*

She thought of the many creatures that scurried about even now as the sun sank below the horizon. All had that awareness and sense of connection. She understood his reasoning as there had always been discomfort consuming the flesh of animals, those beings she could communicate with and feel.

I am glad to be counted as one of your protected, she offered, earning her a curl of his lip like the shadow of a smile.

CHAPTER TWENTY-EIGHT

It was a dream. It was a memory. Danu came to Fiadh as she slept, pulling her from the shell of her body.

You cannot fight what you do not understand, the Great Mother told her, taking her to a castle she had only seen from a distance and dropping her within its walls.

Lord Magnar Baoill sat upon the dais in Felmore Castle. A grizzled beard covered the worst of the scars on his weathered face, leaving only fine trails of puckered skin stretching in webs of pink and white along his cheek to the outer edge of his milky left eye. From the second floor came the sounds of weeping, wails from his barren wife, who'd once again failed to quicken with his child.

"Do not despair, milord," a middle-aged servant said. "The Great Mother may yet grant you a son."

"Damn the Great Mother," Magnar snarled.

She paled.

He barked at her for ale and rubbed his hand over his

face with weariness. Snatching the mug from her trembling hand, he gulped the dark liquid, oblivious as it streamed from the sides of his mouth and into his greying whiskers. Magnar eyed the servant's retreating figure, scowling as another shrill wail snaked its way to his ears. He had tried her and others more times than he could count, but for all that, he didn't even have a bastard child to continue his line.

"Ailis," he bellowed, "tell my wife to cease her howling before my head splits."

Ailis nodded and clambered up the stairs, the soles of her misshapen leather shoes slapping against the stone. Magnar sat brooding as his steward entered, making his way to his lord's side.

"Is that the Lady Grainne?"

"Aye, Great Mother curse her," Magnar snarled.

"My lord?" The man backed up a few paces.

"I need a son!" Magnar yelled. "A son, damn you! And she does nothing but bleeds from her barren womb!"

"The Lady Grainne may yet have a son, my lord."

Magnar waved a hand in Leon's face. "So says the midwife, but I grow weary of her promises." He looked at his steward. "My line shall end."

"Have faith, my lord," Leon said. "My wife did not quicken for nigh on five years, but she went on to have three healthy babes."

Sighing loudly, Magnar settled back in the large chair. "I will not put stock in fantasies, the woman is barren, but I may yet have a son, is it not so? I'll have every maid in Felmore brought to my bed if need be."

Leon blanched and stood awkwardly following that

pronouncement, watching Magnar swipe his hand down his face with weariness. Glancing at the doorway that led to the inner bailey, he cleared his throat.

Magnar looked at him through the gaps between the fingers he had pressed over his eyes. "What is it?"

"You have a visitor, my lord. A woman."

Grumbling, Magnar straightened, tugging at his heavily embroidered tunic to more fully cover his paunch. "What business does she want with me?"

"She would not say, my lord. Though her finery suggests she is from a family of means, she arrived alone and unattended."

Surprise flashed across Magnar's face. "Alone?"

"Aye, my lord."

"And her name?"

"Lady Carmun was all she gave me," Leon said, taking a step back and walking toward the door. "She is quite comely," he offered, giving Magnar a small smile.

"Oh, aye?"

"She is… well," Leon said, licking his lips, "let me just say that she is unusually striking, her face and form even tightening my old loins."

Magnar grunted and bid his steward bring her in.

Leon reentered the great hall, a woman walking placidly behind him. Magnar watched their progress, a look of lust passing over his face as his eyes devoured the divine creature who came to rest at the foot of the dais. She was indeed striking with a ripe body and hair so blond it was nearly white, braided in a thick rope that fell below her waist. Dressed in a gown of deep purple with a neckline and sleeves embroidered in fine silver threads, she swayed as she walked, pulling Magnar's eyes to every curve. Slung low on her trim waist was a thin belt of black leather from which dangled a chain with a red jewel that rested just above her mons. His eye was drawn to it, heat evident in his gaze and the flare of his nostrils.

The gentle murmur of her voice broke his hungry perusal. "My Lord Magnar, I am Carmun of Siska, and I seek your counsel."

Magnar scratched his beard, considering her odd request. "Siska is not known to me, and my steward tells me you arrived unaccompanied. How came you to my land?"

"Your name is whispered across the western reaches, my lord, and I have come to see the man so revered by others."

Magnar puffed his chest. "I can assure you I am every bit the man rumors have portrayed me to be. Now, what can I do for you? What counsel can I provide?"

Carmun smiled, the expression curving her sensuous lips, though her eyes remained cold and calculating. "For generations, you and your people have lived side by side with the Aos Sí, have you not?"

"Aye, their realm lies within Dorcha Wood. They keep to theirs, and I keep to mine."

"And is it not true that your people have suffered of late? That your crops have the blight and your animals have grown sick and weak?"

Magnar's eyes shuttered, and he pursed his lips. "It is no secret that my people have suffered. What is that to you?"

"What if I could bring you and your kingdom wealth and prosperity?" she asked, her voice taking on a sly quality.

"I fail to see how you could do aught but make my loins ache."

Carmun laughed. "Such aches, my lord, could also be tended if you wish it." Her throaty voice was tinged with malice. "But what I offer you first is freedom from the hardships that have plagued your people. I can give you riches and power. I can guarantee the future of your line."

"You are a sorceress to be dangling such things before me!" Magnar's eyes burned with anger and longing.

"I only offer an assurance of the succession of your great line and good fortune to your people. If you do not wish for such things, I will take my leave."

Rising abruptly, Magnar stalked toward Carmun, rage in each step, though the woman stood her ground, seemingly unaffected by his towering presence as he leaned forward and spat in her face. "You are a witch!" His hand moved to the hilt of his blade.

Raising her hardened eyes to his, Carmun said, "What if I could make your wife's womb quicken with a son?"

The color drained from Magnar's face, and he took a step back, swinging away from her. "That is blasphemous talk," he muttered. "The Great Mother has not seen to bless us with babes, and I have no desire to bring her wrath to my house by inviting the sorcery you speak of."

Carmun stepped toward him, reaching out a hand and stroking his arm and then his back, the contact causing his muscles to twitch. "The Great Mother has abandoned you, my lord. Is that much not clear? Did you not see her leaving in the crops that withered in your fields?" Coming to stand before him, she titled her head back and looked up, licking her lips in invitation as her hands rubbed his chest. "I offer you freedom from her indifference. Wealth. Power. Your innermost desire," she purred, letting her hand travel to the hardness between his legs.

He hissed at the contact but made no move to stop her questing fingers as they gripped what she found there. "What…" he said, pausing before grinding out, "what must I do?"

"Kill them."

"Who?"

"The Aos Sí. Kill them all, and I will give you everything."

Fiadh watched the unthinkable unfold as she hung suspended above a scene of callous manipulation. Carmun whispered in Magnar's ear, venomous words, each one infused with power that left Magnar impotent, little more than clay for her hands to mold and twist. Fiadh reached out as though to stop the flow of words, pulling it back when she remembered where she was. When she was. It was too late for Magnar and the world. This was the beginning, where the infection began before spreading to every fief while Rygeil stood blinded.

"Leave your great hall and seek out those whose lands the Aos Sí have tainted. Rally your forces and bring down the race that has been a yoke on mankind's neck for too long," Carmun commanded.

Magnar's eyes glazed over, and he nodded. "And my son?"

Carmun loosened the laces of her dress, letting the bodice slip from her shoulders to the roundness of her breasts. Lust flared as Magnar gazed at her flesh. Commanding his staff to empty the hall, he sat and beckoned to her. She walked toward his outstretched hand, hips swaying in seductive undulations. His eyes tracked her movements like a rabid dog. So caught in her web, he did not see her eyes flash nor hear the low incantations she muttered as she straddled him, taking his seed and imbuing it with dark power.

Magnar sat panting as she drew away, his eyes glazed, head swimming with spells.

"When the moon rises," Carmun purred, stroking his grizzled chin. "I shall return and bless your wife's womb."

Magnar's mouth parted as though to speak, but Carmun leaned over and pressed her lips to his, slipping her tongue into his mouth. It darted between Magnar's lips, forked like a serpent. She breathed into his arrested form, toxic fumes that set him coughing, his body contorting before going limp. Licking Magnar's teeth and bottom lip, Carmun leaned away, a malicious grin of triumph suffusing her face. Spinning on her heels, she left in a flash of purple skirts and white hair.

Fiadh, somehow tethered to the repugnant creature, followed as Carmun sauntered from the hall, walked through the village of Felmore and into fields of crops that withered under her splayed hands as she passed. Stopping, Fiadh watched her turn and look at Dorcha Wood, her lip curling in a snarl. Muttering a curse, she spat into the air, sneering as the wind carried it to the border of the forest, where it struck an oak, causing the ancient tree to shudder and split with a tremendous crack. Cackling, Carmun swept her body into a vortex and spun away from that place, leaving Fiadh staring at the spot where she had stood. The ground was black, riddled with mold and poisonous worms that spilled from the earth in a vile eruption of twisting forms.

The sun arced across the sky in a yellow blur as time passed before her suspended form. Night fell, and Fiadh watched as Carmun reemerged, as though born from darkness itself. On feet that made no sound, she sauntered to the keep, careless of all who may see her as she crossed the bailey and entered the great hall, sweeping up the stairs in a soft swish of skirts. At the threshold of a door, she stopped and laid her hand against the wood, muttering words that sounded harsh and guttural, before pulling on the latch and entering. Fiadh followed, powerless to untether herself, though part of her wished to hide from what she was about to witness.

Lady Grainne lay in the bed, legs twisted in a tangle of sheets. Leaning over the sleeping woman, Carmun lifted and cradled her head, her hand traveling down the curves of her figure, stopping above the woman's womb. She pressed her mouth to Grainne's. A puff of air, laced with words of power and venomous evil, slipped between the woman's lips, filling her lungs and blood, ceasing all movement of her sleeping form as though even her heart had stopped beating. Resting her other hand upon her own womb, Carmun chanted, the power and cadence of her words encompassing both figures. A dark shadow bloomed and began to grow. It curled and twisted, tendrils of the darkness joining the two as something passed from her womb and into Grainne's. The lady's body twitched, and she moaned, never waking, while the magic Carmun wielded reshaped her into a vessel to hold the child that latched itself to its host.

Carmun eased the woman's head onto her pillow. Then rose and bent forward until her mouth hovered above Grainne's abdomen.

"Haegna," she whispered. "You are mine as I am yours."

Fiadh hung motionless above the woman who would bear Lord Darragh's mother, watching the shallow rise and fall of her chest, part of her wishing she could smother her, stopping the heartache in her life before it happened—hating herself for thinking something so vile.

Kaelari had been right to fear Carmun, and Fiadh wondered how different the world would be had Rygeil listened to her warnings and acted. Sadly, she knew the outcome of it all. She had lived with its aftermath.

The air around her incorporeal body stirred, lifting her up and out, back to her bed in Erabel. Back to the present, where forces from all sides were closing in.

CHAPTER TWENTY-NINE

*D*arragh looked on sourly as Haegna darted her tongue along the braid of blond hair he had brought her, the only piece of her gift he would give until she'd told him whatever he'd been summoned for.

"She is ripe, this one," Haegna sighed, pressing the locks to her nose. "You make me hungry."

He watched her with disgust, snatching the braid from her hand. "Enough!"

Pouting, she twisted her body away from his. "You don't love me."

"I am not here to speak of love," he growled. "You called for me, and I have come, bearing gifts should you please me."

She craned her neck and smiled at him, her blackened teeth flashing.

"I know you found your way into his mind." Darragh remembered clearly the moment Gideon's eyes had grown glassy as his mother wheedled her way into his thoughts. He didn't ask how she did it, willing to go only so far to get want he wanted. Let her have her fun and dabble where she would. He had a bigger prize in mind.

Haegna rose slowly from her stool by the fire, straightening her hunched frame to her full height, her dress hanging loosely to the floor. She reached up and patted his cheek.

He pulled away and grabbed her wrist, tightening his grip until he felt her bones begin to give. "Do not touch me."

She snickered, the sound bringing memories from his childhood to the surface. He flinched as a ghostly hand ran across his chest, traveling down his belly while he lay helpless. He slapped her face, her head thrown to the side with the force of it. "Stay out of my head!"

Laughing through her bloodied lips, Haegna hobbled to her rocker and settled herself. "So, you wish to know what I saw?"

Darragh glared at her.

"The girl, an Aos Sí as you well know," she paused, watching his reaction and getting nothing, "was to be brought to Rygeil by Gideon himself."

Unable to hide his surprise, Darragh's eyes sparked. "Oh? And why did he not complete his task?"

"You should be thankful he didn't. If she had fallen into the hands of the elven king, he would have become more powerful than any force mankind could muster... even yours." She laced her fingers and rocked in her chair, the wood creaking in the small cell. "The Cù-Sìth who protects her nearly tore out Gideon's throat. If not for the girl, he'd be dead. It was that beast who thwarted Rygeil."

He stared at her, considering her words. "So, the Aos Sí king is after her. He covets her power," he said, walking in a tight circle until he faced her again, "as do you."

"True enough, but should Rygeil get ahold of her, your future as ruler will be lost."

"Then we must flush her out of that forest she hides in." His head turned in the direction of Dorcha Wood, though he could not see it through the stone of his keep. "I assume you have a suggestion."

She cackled. "I would not be your loving mother if I did not look out for the interests of my son."

He grimaced.

Haegna studied him, this man she had shaped into the ruthless leader he was. She truly would do all in her power to see him control the western reaches. His success was also hers. Of late, she had been scrying in the dark waters of the bowl that sat in the corner, delving into them with an intensity that sapped her strength, reaching into the abyss. And something had reached back. It was an old power, sinister, full of wrath, imprisoned, though the bonds that held him had grown weak. It had marked her wandering eye and saw its own blood in her veins. Dothur, son of Carmun, he had told her as he bade her welcome and called her sister. Through him, the witch's daughter was unmasked, birthing fury at having let the Aos Sí girl slip through her withered hands. But, she mused, Dothur held knowledge she had only begun to plumb.

Focusing on Darragh, she imparted information that

dark being had told her. "The Aos Sí are unmatched in their forests. They draw power and strength from places like Dorcha Wood."

He sat on a stool, rested his hands on his knees, and waited for her to continue.

"Their armies may venture away from their woods, but it taxes them. They grow weak. It is that weakness which we must endeavor to bring about. They know little of siege-craft. They do not build great engines of war. No catapult, siege tower, or trebuchet will ever find its way into one of their armies. They rely on magic and spells, the power of which they gain from the trees themselves. But, remove their source of power…"

Darragh's mouth lifted in a cruel smile. "And we will crush them."

She nodded. "The Lord of Belfirth made the mistake of traveling to them, meeting the forest folk on grounds of Rygeil's choosing. And, as for Lord Crommack, he had but a small force to oppose the elf king."

"We will not make the same mistake and meet them in an open field," Darragh said, warming to the conversation. He looked at the stone that made her cell, the strength of it. "What need have I to expend my own men when I have soldiers from the east and north that I can send out to menace and distract their army. I will keep the bulk of my forces safe behind our high walls and far from the woods."

"Do not forget that they may yet have spells and magics to bring down our walls," Haegna warned. "But, if you bring me the girl to feed my powers, I will be able to block such spellcraft with my own. If Rygeil is to come for us, let him come to a treeless land of iron and stone, where his warriors will be as babes before your blade."

"A treeless land?" Darragh asked.

"Aye. You know what you must do. You must wrest every tree from our domain, rip them all down, every last one. Dorcha Wood must burn."

Darragh left his mother humming with gratitude at the gift of the young girl he'd brought her and made his way to find the Belfirth brat. Although he acknowledged that he should probably be thanking the man for not delivering the girl into Rygeil's hands, he would never admit such. Walking into the fields outside the keep, he found the young lord.

"Lord Hughes," Darragh said, his voice stopping the arc of Gideon's sword as he parried an invisible foe.

"Aye?"

Darragh folded his arms across his chest. "You have knowledge of Dorcha Wood?"

Gideon nodded warily. "Some."

"I have a mind to flush the foul creatures of that accused forest into the blades of my men."

Darragh's words had their desired effect. Gideon smiled expectantly, the expression marring his handsome face with ugliness.

"I'm listening," he said.

"Go to Dorcha Wood with men and axes, torches, and swords." He looked toward the forest. "Burn it. Burn it all."

CHAPTER THIRTY

The rigors of training had left Fiadh exhausted each night, her body falling into bed in dreamless sleep. Danu had ceased to pull her into the past, instead letting her explore and learn her powers with the aid of Veren and Kaelari. Others had come as well, but Fiadh was shy around the newcomers, choosing instead to keep company with Krulan and Rivya much of the time.

"Very good, Fiadh!" Veren said as she blocked his attack with a quick parry. "Your swordplay has improved greatly."

An audience of Aos Sí warriors from many clans watched from a distance, their muffled voices carrying on the wind.

"I have a good teacher," she told him, flexing her shoulders to ease the ache.

The sound of brittle leaves crunching under running feet drew her attention to a cluster of jeboa bushes just beyond where she and Veren practiced. She stood in shock as a púca, the shapeshifter having taken the form of a fox, burst from the foliage, the thick black fur on its back raised in alarm.

It swung its ruby gaze to her. "Dorcha Wood burns!"

Veren dropped to his knees before the creature.

"The Lord of Felmore makes war on the trees and the forest itself," the púca said, eyes darting wildly. "He has men with axes of iron and torches of fire, felling great oaks and elms. Fire and ash stretch as far as the eye can see."

Fiadh called to Dasha. *Fly! Show me where they are.*

He soared into the air. She closed her eyes, becoming one with him, feeling currents of wind beneath his wings as he flew higher and higher. He turned east. Smoke billowed into the sky. Circling, she looked with his eyes and saw men with axes hacking at trees, heard their groans as the trunks split and fell to the earth to be consumed by fire.

Come back to me, she commanded, needing to keep him safe and out of range of any bowmen who may be hiding and watching the skies.

"They are on the eastern border!" Fiadh yelled as she released Dasha.

Veren sprang to his feet, sounding the alarm, galvanizing everyone into swift action. Grabbing Fiadh's wrist, he pulled her toward Krulan and swung her onto his back. The Cù-Sìth burst into a run, his claws tearing huge gouges in the earth. All around her, she heard the feet of others, all racing in the same direction.

As soon as they left the safety of Erabel, she felt it. The forest was screaming in agony, waves of pain radiating from the source of the attack. Creatures of every size and color ran madly in all directions, trying to escape. Fiadh bent low on Krulan's back and took a deep pull of air into her nose, smelling smoke. *Hurry, Krulan!*

I am with you, he told her.

She heard the voices of men long before she saw them. Heat, like a living thing, swept through the air as fire consumed the forest. Ash and cinder covered everything, stinging her eyes and searing her clothes. Krulan darted in and out of the underbrush, barely missing the deer and rabbits, foxes and squirrels, that fled in terror.

War cries ripped through the forest as Aos Sí warriors attacked, cutting men down with wicked blades. Fiadh jumped off Krulan's back and joined them, sword at the ready, muscles knowing what to do after so many hours under Veren's tutelage. But she did not come to kill, only to stop the destruction.

She ran, feeling the blistering heat of the fire. Another body shot past hers, an Aos Sí female, Tainsi, she recalled. Fiadh watched for a moment as she hurled herself into a tree that was yet unscathed, marking her target and then jumping to land on the balls of her feet, sword slicing open a neck before the man could scream. Turning away from the carnage, Fiadh ran to the sound of axes.

It was dying. The forest was dying with every brutal cut and finger of flame. The pain of it slowed her progress, and she had to fight against it, willing herself to run. Fiadh stopped, chest heaving, and reached into the earth with her mind, to the place Kaelari had taught her to seek, and pulled the power of Danu into her body. When she felt it thrumming through her limbs, she harnessed particles of water invisible to the eye, but there if one knew how to find them. Raising her arms, she sang to the life-giving element, calling on it to join together. In moments, a wall of liquid rippled before her. She flung her arms outward, dousing flames that had threatened to devour her and everything in their path.

From a distance, she heard a shout. "Fiadh!"

It was Veren.

"I am here!" she called back.

But her focus shifted as a tree screamed out in terror, its trunk severed. Not waiting for Veren, she took off, following the sound of the oak as it hit the ground. Bursting through the trees, she saw three men, axes in their fists and bloodlust in their eyes. She paused, and they gawked at her for a moment before grinning and stalking toward her. Krulan lunged for them, passing so close to her that she spun and fell to the ground, followed by Tainsi's lithe body as she rent the air with her battle cry.

Tainsi leaped toward the closest soldier, sword swinging in a deadly arc and slicing through his neck before she danced away as two others closed in. Krulan ripped out the throat of one man and tore through the chest of another, his muzzle dripping with blood. Rage filled him, rage like no other she had known before.

A startled cry tore her attention from Krulan.

She turned and watched in horror as a blade pierced Tainsi's chest, the point jutting gruesomely from her blood-splattered tunic. She fell to the ground revealing a soldier who dispassionately ripped his sword from her body. Fiadh fixed her gaze on the man who stared at her balefully, the world stopping as her eyes met his.

"Gideon."

He glared at her, and it was the look of a stranger. Cold. Hard. Unforgiving. "'I might have known I'd find you fighting alongside them. You have chosen your side then."

She could say nothing, only stared, frozen as Krulan snarled, his sights on Gideon's throat, an unstoppable force barreling toward him. She felt the Cù-Sìth's awful power. *I'll kill him this time!*

She couldn't move, only watched as Krulan rammed into Gideon, violently throwing him to the ground. Something within her unlocked then.

No!

It was not a word she screamed at Krulan. It was a Word. Powerful. Imbued with a command Krulan could not fight.

He yelped as if struck and drew back, looking at her with simmering anger.

She ran to Gideon and stood over his prone form while Krulan paced, his will fighting her command, while he growled and flashed his teeth.

Shock, pain, and anger flashed in Gideon's eyes. She flinched from the latter but couldn't look away. And then she saw it, there, in the downward turn of his mouth and the shadow that passed over his face. Longing. Regret.

It was enough.

"Run," she whispered, her heart shattering a little as her eyes devoured his.

He glanced at Krulan, who snarled but kept his distance.

"Run!" Fiadh shouted. "Leave this place before he kills

you. I can't hold him back for long." Even as she said it, she felt the Cù-Sìth begin to edge forward.

Gideon warily got to his feet. She looked up at him, tears pooling in her eyes. She was not a killer. She would not become what he thought her race to be. He began to reach for her, then dropped his hand and turned away. She watched him go, seeing the moment he looked back, the look on his face as Veren and Kaelari broke through what was left of the line of trees bordering the forest. They made to chase him, but she held out her hand, stopping them.

He seemed to say something then, but the roar of the fire and the screams of the dying swallowed his words.

Gazing at the path he took, she realized it was the same meadow she had found him in. So much had happened since that day. So much had gone wrong. But they had come full circle now and left each other in peace.

It was a start.

Rygeil, his face a hardened mask of cruel beauty, stood at the opening of a turret in Oadsera's stronghold and looked to the west. He could feel Fiadh's power from here, as though Danu herself taunted him with the strength of her chosen. Fiadh had grown too strong, too fast. Time was running short. Already, he had been betrayed by Veren and Kaelari, two of his best warriors. More would follow.

He ground his teeth. Damn Lord Ross' brat for failing to bring Fiadh to him! And damn Krulan! That beast should be loyal to *him*, not Threa's spawn!

It galled him to resort to calling on a being he'd consigned to a dark cage centuries ago. But, what choice had he now? Men were flocking to Lord Darragh in droves. If they breached Erabel's borders and killed Fiadh, he would lose his edge, and, once again, mankind would win. Already, their numbers almost dwarfed his own. No amount of birthing spells could change that, and he knew from the

Great War that numbers won wars. He needed to snuff the armies of men out without expending more of his forces to do it. And that meant summoning something with a dark past.

Behind him, scuttling in the darkness, was Crom Cruach, one of the old gods captured and imprisoned long ago.

Without turning his head, Rygeil addressed the male soldier who hovered in the doorway, having delivered the foul being, and said, "Leave us."

The heavy wooden door closed with a thud, and a wet, wheezing filled the small space behind the last king of the Aos Sí as a deformed figure lurched toward him. Rygeil turned slowly, his lip curling in disgust at the sight that greeted him. The malformed creature, body curved so grotesquely he barely reached the height of a human child, was covered in layers of skin that grew thick and misshapen, forming lumps of flesh that twisted his limbs and back. Looking up with yellowish eyes from beneath overgrown brows that jutted unnaturally from a fleshy forehead of mottled skin, Crom Cruach offered a hideous smile.

"Rygeil," he rasped. "You risk much calling me from my prison."

"You are mine to command, wretched thing," Rygeil snarled.

Crom Cruach loosed a grating laugh. "I am no one's slave but will do your bidding should it whet my appetite."

Rygeil looked down at him with a steely gaze. "Long ago, you were a god among mankind, worshipped. I wish for you to reclaim that heritage."

He cocked his head, causing thick strands of hair, the width of a finger, to fall to the side. "Men have forgotten me."

"Make them remember," Rygeil said darkly.

"Why? What benefit is it to you?"

"Draw their eye to you, and they will not mark the movements of my army as I carve through the kingdoms of the north and south."

"But it is what lies in the west that you crave," Crom Cruach said slyly.

Rygeil's stare turned flinty. "I will deal with what hides in Erabel."

Crom Cruach lumbered over to a stool that sat in the corner of the room and eased himself onto it, his deformed legs sprawled at awkward angles above gnarled feet. "There will be a cost for my aid, Rygeil."

"Name it."

"Men once laid their firstborns at my feet," he said, eyeing the powerful king. "I will not ask the same of you, though it would be my right to do so."

"Spit it out, wretch. What is your price?"

He leaned forward, gangly arms with twisted fingers resting on knobby knees. "I wish to split her skull upon the altar where the heads of a thousand babes were dashed."

Rygeil's mouth twisted in disgust. "When I have drained Threa's spawn, you may have her."

Vile laughter bounced off the stone walls as Crom Cruach's body rocked. "How far you have fallen, my king!"

"Crawl back into that hole I consigned you to, monster,"

he spat, towering above the repellent figure. "I will summon you when my armies march."

Crom Cruach rose slowly, bones cracking along his spine as his muscles contorted, straightening his hunched back until he stood to his full height and met Rygeil's eyes. "Yours is not the power to command me at your whim. That rests with *Her*, and none you consume will grant you strength to surpass that of the Danu's chosen. You ride to your death if you seek her in the womb of the Great Mother."

"She will come to me, foul one, and when I am done with her, you may sup what is left."

Smiling, Crom Cruach walked to the door, leg dragging on the floor behind him. "If you draw her out, her power is yours." Stopping at the threshold, he muttered, "Fail to pull her from Erabel, and it is your skull I will bash against my idol."

Rygeil grew rigid, teeth flashing wickedly. "Remove yourself from my sight before I have you gutted."

He pulled open the door, startling the male guard who stood in the alcove just outside. "I will await your summons…" he started before adding snidely, "my king."

Slamming the door, Rygeil stalked to the opening in the wall, once again casting his eyes to the west where his granddaughter took refuge. His spies had informed him that she was much like her mother, blind to the blight of mankind. Fiadh had lived too long in proximity to them to see that they were a plague upon the earth. Vermin. Nothing more than squalling rats who would cower under his wrath when he loosed his power into every realm.

Perhaps, he mused, he would let some live, those who

proved useful—slaves, and the like. Though not as strong, her twin brother had provided much, enabling him to harness forbidden magic. But it was limited. As long as Fiadh lived under Danu's shadow, he would remain weak next to her strength. From a distance, a dark shape grew, becoming clearer as it neared. Rygeil held out his arm, catching the talons of a hawk on the thick pad of his tunic as it landed.

Stroking the bird's chest, he purred, "What news have you brought me, Creaba?"

The bond sparked as he looked into the bird's eye, seeing what she had flown over in her travels into the heart of Dorcha Wood. From her mind, he drew out images of Fiadh in the large arena that once held the festival of Tailteann. A low growl ripped from his throat as he saw Veren and Kaelari at her side. The vision didn't last as the bird whirled in the sky and made her way back to her master, but it was enough. The time was growing near for his next move, one that Kaelari had likely warned Fiadh of. Whatever warning she may have given would be useless. Some bonds were too powerful to resist, forged so deeply they withstood all efforts to sunder them.

He left the tower and made his way to the great hall, where Calum sat before the hearth, the flames of the fire reflecting off his pale face. He was a shell of the boy Rygeil had taken from Darragh, emptied of power that had been rooted in his being until Rygeil had drawn it out like a dearg-due drains the blood of its victims. But the twin-bond remained, untouched, to be hoarded and used when the time came. He dragged a chair next to his grandson, smiling when he saw him track his movements.

"It is time to go on a journey."

Calum cocked a brow. "To Erabel, no doubt."

"You need to fetch your sister and bring her to me."

He nodded, shifting his face back to the flames. "I have waited a long time to hear those words."

Fiadh's story will continue in
A Storm of Wrath & Ruin

AFTERWORD

Celtic mythology is filled with dark creatures. From the Cù-Sìth to Crom Cruach, there are dozens of frightening figures to haunt your nightmares. Throughout the Daughter of Erabel series, I bring many of them to life. Some are not the horrible beasts of legend, while others are indeed as gruesome as those tales suggest.

The Merrow are the Celtic version of mermaids. While many stories portray them as friendly, there are plenty of tales that speak of female Merrow dragging sailors into the sea where the captive could live for years. You will see more of Eradar, guardian of the Merrow, in book three, *A Storm of Wrath & Ruin*.

Crom Cruach, whose original name means crouching darkness, is one of the more frightening creatures from Celtic mythology. He was said to have been an old god who was worshipped by mankind. People feared him and would offer human sacrifices in exchange for good yields of crops or milk. Crom Cruach returns in book three.

Each book in the *Daughter of Erabel* series features unique Celtic knotwork. In *Blood of the Lost Kingdom*, you see the triskele symbol. This spiral shape is one of the oldest symbols in history. At its heart, the symbol reflects motion. This could be the constant change one goes through in life or the cycles of the earth. There are many interpretations of this ancient design: life-death-rebirth, mother-maiden-crone, earth-water-sky, and past-present-future. The Celts were not the only ones to use this symbol, and it has been found on artifacts from around the world.

ACKNOWLEDGMENTS

Books are true magic, and writers, the magicians. We create worlds and characters that never existed until our minds birthed them onto the page. As an author, I pour my heart and soul into my books, nurturing the story and characters over months until they are ready to introduce themselves to the world. It is a great privilege to share them with you.

But, the work of a novel is not done purely in my head. I have spent countless hours prattling on about the series to family and friends who, most of the time, humor me and, some of the time, roll their eyes and attempt to slink away. My husband and sons remain my biggest and most loyal fans. They cheer me on as I spend hours—yes, hours—in a chair that starts as a comfortable seat and inevitably becomes a source of aches and pains. They show their support and pride in so many ways, and I am truly grateful.

I can tell you with utmost sincerity that this book would have been colorless without my amazingly talented editor,

David. He can tap into my soul as a writer and draw out the best in me. I could never do this without him.

I reserve my final note of appreciation to you, dear reader. Thank you. Thank you for taking a chance on this indie author. I hope you love the characters and stories as much I loved creating them for you.

Kristin Ward is an award-winning young adult author living in Connecticut. A science and math teacher for over twenty years, she infuses her geeky passions into stories that meld realism and fantasy. Kristin embraces her inner nerd regularly, often quoting 80s movies while expecting those around her to chime in with appropriate rejoinders.

As a nature freak, she can be found wandering the woods - she may be lost, so please stop and ask if you see her - or chilling in her yard with all manner of furry and feathered friends. Often referred to as a unicorn by colleagues who remain in awe of her ability to create or find various and sundry things in mere moments, in reality, the horn was removed years ago, leaving only a mild imprint that can be seen if she tilts her head just right. A lifelong lover of books and writing, she dreamed of becoming an author for thirty years before publishing her award-winning debut in 2018.

Her first novel, **After the Green Withered**, is one of many things you should probably read.

https://www.kristinwardauthor.com/